DARK
HEARTS

BOOKS BY D.K. HOOD

D.K. HOOD

DARK HEARTS

bookouture

Published by Bookouture in 2024

An imprint of Storyfire Ltd.
Carmelite House
50 Victoria Embankment
London EC4Y 0DZ

www.bookouture.com

ISBN: 978-1-83525-200-0
eBook ISBN: 978-1-83525-199-7

To my son, Wesley, who ignited my interest in serial killers.

PROLOGUE

SUNDAY

Roaring Creek

The bell over the convenience store door tinkled and Cassidy Wilder stared in horror at the man coming through the door drawing a weapon. He casually screwed on a suppressor and aimed it at the spotty-faced, red-haired youth behind the counter. Two other people in the store moved away and ducked down out of sight. Heart pounding in her ears, she backed away, dropping down to hide between a display of sunglasses and toiletries. Had he seen her?

"Fill a bag with money." The male voice was just above a whisper. "All of it—and those scratch games."

A man who was close by shuffled forward a few inches and pulled a pistol with trembling fingers. The thief moved like lightning, turning his gun and firing.

Bang!

The customer slumped to the ground, his pistol spinning away across the tile. Blood oozed from a hole in his chest and pooled around him. His mouth worked but no sound came from his pale lips. Cassidy crawled toward him, and he stared at her, blinked twice, and then his stare fixed in death. Panic gripped her and she shuffled backward, peering at the gunman between the shelves. He was tall, maybe six feet, and wearing a balaclava, leather gloves, and a long dark coat. His polished boots stuck out from Wranglers, and he didn't resemble the usual desperate type that held up a store. She heard a voice, a woman asking about the noise.

"Stay back, Mom." The youth behind the counter pressed himself against the shelves behind him.

A woman appeared from out the back.

Bang! Bang!

Even with the suppressor, the sound of the shots blasted the silence and echoed around the room. Cassidy flinched, terrified and sickened at the sound of two bodies hitting the floor. He'd shot the people behind the counter. Who was next? A woman hiding in the next aisle panicked and ran screaming for the door. Two more shots rang out, and she fell to her knees and crawled, slipping in her own blood, trying to get away. The gunman shot again, and she lay staring into nothingness.

Trembling with shock, Cassidy wrapped her arms around her knees and kept her head down. The store was so quiet she didn't know what was happening. The stink of gunfire filled the room, mixed with the smell of blood and death. Footsteps, slow and deliberate, came toward her as if the gunman had all the time in the world. Frozen with terror, Cassidy stared at the floor.

"Get up." The man poked her with his gun. "Don't make a sound or I'll spread your brains all over the coffee machine."

The heat from the suppressor burned through her clothes and she jerked up her head and stared into cold eyes. The muzzle of the gun was aimed at her forehead. Shaking, she staggered to her feet. A bag of money was thrust into her hands and she took it without thinking. The man waved the pistol toward the door. She stared at him, too scared to move.

"See the truck out front? Walk out, nice and calm, and climb inside." He pressed the gun against her forehead. "One sound, one wrong move, and you die." He chuckled. "We're going for a little ride."

ONE

MONDAY

Special Agent Beth Katz sat at her desk at the Rattlesnake Creek FBI field office engrossed in a homicide case file. It was abundantly clear to her that a serial killer roamed the communities in the nearby county of Mischief. It was a case that triggered her carefully disguised dark side. This one she'd investigate on her own, keeping all of her involvement secret, and if the perpetrator proved to be unstoppable, she'd allow her alter ego to rise and take him down. It had been a time since she'd given in to her dormant impulses, and ignoring them hadn't been easy. She understood her triggers, and this string of unsolved murders was begging her personal attention.

Three deputies worked the case at the Mischief Sheriff's Department, and they'd created a list of suspects, but the men involved had produced alibis for the times of the other murders. She scratched her head and leaned back in her chair, staring at the long list of young women and girls found dumped all over the communities of Wolf Valley, Buffalo Pass, and Second Thought. The murders all had similarities. The young women and girls were between thirteen and twenty and had seemingly vanished from the streets and showed up miles from their homes, raped and strangled. Bodies had been found in dumpsters, alleyways, deserted buildings, construction sites, or just alongside the highway.

She checked out the Mischief Sheriff's Department, and although it was more than obvious these murders were the work of a dangerous serial killer, no assistance had been requested. In fact, in a recent media statement the sheriff had said he was interviewing suspects and suggested a local gang might be involved. The case intrigued her, mainly because the local law enforcement must have been blind not to have noticed the method of killing was identical. It wasn't a group of men, but one man who had committed these crimes. Not only that, they'd used their local doctors to examine the bodies. The medical examiner for the region, Dr. Shane Wolfe, hadn't been called in for his opinion. The entire investigation stunk on ice, but it wasn't a case she wanted to explore with her partner, Agent Dax Styles. Although Styles knew Cutthroat Jack was her father, he had no idea of her dark side—and she needed to keep it that way. He wouldn't understand that taking out monsters was personal. The Mischief serial killer needed to be stopped and she just happened to be the one to take him down. It might take her a little time, but she'd eventually find him. After taking one last look at the files, she closed them, and using her cyber-crime skills, removed any trace she'd been snooping in the Mischief Sheriff's Department database. She smiled to herself as Styles walked into the office, his K-9, a Belgian Malinois by the name of Bear, at his heels. *This one is mine.*

Before Beth could greet him, Styles held up one finger and went to the kitchenette to dump takeout bags on the counter. As be bent to push things into the refrigerator, it was obvious he was taking a call from the director of the FBI. Styles was a maverick—he ran by his own rules—and the director was the only person she'd ever heard him refer to as *sir*, so she leaned back in her chair and watched him with interest.

Styles was all tough cowboy, six-two, muscular without an ounce of body fat, light brown hair that curled at his collar. His work attire was usually Wranglers, cowboy boots, and a Stetson. He was good looking, with soft eyes and a scar on his chin, and she'd seen many more battle scars on his body during their daily workouts. In his holster he carried a Magnum, but she'd rarely seen him draw down on anyone. He had the old-school way of dealing with unrest: he talked some, and if that didn't work, he'd usually wait for a mess of guys to attack him. That was their big mistake. As a military cop, he'd been trained to take down the most experienced soldiers, so a few hometown boys were just a workout to him. When he disconnected and pulled the wireless earbud from his ear, she stood and went to set up the coffee machine. "So what's up?"

"That was the director. He has a case for us." Styles shrugged. "You recall the convenience store robberies over the past few weeks?"

Beth turned on the machine and leaned against the counter. "Only what's on the news. Holdups are happening all over. The store clerk was shot, I believe. That's not the type of case we usually take. Can't the local sheriff handle it?"

"That's the point." Styles scratched the scar on his chin, something he often did when he was thinking. "It's three remote communities. All have their own sheriffs, and there's not too much cooperation going on between them. It's not the robberies, although the number of innocent people being shot by this guy is growing, it's the kidnap and murders that make this different."

This was the first time Beth had heard anything about an abduction. She frowned and peered into the takeout bag Styles had left on the counter. Smiling, she pulled out an egg salad sandwich and handed a second one to him. It used to be donuts, but he'd come around to healthier eating since she'd arrived. "They never mentioned that on the news."

"No, because it's been kept under wraps." Styles dropped the sandwich on his desk and leaned against the counter beside her. "The robberies have occurred in Roaring Creek, Broken Bridge, and Rivers Edge. He's hit the Roaring Creek one twice now. The new owners reopened last week, and yesterday someone walked inside, killed four people, and abducted a young girl only sixteen years old." He sighed, removed his hat, and ran his fingers through his hair. "She's still missing. CCTV footage shows the same guy, wearing a balaclava and gloves and carrying a pistol with a suppressor. From the footage, the gun has been identified as a Beretta M9A3, the slugs pulled from the victims nine-by-nineteen-millimeter FMJ M882."

Beth digested the information as the coffee pot steamed behind her, filling the room with the aromatic delight of freshly brewed coffee. "Is he the same person in each case? Have they CCTV footage of all of the robberies?"

"Not all of them, but in the ones they have, the guy looks the same." Styles headed for the kitchenette and took down two cups. "The problem is that the footage is grainy in all of the robberies apart from the last one. Being new owners, they replaced the old camera, but we don't have any firsthand witnesses because he killed everyone and then took the girl with him. She wasn't a willing participant, from what the director just informed me. She was scared to death."

Nodding, Beth took out the fixings and placed them on the counter. "You mentioned he abducts young women from the stores during the robbery. Have any come forward afterward?"

"Nope." Styles poured coffee, added the fixings, and carried his cup to his desk. "They've all been found dead, miles from town, usually dumped on the side of the road. They'd been sexually assaulted and then shot in the head execution-style."

Stirring her coffee slowly, Beth looked at him. "How many murders to date?"

"Ten in the stores, plus three girls and one missing." Styles dropped into his chair and bit into his sandwich. He chewed and swallowed. "Going on the usual timeline, he kills them the following morning after the abduction." He sipped his coffee, looking at her over the rim of his cup. "Another thing, all of them are carrying a one- or two-dollar scratch game. It's not clear if he leaves it behind like a signature or not."

Beth had mixed feelings about the case. "Interesting. Are they sending the case files and local law enforcement contacts for each case?"

"Yeah." Styles leaned back in his chair, eyeing her with interest. "I can see your mind working from here. What are you seeing that I'm not?"

Laughing, Beth shook her head. "You just gave me the bare facts in a homicide slash robbery slash abduction slash murder and no conclusions. I'll need to read all the information before I can hazard a guess as to what's going on in this person's mind."

"They don't have any suspects." Styles leaned back in his chair, his large hand wrapped around the sandwich. "They assume he arrived in a vehicle, but no one saw anything. The only witnesses are dead, including a guy walking his dog past the store. No one seems to hear anything either. It's beyond weird."

Beth thought for a beat. "So he's not local to any of the communities he hit or someone would recognize the CCTV footage of him entering the store."

"He's covered up, balaclava, cowboy hat, long coat, he wears gloves and is cool, calm, and collected." Styles waved his egg salad around, and his dog followed the movement, just waiting for him to drop a morsel. "I figured a random hit, but it doesn't sound like that to me."

The signal for an email sounded on his computer and then

on Beth's. She went to her desk. "Ah, that will be the files. We'll need to print out all the images and get them onto a whiteboard for comparison. I'm especially interested in the girls he kidnapped."

"How so?" Styles bit into his sandwich and tossed the remaining portion to Bear.

Beth scanned the files and sent images to the printer, which buzzed and spat out paper. "From what I'm hearing, this killer has two angles or two fantasies, which is unusual." She glanced over her screen at him. "Give me time to look at the files and see if I can discover the nature of the beast."

TWO

Pondering over what the director had said, Dax opened the files. He scanned a few of the reports and sipped his coffee, his attention drifting to Beth. She'd arrived from DC under a cloud. It fast became glaringly obvious that the slim-built beautiful blonde was a contradiction. She didn't resemble any FBI agent he'd met before and she sure as heck didn't back down from anyone. After watching her in action, he felt sorry for anyone stupid enough to attack her in a dark alleyway. The report had mentioned her lack of compassion and yet he'd seen her put her life on the line to save kids. She willingly walked alone into situations with nothing but her bare hands and yet managed to bring down the bad guys.

He found her eccentric way of doing things unnerving at times. She straddled the law, but then so did he. In Rattlesnake Creek, with only one sheriff and no deputies, he was often called upon to help out, and he wasn't the type to draw down on anyone when he could reason with them. If they attacked him— it only happened once—he didn't like or want to kill people or haul them in for drinking too much and brawling.

Beth didn't depend on him. She liked her alone time, which

suited him fine. She lived in the same building as he did, but they both owned cabins in the forest. He liked to get away on his downtime and go fishing, but Beth had many hobbies. She painted landscapes and collected antiques. She could be anywhere and everywhere at any one time, visiting stores or out painting a masterpiece, although he never had a problem helping out if she needed assistance moving furniture, but that wasn't often. It seemed she was taking her time furnishing her cabin and finding the right pieces was all part of the enjoyment.

When she met his gaze over the top of her screen, he realized he must have been staring at her and cleared his throat. "I know you must be disappointed being given this case. I did try to convince the director we planned on chasing down the Tarot Killer."

"What did he say?" Beth slid her chair away from her screen to look at him.

Styles shrugged. "He said every man and his dog were on the case. Chasing a shadow was a waste of taxpayer's money and we should concentrate on crimes we can actually solve."

"Ah, I see." Beth smiled at him. "He never changes, does he? We're all bricks in a wall to him. Do the job, get results. He must have that on a plaque on his wall." She sighed. "However, this is a good case for us because we have a different way of doing things. We both come into them from different angles. While the printer is doing its job, I've taken the image from the latest CCTV footage and it's currently running through the FBI face-recognition software."

Standing to refill his coffee cup, Styles looked over his shoulder at her. "Yeah, but that only covers people who have been arrested and you need a complete face."

"Ah, well, technology is moving forward at a sizzling pace." Beth held up her cup and jiggled it at him. "I can set up the program to run through every CCTV camera in the towns where each crime occurred. I've rewritten the software to focus on eye shape and color. Which means every person who walks by, if they resemble the man in the balaclava, we can get a list of suspects. Most people have ID, and any matches are immediately routed through various databases that carry images."

After refilling both cups and taking one to Beth, Styles returned to his desk. Beth's time in cybercrime gave her an edge most agents didn't possess, and she was up to date to the second. "You did that already? How so?"

"It's my specialty." Beth gave him a long look. "I've been manipulating codes since I first sat in front of a computer. For me it was natural, like talking, and I picked it up real fast. I was writing games by the time I was twelve. I see the code as you would read a book. This is one of the reasons I was useful to the FBI. They don't think of me as a fighting machine who takes down bad guys. They look at me as a nerd, so when I started taking down bad guys in the field, for them it didn't compute. I know this by the way they speak to me—have spoken to me, I should say. You're different. You see me as an asset even if I'm a little unconventional. I get the job done and that's the whole point of why we do this work."

Understanding flooded Styles and he nodded. "Yeah, I figure we make a good team. Sometimes you need to walk close to the line between legal and illegal to stop a killer." He sighed. "So is this new technology all about AI or is this different?"

"Different." Beth smiled. "If you mean, can we ask an AI how to solve this crime, well, we could, but it could only scan similar cases and come up with a variety of possibilities. Most of them would be like a bad fiction novel because we use our brains to think like a killer. An AI doesn't have the capability to do that, and if they advanced to that level, there will already be a failsafe built into the system to prevent them from delving into a psychotic mind." She grinned. "I'm sure we've seen enough movies about evil robots to stop them taking over the world just yet. The problem is, if they make them too smart, they'll start thinking for themselves. If that happens, well, to them we'll be redundant and a waste of energy. Let's hope it never happens and the technology is used for good not evil."

Shaking his head, Styles raised both eyebrows. "Amen to that."

She always amazed him the way she explained technology. He'd believed he'd been up to date on most things until she'd arrived. Her mind was super fast, and he admitted to himself he envied her skills just a little. He walked to the printer and scooped up the images and tapped them into a neat pile. "Okay, these images all have the names of the victims and dates of their murders. The last three in the pile are the kidnap and murders and an image of the missing girl."

He walked to the whiteboard and pinned them up. He placed the shooting victims in the convenience stores on one side, and the rest he arranged in a line down the other side. He looked them over, hunting for comparisons of type. Many killers picked the same type of victim. "I did a quick scan of the case files, skipping over the murders, and went to see if any of the victims were linked... as in from town to town."

"You wanted to eliminate a vendetta?" Beth went to the whiteboard, and Bear walked to her side and leaned against her. She stared at the images, absently rubbing the dog's ears. "Did you find anything?"

Nodding, Styles picked up a pen from a holder attached to the board and placed a cross beside two images. "These men are cousins. One lives in Roaring Creek, the other out at Broken Bridge." He looked at her. "These are all close-knit communities, there would be many family members spread across those areas, but it is a similarity."

He glanced at Bear and smiled to himself. His dog had come to him after his handler died in action. Bear had been wounded and he was the only person who knew the dog. It was him or euthanasia, but true to his nature the dog had stayed by his side and he enjoyed his company. Bear hadn't attached himself to anyone else until Beth arrived, something he found to be very unusual.

"What about the girls?" Beth went to her desk and picked up her tablet. She scrolled through case files. "Nope, they didn't know each other, but they're all within the same age bracket. All were in the store alone at the time of the shootings. In each case covered by CCTV cameras, the killer hands the girl the bag of money and sends her out of the store before him. The thing is, did he take them as a hostage or did he have another motive?"

Styles went back to his desk. "We'll need to look at the autopsy reports."

"What reports?" Beth pulled a face. "These are useless. We can't base a case on a local doctor or, in one case, a local mortician's report on the victim of a crime. How long ago was the last victim abducted before the current missing girl?"

Frowning, Styles recalled the conversation with the director. "That would be four days ago out at Broken Bridge. Last Friday, Arizona Carson was taken after a shooting at the convenience store but found dumped alongside the highway the following day between Broken Bridge and Roaring Creek with a gunshot wound to head. The most recent shooting was out at Roaring Creek yesterday. Cassidy Wilder remains missing. That's the second shooting in the same store over six months."

"We'll need to see the body of the last girl he abducted. He might have left some clues." Beth glanced up at him. "And view the crime scenes of both shootings. Can we do that—like today?"

Styles nodded. "Yeah, but the medical examiner will want to be there as well. I figure first we locate the remains of Arizona Carson." He watched Beth as she scanned pages of documents, her eyes flashing back and forth. He sipped his coffee. "The three communities are serviced by the hospital at Roaring

Creek. They have a morgue, so it's likely they took the shooting victims there."

"Ah, yes, here it is: Roaring Creek General." She went back to her desk and grabbed her phone. "The report says the body was discovered alongside the highway and taken there for examination." She made the call and placed the phone on speaker.

After introducing herself, Beth asked the hospital administrator, Trudy Newman, for the whereabouts of the body of Arizona Carson.

"It's currently in the hospital morgue, waiting for transfer to the undertaker for burial." Ms. Newman cleared her throat. *"Is there a problem we should be aware of, Agent Katz?"*

"Yes, Arizona Carson's death was a homicide and under investigation." Beth stared at Styles and shook her head in dismay. "Who ID'd the body?"

"Well, the mother identified the shoes. Arizona Carson was shot in the head and the face is unrecognizable."

"I see." Beth drew in a deep breath. "We'll require DNA testing to establish identity. I'll contact the medical examiner, Dr. Shane Wolfe. He'll likely want the body taken to Black Rock Falls for examination."

"I don't have the authority to hold the body or release it to anyone else but the next of kin." Ms. Newman tapped away on her computer. *"I'll need paperwork."*

"That's not a problem because until we identify the body there is no next of kin. I'll need the name of the doctor who issued a death certificate for an unidentified body, and did they perform an autopsy? If so, who ordered it?" Beth was making notes as she spoke.

"That would be Dr. Michelle Barnes. There wasn't an autopsy. It's clear how Arizona died."

"That's for the medical examiner to determine." Beth looked at Styles and rolled her eyes. "The body isn't to be released without the permission of the medical examiner. In fact, it shouldn't have been removed from the crime scene, but that's not your concern. I'll take that up with the local law enforcement. Please notify the family that the medical examiner will be performing an autopsy to determine cause and time of death and hopefully give us a clue to catching her killer. He'll need Mrs. Carson to give a DNA sample. Will you please contact her and have her go to the hospital?"

Styles twirled his fingers and mouthed the word *helipad*.

"Does the hospital have a helipad?" Beth tapped her pen on the table.

"Yes, there is room on the roof for four helicopters. We service four of the local mining communities."

"Okay, send me the coordinates. Thank you for your assistance. We'll be there soon." She disconnected and stared at Styles. "Is it usual to skip a formal ID in these parts?"

Rubbing his scar, Styles shrugged. "Not that I'm aware. If you contact Wolfe and give him the coordinates and bring him up to speed, I'll go and do a preflight check on the chopper."

"I'm on it." Beth picked up her phone again. She smiled at him. "I'm looking forward to visiting a new town."

Styles pushed on his Stetson. That was Beth. Of late, she always came up with a positive to smooth out the horrific crimes they handled. She was one unusual woman. Murder and mayhem all around her, and for her it was just another day at the office.

THREE

Roaring Creek

Numb from shock, Cassidy Wilder stared at the man acting so casually, as if he honestly believed she enjoyed being held prisoner in the cellar of a deserted building. Cold bit into her bare flesh and her teeth chattered. The blanket he'd tossed over her smelled musty, but it was better than nothing. The images of the faces of the people he'd shot moved across her mind in a constant stream of horror. He hadn't cared or reacted when he'd shot them, no more than if he'd been swatting flies. His cold persona had changed in the truck and he'd made casual conversation as if they were on a date, but he'd kept the pistol across his thigh with a warning that she'd be next if she made a fuss. He'd promised to let her go first thing in the morning, but only if she behaved herself. Wanting to live, Cassidy had followed his instructions and survived a night of torture by his hands. Each time she cried out, his brutality increased as if he fed from her pain. She'd sobbed with relief when he'd left early this morning. He'd been gone for a long time. Would he come back or would she die here?

She sat hunched on a mattress on the floor, one hand tied to a pipe using a zip tie. Hunger gnawed in her belly, but he'd left her water and allowed her to use the bathroom before he left. It was a dilapidated room, with cracked tile and brown stains covering the basin and shower cubicle. The toilet flushed and in the back of her mind she tried to picture the building when they arrived. It had been dark and she'd seen other structures, and yet on entering they'd walked through what looked like an old redbrick office building and taken stairs down to what could only be described as a cellar. At first there were no lights, and he'd used a flashlight to guide them. Once he'd secured her, he'd left her in the dark, but not long after, a light flooded the room and he returned.

Footsteps sounded on the steps outside, and Cassidy cringed as the door opened and he walked inside. He'd showered and changed. His hair was still damp. He said nothing but turned his back on her and went to stoke the old furnace. Overnight it had warmed the cellar, but now an icy chill filled the room and he cursed her for keeping him so busy he'd allowed the furnace to go out. He walked over to her and took a knife from his belt. Terrified, she cringed away in terror.

"If I'd wanted to kill you, I'd have done it already." He bent and cut the zip tie and then handed her a peanut butter and jelly sandwich in plastic wrap. "Eat."

She stared at the sandwich, wondering how she could fit anything between her swollen lips. The need to survive gripped her and she met his amused gaze. "Thank you."

"When I was a kid, my pa would always give me a peanut butter and jelly sandwich as a reward for being good." He looked her over. "He'd often sneak me out of the house and take me to work with him at night. I'd be on a cot out back and people would come in and buy stuff. I had to keep quiet and not tell anyone."

Cassidy broke off small pieces of the sandwich and pushed

them into her mouth. "What about your mom? Didn't she worry about you?"

"No. I did tell her, and she beat me for telling lies." In a second, his calm demeanor changed. His expression grew hard and his mouth turned down. He stared at her without blinking. "When Pa left, she blamed me. She blames me for everything. If it darn well rains, it's my fault. She was never fat before she had me. I can't do anything to please her. You know, when I was six, she broke a broomstick over my back. I hate her." He scratched his chin. "I don't know why she turned nasty. My grandma told me she was a lovely girl until she married my father at seventeen."

Unable to believe he was holding a conversation with her as if they were close friends, she washed the sandwich down with water, wincing at the pain of her cut lip. "Did you tell your grandma you were being abused?"

"No, I smothered her with a pillow." He raised both eyebrows and stared at her as if waiting for a reaction. "I was twelve and my mom sent me over next door—that's where she lived—to take her some soup. I left the soup beside the bed. She wanted me to feed her and she smelled like shit. I hated her too." He smiled. "It was the best day. My mom went over to get the plate and found her dead, the soup untouched beside her. End of story. Seems when I put the pillow over her face, she suffered a heart attack." He chuckled. "Trust me, she didn't have a heart." He looked at her again. "Finished? Go and take a shower." He pulled a plastic spray bottle out of his backpack and handed it to her. "Use this. Wash all over and your hair. I'm going to watch to make sure you do it right."

After a humiliating shower, using a lotion that burned her skin, he allowed her to dry herself on paper towels and dress, but he kept her underwear. Trembling with fear, and flesh burning, she stood staring at him, waiting for his next command. He seemed to enjoy giving her orders. After pushing everything she'd used into a garbage bag, he marched her outside and back into his truck. "Where are we going now?"

"I already told you." He gave her a long look and shrugged. "I'm going to let you go."

They drove for miles and Cassidy had no idea even which county they were in by the time he stopped on the deserted highway and pointed to a clump of trees. "Head to the trees. There's a house on the other side. You can call your mom from there." He pulled a scratch game from his pocket and handed it to her. "This is your lucky day. Wait there I'll come around and open the door for you."

Bewildered, Cassidy took the card and scrambled out of the door. Looking around, she scanned the blacktop way into the distance, hoping to see another vehicle, but the highway was empty both ways for miles.

He took out his pistol and waved it at her. "Run."

The sound of a bullet being chambered seemed loud in the silence. Terrified, she took off running toward the trees without a backward glance. The trees seemed so far away, and she couldn't run fast enough. Behind her a gun fired, and the grassy lowlands spun away into darkness.

FOUR

As the FBI chopper descended onto the top of Roaring Creek General, Beth surveyed the town. It was spread out over miles, with the usual mountains, rivers, and ranches dotted out across the lowlands. Redbrick and wooden buildings lined Main. As they flew, she took in the immediate area. The highways joining the communities went long and straight for miles in all directions across the lowlands or wound through mountain passes like long black snakes. Mining was evident, with mining camps peppering the landscape like clumps of mushrooms or with bare patches cut out of the green vegetation and filled with massive pieces of machinery. She shook her head, wondering if the land ever managed to return to its natural state after so many trees had been stripped away.

She appreciated beautiful scenery, loved painting it, and it soothed her soul on days like these filled with bloodshed, but she hated seeing the land destroyed. That part of her appeared to be untouched by her psychopathy, and she loved animals, another anomaly. She often compared herself to science-fiction characters who by no fault of their own had been the issue of two opposite species. In her case, both sides of her had different ideas of how to deal with monsters and each had a convincing argument for being themselves. Yes, she often referred to herself as two people because in reality that's what she'd become. She gripped the seat as the wind increased, making the landing difficult. The chopper swayed dangerously before setting down. She turned to Styles when he cut the chopper's engine and removed her headset. "I'm not seeing any land reclamation. Isn't that part of the agreement for a mining lease of natural resources in these parts?"

"What you're seeing are ongoing concerns." Styles hung up his headset and looked at her. "Yeah, you have it right. Any land disturbed during excavating must be returned to how it was before the mining. Not that they can replace trees they cut down, but I guess it's okay if they plant young ones. It's not my field of expertise, to be honest." He gave her a long look. "We're going to see the body of a young woman brutally murdered and a number of gunshot victims, and you're worried about trees?" He snapped his fingers and smiled at her. "Oh, right. This is a coping mechanism you use to deflect the horrors of murder."

Sighing, Beth nodded. "Yeah, it distracts my mind for a time. I find it difficult knowing that someone is close by killing young women, and right now we can't do a thing to stop them. Viewing victims of crimes is horrific. I need to take in some beauty to cope sometimes." She glanced at him. "It's not idle chatter either. I really do care about the land. That's something I can help conserve. I can only bring the girl's killer to justice, but I can't bring her back to life. The land can be saved."

"The land is owned by someone, Beth." Styles gathered his things. "Leave them to care about the land and you concentrate on profiling this killer."

Nodding, Beth climbed from the chopper and watched Styles tether the skids securely to the helipad. It was something she'd never seen him do before. As she headed for the door, a blast of wind almost swept her off her feet. Styles grabbed her by the arm and steadied her, his feet spread wide apart and one hand on his Stetson. She smiled at him. "Wow, it's windy up here. I figured after the melt the weather would improve."

"It's always windy here." He pointed to the mountains and a gap. "It comes through that valley and blasts the town most times. That's why they've built tethers into the roof for the choppers." He stared into the sky. "Did you get an ETA for Dr. Wolfe?"

Nodding, Beth gripped the doorframe and pushed open the door to the building. "Yeah, I figure he'll be here withing ten minutes. He told me his chopper was ready for takeoff as he was planning on heading out to Helena. It's nothing urgent, so he got his team organized and left at once."

They walked down a flight of steps and came to a bank of elevators. Beside them on the wall was a directory. They headed inside and hit the button for the morgue. The car dropped fast, not stopping at any other floor, and the doors opened with a whoosh, immediately filling Beth's nose with the strong antiseptic odor of hospitals. Outside they found a corridor and a desk with a bell beside a notice: PRESS IF COUNTER UNATTENDED.

Beth rang the bell and they waited for at least five minutes before a woman came out from the swinging metal doors. She had a name tag attached to her jacket that read MINA SOARES. Composing her face into a neutral expression and putting her hard-nosed cop persona into place, Beth approached the counter. "I called earlier. Agents Katz and Styles. We're here to see the body of Arizona Carson. The medical examiner, Dr. Shane Wolfe, and his team are in transit."

"Yes, we've been expecting you." Ms. Soares raised both eyebrows. "We've been advised by the local sheriff to wait until Dr. Wolfe arrives before we allow anyone to see the body."

Obviously, her hard-nosed cop attitude wouldn't work with

this woman, so Beth reverted to using charm. During the ride from Rattlesnake Creek, she'd read files and made a few assumptions about the killer. It was very rare for a psychopathic killer to leave a victim without taking a trophy. This could be anything that reminded him of the kill and allowed him to relive them in his mind. The reason behind trophies was easy to understand. Once the person is dead, the memory vanishes from their minds. Not like amnesia but more like a soda can. Who cares about a soda can once it's empty? The memory of the sweet drink is still there, and if they'd kept a reminder, they could bring back the memory of indulging in an instant. She smiled at the woman. "Yes, of course, I understand completely. Would it be too much trouble to see her personal effects? Have they been preserved?"

"Well, if you mean have they been handled by someone without gloves? The answer is no. They were cut from the body and bagged. I'll be able to get them for you."

Beth nodded. "Thank you so much. Is there a room we could use to examine them?"

"Yes, we have an empty office." Ms. Soares indicated to an open door across the passageway. "I'll go and get them for you." She turned away.

"Who are you and what have you done with Agent Katz?" Styles stared at her, his eyes dancing with amusement. "Is this good cop, bad cop? Should I start to raise my voice or threaten to take them in for impeding a federal officer in his duty?"

Shaking her head, Beth searched her pockets for examination gloves and pulled them on. "Ah, come on, you know all this tough image is just for show. I'm all sweetness and light underneath, right?" She smiled at him. "They say you get more flies with honey than with vinegar. She has her orders and doesn't want to be fired for making a mistake, is all."

"She didn't ask to see our creds." Styles shrugged. "Handing over evidence to just anyone is a big mistake. She doesn't know who we are. We could be the killers wanting a little more time with the corpse for all she knows." He pulled on a pair of examination gloves with a snap and grinned at her. "I figure we could pass as a couple of psychopaths, what do you say?"

Beth snorted. "You say the nicest things, Styles."

FIVE

The clothes arrived, all shoved into a big plastic bag and sealed with a name tag. Beth took it and led the way into the office. A desk and one chair sat in the middle of the room. On the desk was a box of tissues. Beth passed the bag to Styles and took a small bottle of PCR Clean from her purse. She never left home without the DNA remover, but Styles didn't need to know that. She held it up and smiled at him. "I brought this as an afterthought, just in case we needed a clean area." She liberally sprayed the desk and wiped it dry with a handful of tissues. "There, now open the bag and dump everything on the table."

Surprisingly, the clothes were not covered in blood. There was a small pattern of spatter across the shoulders of a jacket and down the front. Beth took each piece of clothing, examined it, and then, after photographing it, returned it to the bag. The shoes were in a separate bag and Beth didn't touch them for fear of destroying trace evidence. "I see leaf fragments, pine needles, and blood traces." She blew out a long sigh. "What do you see?"

"Arizona Carson was fifteen, from her photograph a normal size for her age." Styles' brow furrowed. "The underwear is missing. The bra is there but no panties. We'll need to ask the parents if she wore them."

Beth rolled her eyes. "You can't just ask a parent that, Styles. We'll need to ask them to make a complete list of her clothing right down to her socks and shoes." She sighed. "We'll make some excuse about it being needed for a positive ID. It will make it easier on them. She might not have been sexually assaulted like the others. Can you imagine the trauma it would cause, knowing a killer has their daughter's underwear?"

"Yeah, it would be another punch in the guts." Styles raised both eyebrows. "So why take the panties?"

Beth thought for a beat. "I've read about other killers taking their victim's panties as trophies. They're especially good evidence when we find their stash. There's always DNA on panties. When we find his stash, it will make it easier for us to make a case against him."

"I'm aware." Styles sealed the bag and dropped it onto the table. "Any other insights? This guy seems to be crossing lines between a holdup with a deadly weapon to kidnap and rape and murder." He sighed. "He's like two people. Is that possible?"

It had been something Beth had considered. "Yeah, they can follow any pattern or no pattern. Trying to link the two independent actions is the problem. We have a motive. The money stolen from the store is one. The abduction is sketchy. Why is he taking the girls when he seems to get away without anyone seeing him? No one is chasing him. Why does he need a hostage?"

"Do you figure we should run it past Jo Wells, the behavioral analyst out at Snakeskin Gully?" Styles raised both eyebrows in question. "She did mention we could call on her at any time for assistance in a case. Her partner, Ty Carter, is a great asset as well. I like them."

Trying to appear enthusiastic, Beth nodded, but her

stomach dropped. She looked at him. "I like them too." She did like them in her way. She appreciated Ty Carter's frankness; he was only just in control of his filter and it showed. Jo, on the other hand, missed nothing and was as smart as a whip.

Wanting to groan, Beth turned away, busying herself with her phone. She could just imagine the complications of having two more FBI agents breathing down her neck when she might need to sneak away to deal with the case eating her up inside out at Mischief. She'd met Jo Wells, and although Jo was at the top of her field, Beth believed she hadn't sent up any red flags with "I'm a serial killer" written all over them just yet. During her time working with Styles, and watching him deal with his particular brand of anger by hitting balls in a baseball net, her control over her dark side had increased. She used physical exertion when life became complicated, and so far, it had worked.

The elevator chimed and the doors slid open to reveal Dr. Shane Wolfe, his daughter and ME in training, Emily, and his assistant and badge-holding Black Rock Falls deputy, Colt Webber. Beth smiled. "Dr. Wolfe, Emily, Colt, good to see you again."

"I'm hoping the attending physician hasn't destroyed evidence." Wolfe's gray eyes moved to Styles and he held out his hand. "Good to see you again, Styles. What have we got?"

Beth waited for Styles to give him a rundown of the personal effects and then turned to Wolfe. "This is our first hour on the case. We wanted to secure the victim's remains and take the personal effects into custody. We'll be viewing the crime scene as soon as possible."

"Styles mentioned four gunshot victims from yesterday, plus three and an abducted and murdered girl taken from a different location." Wolfe's face was grim. "I'm assuming your priority is the missing girl, so we're looking at the previous victim's remains for clues?"

Nodding, Beth looked at him. "That's the plan. Right now, we have positive IDs for the Broken Bridge murder victims, apart from the abducted Jane Doe, who we assume is Arizona Carson." She glanced at her notes. "We have nothing on yesterday's Roaring Creek shootings, apart from the sex of the victims and the abducted girl, who we assume is Cassidy Wilder. Her mom came forward after she heard about the shooting on the TV. She'd sent her to the store to buy milk."

"Okay and, please, will y'all call me Shane or Wolfe?" Wolfe smiled at her. "We'll be working together in a close-knit team, and I prefer to keep it casual between us. Unless that's a problem, Agent Katz?"

Astounded, Beth returned his smile. She like the tall, blond, rugged man. He was dependable and ultra talented but ran a tight ship. She, it seemed, was surrounded by ex-military, and Wolfe, like Styles, ran to a different rhythm than her. "That would be nice, thank you, Shane."

"Good." Wolfe went to the counter and pounded on the bell. When Ms. Soares came into the room, he gave her a hard stare and held up his creds. "Dr. Shane Wolfe, medical examiner. Take me and my team to the body of the Jane Doe you refer to as Arizona Carson, and I want the attending physician here at once."

"Yes, of course." Ms. Soares unlocked a door beside the counter and waved them in. "Come this way."

They followed Wolfe into the bowels of the hospital. It was so quiet their footsteps sounded like gunshots ricocheting along the empty corridors. They reached a set of metal doors with MORGUE written above them in black letters. Inside, they all changed into scrubs, masks, and gloves before being escorted into an examination room by an orderly. All morgues have the same sour smell of death, overlayed with a miasma of chemicals. Even with her wearing a mask, the odors permeated Beth's nostrils and she wished she'd availed herself of the mentholated balm the members of Wolfe's team used. A stainless-steel gurney was pulled from the wall refrigerator. A body covered with a sheet, with only the toes showing, complete with a name tag. Why was that the same in every morgue Beth had visited?

"There is massive facial damage, Dr. Wolfe." The orderly frowned over his face mask. "A warning if anyone is squeamish."

"I'm sure everyone here has seen a gunshot wound before." Wolfe frowned. "Where are the other victims? The ones from Broken Bridge and the shooting yesterday?"

"They're not here." The orderly shrugged. "I don't know."

"Do you have an undertaker in town?" Wolfe raised an eyebrow. "Or some place that has refrigeration for remains?"

"We have a mortician, right here on Main." The orderly frowned. "There's a meat-processing plant that has a cold room. When we had a mine accident some years back, they took the bodies there." He shrugged. "Sheriff Bowman here or Sheriff Weston out of Broken Bridge will know."

"Thank you. Please wait outside. I'll call you if I require assistance." Wolfe waited for him to leave and then slowly removed the sheet. He did a very cursory examination and frowned. "I'll need to take her back to my office. There's so much evidence here and this hospital won't have the equipment I need to record it."

Beth scanned the body, taking in the injuries, ligature marks, and bruising. "What can you give us?"

"The gunshot wound is the death blow, almost an afterthought, but this girl has been beaten and sexually assaulted." Wolfe covered the body with reverence. "Heaven knows what happened to her, but I'll find out. I'll have the body prepped and ready for transport. I need to see the crime scene, and as another incident occurred close by yesterday, I'll need to see that first." He looked at Styles. "Can you get me the coordinates of Thursday's robbery? The one that goes with this crime?" He thought for a beat. "We'll need transport to and from the local crime scene as well. Contact the Roaring Creek sheriff to organize something, same with the sheriff out of Broken Bridge. See if you can find out what happened to the other victims in both cases. If they're not here, where the heck are they?"

"I'm on it." Styles nodded and left the room. "We'll need to speak to the first-on-scene responders as well."

"Good." Wolfe removed his gloves and tossed them into the trash. "I'll speak to the physician and make arrangements for the transport of the remains. I'll swing back this way after we've processed the crime scenes and collect the body." He looked at Beth. "Can you make arrangements for the assumed mother to come here for a DNA swab?"

Beth nodded. "She should be on her way. We'll meet you at the front desk." She hurried outside and met Styles in the hallway.

"Wow!" Styles walked beside her. "Wolfe doesn't waste any time, does he?"

Wolfe had impressed Beth too. She pressed the button for the elevator. "With his caseload, I'm not surprised."

SIX

Mischief, Montana

I like my job and being able to do just about anything I want is a powerful drug. They say that power corrupts people, but I'm not corrupt. I'm living the dream. I see guys walking along the sidewalk, mouths turned down, or sitting drinking alone in bars because they can't get a woman. Those men are fools. I can get any woman I want. I can take another man's wife, daughter, or sister, and no one stands in my way. I just drive around and when a ripe fruit appears on the vine, I pluck it for my pleasure.

I have no fear of the law. They'll never touch me. You see, I blend into society without a crease, and when I indulge my desire to take a woman, it doesn't make a ripple on the water of my pond. In this world, people rely on each other to make things happen. Laws can't be passed by one man and the milk doesn't get to thousands of breakfast tables by one man—right? The thing is, it only takes one man to prevent a chain of events happening.

I'm the broken cog in a wheel. The black hole of information. This is why I can take my time and indulge my desires with any woman I choose... or girl, for that matter. The age isn't a factor for me. It's the look in their eyes when they know I'm killing them.

SEVEN

Roaring Creek

After discovering the Roaring Creek Sheriff's Department was a stone's throw from the hospital entrance, Styles left Beth chasing down Mrs. Carson for a DNA swab and headed down to meet Sheriff Bowman. The office was large, with a receptionist who introduced herself as Sharifa Hagstrom and offered him coffee while he waited for the sheriff. After five minutes or so, a haggard, fifty-plus, gray-haired man, carrying far too much weight to be able to run and apprehend a criminal, waved him into his office. Styles held out his cred pack. "I'm Agent Dax Styles from the Rattlesnake Creek field office. As you're aware, the convenience store killer has spread himself out across three or four counties, and we've been called in to take over the investigation. I believe your store was hit the second time in six months? Have you made any headway with the case?"

"Can't say that I have." Bowman waved him into a chair and sank with a sigh into a large padded chair behind the desk. "No witnesses, no evidence, and another girl missing. I've had my deputies driving all along the highways searching for a body since sunup. We're assuming from the other incidents she is dead by now. He doesn't keep them for more than one night."

Styles nodded and placed the cup of coffee on the table. "I have the files but there isn't anything to go on at all. For instance, the same crime happened six months ago. It's obviously a homicide. Why wasn't the state medical examiner notified? If there was evidence, it's lost forever now." He gave Bowman a long hard stare. "For instance, where are the bodies of the victims from yesterday's shootings?"

"They are at the undertakers. He's preparing them for burial." Bowman's forehead creased into a frown. "Our local doctor examined the bodies, pronounced them dead, and gave their cause of death as gunshot wounds."

Horrified at the thought of the victims already being embalmed, Styles gaped at him. "Call the undertaker and make sure he stops any preparation. Did the doctor at least remove the bullets for identification?"

"I believe so." Bowman wiped a hand down his face. "I've been busy concentrating on finding the girl."

Nodding, Styles took out his notebook and pen. "I'll need the doctor's name and details. Also the names of the first on scene and their contact details. How far away is the crime scene?"

"A mile or so from here." Bowman raised both eyebrows.

Thinking for a beat about the time needed to complete everything over such a wide area, Styles blew out a breath. "The medical examiner will need transport for his team and myself and Agent Katz to the crime scene, the undertakers, and then back to the hospital. Five of us in total. How far is it to Broken Bridge from here by road?"

"Maybe half an hour, forty-five minutes." Bowman gave him the details and then looked at him with unfocused eyes. "How did you get here?"

Styles made notes and then looked at him. "We have a

chopper. We'll fly to Broken Bridge. Is there a place close by to the convenience store large enough to land two choppers?"

"Yeah, there's a park opposite." Bowman sighed. "Do you want me to call Sheriff Weston to meet you there? He can arrange transport if you need to move around Broken Bridge." He sighed again. "I'll call in one of my deputies, and between us, we'll be able to give you a ride where you need to go."

"That would be good. We'll meet up outside the hospital." Styles looked up from his notes. "Give me Sheriff Weston's number. I need to know what happened to the bodies from the shooting last Friday and who was first on scene."

The sheriff gave details, excused himself, and made a call. Styles listened as he explained the situation to Weston. Once he'd disconnected, he stood sliding his chair back on its wheels. Styles folded his notebook and slid it inside his pocket. "Has he still got the bodies?"

"He has." Sheriff Bowman rubbed his chin. "He sealed the crime scene and the bodies are on ice in the spare cooler at the meat-processing plant. It's never used, apart from disasters. It's old and not up to the hygiene standards for human consumption, so was perfect for the victims while they work out the identities." He sighed. "He'll meet you at the park with transport for five people."

Styles nodded. "Who called in the shooting?"

"The first on scene in the Roaring Creek case was a guy delivering newspapers. He didn't enter the premises." Bowman shook his head slowly. "I was on scene directly after. I'd received a 911 call about Cassidy going missing moments before."

Considering the evidence to date, Styles ran the case through his mind. "Do you have a copy of the footage of the murder from the CCTV camera inside the convenience store?"

"Yeah, I checked back over the previous few days as well, to see if anyone in particular frequented the store, but the people dropping by were random. A ton of teenage kids go back and forth running errands at all hours, for their folks, I guess." He heaved a sigh. "The missing girl, Cassidy Wilder, dropped by frequently, most times between nine and ten at night. Both her parents work late, so maybe they're the forgetful types and need supplies. She usually buys milk, bread, and things like that."

That made her an easy target. Styles looked at him. "How did she get to the store?"

"She walked." Bowman sighed. "Her home isn't far, maybe five hundred yards or so from the store."

Nodding, Styles held out his phone. "Send the CCTV camera files to this number." He waited for Bowman to comply. "Thanks."

Standing, Styles pushed down his Stetson. "I'll head back to the hospital. Can you arrange transport ASAP? We'll need to process both crime scenes this afternoon and examine the victims' remains. It's gonna be a long day." He headed for the door and, as he walked past the counter, tipped his hat to Sharifa Hagstrom.

Back at the hospital, Styles found Beth feeding coins into a coffee machine. He shuddered. "You must be desperate to drink hospital coffee."

"Yeah, well, after dealing with a hysterical mother, I needed something." Beth raised both eyebrows. "Find out anything interesting?"

Styles explained and watched the horrified expression cross her face. "Yeah, I figured Bowman would have more sense. Two mass murders and abductions within six months and he didn't call for assistance and then he sends the bodies to be embalmed. We're lucky the killer dumped the girl's body on the county line, or she'd be six feet under by now." He plucked the cup from her hand and tossed it into the trash. "There's a diner about fifty yards from here." He went to the counter. "Can you tell the medical examiner we've gone to the diner for coffee? He'll be along shortly."

"Sure." The receptionist looked up from her computer.

Waving his hand toward the door, he followed Beth outside. "From what I've heard, there's a good chance that they'll find Cassidy Wilder's body dumped on the side of the road in the next twenty-four hours. We need to be on scene when that happens. I figure we find a place to hole up for the night or however long this takes and wait. I'll need to go home and get Bear and I figure you'll want a change of clothes."

"Yeah, after dealing with dead bodies and crime scenes all day, I'll need to scrub myself clean." Beth pushed open the door to the diner. "I'll order coffee to go for everyone and ask where there's a decent motel. Preferably near somewhere we can park the chopper."

As he waited, Styles scrolled through the case files and shook his head at the lack of evidence. He searched the files and found a list of personal effects from the abducted girls, and they were all the same. The killer had taken their panties. These shootings were connected and by someone who knew the three counties like the back of his hand and could move through them practically unseen.

EIGHT

The convenience store in Roaring Creek was situated near the corner of Main and Riverside and set between the local library and an empty building. Beth climbed from the front seat of Sheriff Bowman's vehicle and scanned both ways. "So which way is Cassidy Wilder's home?"

"The end of Riverside." Bowman pointed along Riverside and shook his head. "This has always been a secure town. Sending a kid to the local store was safe. Now that enjoyable part of small-town life is over."

Riverside ran straight for as far as the eye could see. It was a rural mining town. Houses sat in clusters of threes and fours along the sidewalk. She noticed the streetlights were few and far between. It would have been dark at nine at night, and deep shadows would have covered the sidewalk. Chills crept up Beth's spine. In a town stalked by a serial killer, it would have been like running the gauntlet. She turned to look at the convenience store. They waited for Sheriff Bowman to open the entrance with keys. They pulled on booties, gloves, and masks before entering and plastered themselves along one wall to avoid the blood spatter. The smell inside the confined space was abhorrent. The metallic smell of congealing blood and putrid human waste permeated Beth's face mask. Before heading for the convenience store, they'd all viewed the CCTV footage of the murder and waited for Wolfe to forensically process the crime.

Beth could clearly picture the shootings in her head. The elements of the crime scene had been left in situ, with bullet casings spread out all over the floor but none of the usual paraphernalia seen in a crime scene. All the victims had been pronounced dead at the scene and taken away in body bags, so the usual discarded bandages and gloves were missing. It surprised her to see the care the paramedics had taken to preserve the crime scene before removing the bodies. It was obvious from the few footprints that they'd been wearing booties. Only one set of distinctive footprints went from the chalk outline of a fallen man to the front door. After viewing the CCTV footage, Beth identified the prints as belonging to Cassidy Wilder. In the footage, the girl had tried to avoid the blood spatter, but one side of her shoe had left a distinct footprint.

One thing Beth noticed was there were no bills on the floor. Often during a robbery, the person behind the counter would drop bills in their hurry to comply. From the audio attached to the footage, the perpetrator appeared to be cool, calm, and collected. She had seen many robberies in her time, and the perpetrator was usually agitated and out of control. Most would know they were under surveillance, and the need to get in and out as fast as possible would be paramount. This man was on a mission. He was way too relaxed. It was obvious to Beth that he'd planned the holdup to the second. She found it hard to believe that he'd entered the convenience store to rob it. No, this man's thrill came from the killing. His disguise was perfect and the people so terrified that any chance of him being identified would be remote, and yet he

gunned them down without mercy. The money meant
nothing to him.

"With all the witnesses dead, why did he take the girl?"
Styles moved to her side. "And why does he leave a scratch
game with each of his victims?"

It was easy for Beth to climb inside the killer's mind. She
understood his reasoning, but to divulge it at this point would
make her look suspicious. Although she'd admitted to studying
psychopaths, what she knew about this particular killer wasn't
in any books. She waited for Wolfe to stop speaking to his team
and then turned to Styles. "I'm looking at the other evidence at
this crime scene." She gave him her thoughts on the perpetrator.

"Yeah, well, I agree he appears to be calm and controlled
during the robbery, but then he's done this a few times before.
'Walk into a place like you own it' works for him. He controls
the room in an instant." Styles pulled out his phone and
reviewed the footage again. He scratched his head. "Although
he doesn't seem too interested in the money. In all the holdups
I've seen previously, the robber's attention is always on the cash,
so much so people often manage to escape the building. He's
not watching the clerk behind the counter at all. His attention is
fully on the people in the store. It's as if he's deciding which one
to kill first."

Nodding, Beth looked over his shoulder as the footage
played on his phone. "Yeah, that guy behind the counter could
have had a gun for all he knew, but he wasn't worried." She
needed to give Styles a glimpse of the workings of this particular
psychopath's mind. "This scenario reminds me of something."
She paused a beat as if thinking. "Have you ever seen a cat
watching a mousehole? They sit there watching and if a mouse
makes a single move, they pounce. If the mouse doesn't move
and remains frozen, the cat will lose interest." She raised both
eyebrows and smiled at him behind her mask. "Watch him. He
doesn't shoot unless they move. The only exception is the

woman coming from the back room. At this point, he doesn't know if she's armed, so he takes her down. He pauses just long enough to get the reaction from her son and then pulls the trigger."

"Ah, so you're saying he's giving them a reason to kill them?" Styles frowned. "Yeah, I remember Jo Wells mentioning something about psychopaths needing their victims to give them a reason to kill them, or to blame them for killing them." He gave her a long look, and she could almost see the wheels turning in his head. "He didn't come here to rob the place, did he? He came here to murder people. Oh, what did Jo call this type of killer?"

Bingo. "Opportunistic." Beth shrugged. "I'm open to suggestions, but I'm not sure if this description of the killer fits the crime."

"How so?" Styles cleared his throat.

She sighed. "I figure you're correct about him not coming here to rob the place, but he's too calm and collected to have picked this place at random. He's been here before six months previously, but the store has been remodeled and he wouldn't know the new layout unless he'd been here. The sheriff said that Cassidy Wilder frequented the store many times a week. If she was his ultimate target, maybe he's covering up the fact by robbing the store? For all we know, he could have been stalking her for weeks."

"You've nailed it, Beth." Styles eyes sparked over his mask. "He's trying to outsmart us by disguising his real motive. Ingenious. These serial killers never fail to impress me with their devious minds." He shook his head slowly. "No wonder so many of them get away with murder. It's impossible to work out their next move. I don't know how you do it."

Swallowing hard, Beth avoided his gaze. "I have an analytical mind. I just look at the facts, is all, and try and come up with a solution."

"I'm done here." Wolfe moved to their location. "I'll be asking the sheriff to conserve the crime scene for a little longer, just in case we need to come back." He indicated with his thumb over one shoulder. "From the trajectory of the bullets, the shooter remained in the same position as we viewed on the footage. We see his hand moving, but not his body. There were no missed shots, even when he aimed between the counters, he hit the man directly in the chest. The woman who came from the back room surprised him, and yet his head shot was absolutely textbook. From my observation, when he shot multiple times the woman running for the door, it was either because she annoyed him or he enjoyed it. From what I've seen on the footage, the shots were well placed and far apart. He could have finished her quickly with one headshot but took his time, inflicting as much pain as possible. I'm sure these findings will be proved during the examinations of the victims."

"So we're dealing with a man who knows how to shoot." Styles sighed and followed Beth out the door. "In Montana, we might as well pull in every man walking past at any one given time."

NINE

After leading the way from the crime scene, Beth walked toward the waiting vehicles. She looked at Sheriff Bowman. "Next stop, the mortician. Did you call and tell him not to touch the bodies?"

"Yeah, he had a corpse to prepare for a funeral in the morning, so you're in luck." Bowman swung into his truck and waited for her and Styles to climb in along with Wolfe.

"Did you speak to the doctor at the hospital who issued the death certificate for Arizona Carson?" Styles turned to Wolfe.

"Yeah, I explained in detail the ramifications of issuing a document without proof of identity." Wolfe shook his head. "I figure she got the message." He sighed. "The body will be ready for transporting by the time we're through with the crime scenes and victims. If they're all open-and-shut cases of gunshot murders, I'll collect evidence and sign off on them to give their families closure."

"The missing girl will be crucial to the investigation." Styles removed his Stetson and smoothed his hair. "There are deputies in both counties searching the highways for signs of her. The locals are searching their outbuildings and looking out for signs she might be lying dead somewhere."

"That's the best we can do." Sheriff Bowman looked in his mirror at Styles and Wolfe. "We don't have the resources to search the entire county. We're doing the best we can with what we have."

Beth turned in her seat to look at him as they stopped in front of the local undertaker's. "When we're done here today, we'll be heading back to our office, but we'll be back. We're staying in town until Cassidy Wilder shows." She met his glance. "I'm told the motel on Bison is okay and has a decent restaurant."

"It's popular with the miners who come into town to let off steam. That can be anytime. They work odd shifts." Bowman shrugged. "They expect good food, and you shouldn't be disturbed during the week, but weekends can get rowdy."

"We're used to miners." Styles barked a laugh and climbed out of the truck.

Keeping the sheriff's attention, Beth met his gaze. "It's fine you giving us a ride, but not practical. Is there anywhere we can rent a vehicle for a couple of days?"

"Yeah, the local gas station has loaners for customers getting work done. They have rentals available." Bowman scratched his cheek. "It's opposite my office. I'll drop you back there if you'll be wanting something for this afternoon."

"Great." Beth pushed open the door and headed after the others.

They followed Sheriff Bowman into the undertaker's and waited for him to make the introductions. As they walked into what the mortician called his "cold room," she stared at the bodies covered in white sheets. The room smelled of formaldehyde and decaying corpses, and she reached in her pocket for a face mask. She gaped in surprise at one of the victims when Wolfe removed a sheet. The man was fully dressed. She looked at Wolfe. "I was led to believe these victims were identified and bullet fragments retrieved from the body."

"So was I." Wolfe pulled a folder from his forensic kit and opened it. "They all have death certificates and I have a list of next of kin who identified the remains." He turned to the mortician. "Did you conduct the identifications of these people?"

"Yes, sir, I did indeed." The mortician opened a drawer in a filing cabinet and took out four large plastic bags, labeled and sealed. "These are the personal effects. I contacted the next of kin and they came down and identified the bodies. The head-shot victim had a distinctive birthmark on her neck. The others I managed to make presentable for viewing this morning. Dr. Bligh came by and issued the death certificates. He did a cursory examination, but the paramedics had already given an approximate time of death in their report."

"I'll need the use of your preparation room." Wolfe removed his coat and shook his head. "I want to examine each body and remove the bullets." He looked at his daughter Emily. "You'll be assisting me. Webber, collect what we require and then help us to remove the clothes."

"I can help with that." Styles pulled gloves from a box on the counter. He turned to the mortician. "We'll need bags for the clothes and your assistance. Hurry now, we have another crime scene to process out at Broken Bridge before nightfall."

"Yes, of course. I have three rooms available that you can use." The mortician pulled on gloves and went to the first victim. "I'm happy to assist."

Beth took charge of the garments. Matching each set of clothes with the correct personal effects and attaching labels. As Wolfe wheeled the first victim into the preparation room, she went to his side. "I can assist you if it will leave Emily free to work on one of the other victims."

"I'll be examining all the victims first and she is more than qualified to remove the bullets, and that will save time." Wolfe's eyes brightened above his mask. "I would welcome your assistance. I'll record my findings." He took out a recording device and set it on the counter.

It amazed her how Wolfe's team moved like a well-oiled machine. Colt Webber had waved his magic wand and a metal dish with instruments laid out was set on the counter, ready for use. Small containers for the bullets and various-size evidence bags sat on the counter too, complete with a pen for the labeling. Beth pulled on gloves and then gave him a nod. "I'm ready." She turned on the recorder.

"Victim one is a man in his late forties, heavy build. He has been identified as George Pittman." Wolfe made an incision on each side of the gunshot wound. He inserted his fingers and felt around and then looked up at Beth. "This man suffered a gunshot wound to the sternum. The projectile fractured the sternum and entered the heart. Death would have been immediate. Cause of death: gunshot wound to the chest. Time of death: as noted by the paramedics." He stripped off his gloves and stopped the recording. "We'll head to the next room." He led the way outside. "Emily, take Webber and remove the bullet fragments from the first victim. When you're done, follow me and do the same to the others." He looked at the mortician. "Once Emily is finished, you can start to prepare the bodies for burial."

Fascinated by the way Wolfe worked, Beth moved with him from victim to victim, offering what assistance she could and listening with interest to his commentary. He moved swiftly and removed the bullets from the last victim himself to save time. Beth collected the bullet fragments as they removed them from the body, placing each in a container and then labeling them. Once they'd finished, she collected all the evidence bags and stored them in a container. It had taken two hours from start to finish. The bodies would be laid to rest, but she still needed to hunt down their killer.

A short time later, they were in the choppers and flying to Broken Bridge. It wasn't a long journey, but the scenery was spectacular, taking them above snowcapped mountain peaks. As the mining town of Broken Bridge came into view, blue and red wigwag lights could be seen in the distance. "That must be the park." She pointed ahead. "It looks like they're expecting us."

The chopper descended and Styles put it down in a large parkland area. Beth looked around and spotted a diner on the opposite sidewalk. "Hungry?"

"Starving." Styles smiled at her. He pointed into the distance. "Wolfe is on our tail. We'll wait for him to land and see if he wants to take a break."

Beth nodded. "Sure. I like Wolfe. He is so respectful toward the dead. He doesn't just lay them bare. He preserves their dignity. He really cares and that's good to know. It's not just a job to him." She sighed. "I've been to many autopsies in my lifetime, and I've never seen anyone work as fast as he does. He's very thorough too. I doubt he ever misses a thing."

"He's at the top of his game, that's for darn sure." Styles stretched and yawned. "It's just as well we have a professional on hand. Mistakes with serial killers cost lives."

Beth tidied her windswept hair, pulling it back into a low ponytail at the nape of her neck. "That happens too often, and they get away with murder for years or forever. I believe the serial killers we hear about are only the tip of a very deep iceberg." She gave him a long look, gauging his reaction. She really wished she could tell him about her dark side. Would he understand her need to seek justice or would he drag her off to jail? "Thousands of missing people vanish each year... each year, Styles. Where do you think they are and what's happened to them? We know some people disappear intentionally for many different reasons, but not kids. It has to be serial killers.

I'm convinced they're responsible for the majority of missing persons."

"Trust me, I know." Styles wearily ran a hand down his face. "My sister went missing. I was out playing with her and ran away. I never saw her again. She was abducted and although a search went on for weeks, they never found her." He blew out a long breath. "I've always blamed myself. If I hadn't run away, she'd be safe. Her going missing set up a string of chaotic events in my life."

Surprised Styles had divulged such a private part of his life, she squeezed his arm. Right now, he needed compassion and support. "You should feel differently about this now, after working with serial killers. Someone could have been stalking her for weeks and you were lucky to get away with your life. Often those who hunt for little girls don't have too much time for little boys. You'd have become a victim immediately. You know that, don't you?"

"Yeah, it has crossed my mind." He shook his head slowly. "So has what might have happened to her. As we've never found a body, she could have been kept by someone for many years. It's not knowing what happened to her that eats me away."

Beth considered the ramifications of helping him solve the case. Setting aside her expertise in cybercrime, she also had many skills she hadn't divulged to the FBI. She'd established a good relationship with Styles. She trusted him to have her back and owed him for turning a blind eye to her eccentricities. Many in his position would have reported her to the director of the FBI for assessment. At this point in time, it was a "you scratch my back and I'll scratch yours" situation. She took a deep breath. "If somebody kept her, there's a chance they became attached to her. You do understand that children who are taken away from their parents and told their parents are dead or whatever often become attached to their abductor. You've heard of Stockholm syndrome?"

"Sure." Styles' brow furrowed. "It's been decades. She'd have looked for me if she'd been alive. We were very close."

Shaking her head, Beth looked at his sad expression. He carried a huge burden. "Not if she believed you were dead." She sighed. "They wouldn't be able to hide her forever. They'd have found a way to make her belong to them—false birth certificate or whatever. It's not that difficult to obtain fake documents. Do you want me to look for her?"

"So how, after all these years, would you be able to find her when no one else has found even a trace?" Styles gave an agitated roll of his shoulders. "You're good, I know this, but after so long any leads would have dried up."

Thinking it through, Beth shrugged. "I don't know if I'll get a result until I try. First up, I'll need a photograph of her. I'll run it through some software I've developed over the years and see what shows. If we don't get a hit with an image or by running your DNA for a sibling comparison, you'll know she likely died the day she was abducted. You know as well as I do that murder victims are sometimes never found. The thing is, Styles, is this something you want to lay to rest? Because if you do, I'll break my butt getting you answers." She met his gaze. "Can you handle the truth? It might be hard to accept."

"Let me think on it for a time." Styles smiled at her and sighed. "I do need to move on and what you said about me becoming a victim is valid. I've never looked at it that way before and about her being stalked. Yeah, that's possible. I recall her mentioning something about being followed home by a man. She told my mom, who waited at the bus stop for us each night and walked us home."

The sound of a chopper filled the air and the ME's chopper dropped down into the park. Beth looked at Styles. "Time to go."

TEN

Distracted, Styles mulled over what Beth had said and didn't notice the angry crowd gathering on the opposite side of the park. His mind snapped back to the now the moment Wolfe's raised voice pierced his thoughts. He scanned the milling crowd opposite and immediately stepped in front of Beth and Emily.

"Now what are y'all doing here?" Wolfe marched across Main as if he owned it. "Can't you see we're trying to conduct an investigation?" He stared down the crowd. "Have y'all lost your minds?"

"We want action." One man in a brown Stetson, with his mouth turned down, stepped out front as a spokesperson. "People are being murdered all over, girls kidnapped, and nobody is doing anything."

"Why do you figure we're here?" Beth stepped out from behind Styles, head held high, and walked across Main and right up to the angry man. "You have the state medical examiner and the FBI, what more do you want? Unless you've witnessed the murders, return to your homes and allow us to do our work."

"You ain't doing enough or Arizona wouldn't be lying in the morgue out at Roaring Creek General." A young man in the crowd stepped forward and shoved Beth to one side. "Maybe we need to take the law into our own hands." He raised a fist in front of Beth's face.

"Don't do anything you'll regret." Beth had grabbed the man's hand and savagely bent the wrist back. "Laying hands on a Federal officer is an offense. Maybe I need to hand you over to Sheriff Weston for some jail time?"

The young man whimpered in pain, but Beth held her ground.

"Let go, this is police brutality." The young man pulled hard to break Beth's grip and then his other hand balled into a fist.

Seeing a potential disaster about to unfold, Styles stepped to Beth's side. Not wanting to be seen rushing in to protect her, he stood a pace behind her and stared down the young man. "I wouldn't do that. You wouldn't like to see her angry."

"No, you wouldn't." Beth gave the young man a lazy smile. "I fight real dirty."

Styles stared at the hostile crowd and lifted his cred pack to show them. "Agent Katz instructed you to disperse. I suggest you comply, or we'll be taking names for obstruction of justice. We've only just arrived and the longer you hold us up, the longer it will take to conduct our investigation." He gave Beth a look, which he hoped calmed the wildness in her eyes.

Anyone who challenged or threatened her released the beast. Once cornered, she was unpredictable. He figured it went back to her horrific time spent in foster care, not PTSD but the will to survive. As the months passed by, his understanding of her sometimes bizarre behavior and mood swings had solidified. He'd coped with a very unstable wife and had sought to work out their problems without success, but Beth he could help. She'd been coping alone for way too long and fighting her demons. A serial killer for a father and being tossed from one abusive foster home to another had left deep scars, but he'd gotten to know the person underneath the façade she'd built around her for protection. In the chopper she'd shown compassion for his problems and offered him a way to redemption. He owed her the same.

"Go home." Beth dropped the young man's hand. "You get only one chance. Impede our investigation again and I'll send you to jail." She stood hands balled on her hips and stared down the crowd.

"If we get any clues about who is responsible for these crimes, the sheriff will let y'all know in a media release." Wolfe scanned the crowd. "We don't have time for this stupidity."

Styles stood beside Beth with Wolfe on the other side like a wall of justice. The men's eyes flicked from one to another, and the spokesperson nodded and turned away. Blowing out a long breath, Styles waved at Emily and Colt Webber, who had one hand resting on the butt of his weapon, across the road. He looked at Beth. "I guess we can eat now?"

"I guess so." Beth headed for the diner and marched inside.

Styles pushed two tables together and they all sat down, peering at the menus. "What the heck was that all about?"

"I figure the townsfolk hereabouts are scared." Wolfe leaned back in his chair. "Now that the convenience store over at Roaring Creek has been hit twice, they believe they're not safe."

"It would be hard to go from a no-crime town, apart from some drunk miners, to holdups with violence." Emily's eyes flicked from the menu and then back. "How long have we got to eat?"

"We'll grab a snack and get back to it." Wolfe sighed. "I called ahead and spoke to the local doctor. He's already examined the bodies, collected all the personal effects and bagged them as per procedure, removed the bullet fragments, and arranged for viewings of the next of kin. All have been positively identified by close family members. He is ex-military medical, and I checked him out. He has an outstanding record, so I don't figure we'll have much to do with the bodies. I'll examine them and get copies of the reports, but I imagine they're fine and we'll be able to release the bodies."

Nodding, Styles gave his order to the server and looked at Wolfe. "So we process the crime scene and get the hell out of Dodge?"

"Something like that." Wolfe raised both eyebrows. "You're planning on staying in Roaring Creek?"

"Just until we find Cassidy Wilder." Beth folded her hands on the table. "Going on the other cases, this killer doesn't keep them for more than one night before disposing of their bodies. If she'd been out there wandering around, someone would have spotted her. Two local choppers have been searching all over the county." She looked at Styles. "The mortician told me that his cousin lives hereabouts, and every man and his dog have been searching alongside the highways... as that's the killer's MO for his favorite dumping areas."

"I have the CCTV footage of this shooting." Wolfe pulled out his phone. "I'll send it to y'all. It's much the same as the previous one: he goes to the counter, asks for cash, kills the people in the store, and last, the cashier. He takes the girl. On leaving, an old guy must have been walking by with his dog, and he shoots him as well. I can hear gunshots and we know about the victim and his dog. Same as with the other footage, the CCTV is angled from the front door to the counter. It takes in the aisles but gives us nothing that happened outside." He sighed. "Same as before. No one saw anything."

When Styles' phone chimed a message, he opened the file and viewed the grainy footage. "It's practically useless, but yeah, it looks like the same guy. Why don't people update their equipment? This is useless to identify anyone."

"It's just a deterrent for shoplifters." Beth sipped coffee the server had just delivered and sighed. "They don't know they're not state of the art, do they?"

Styles shrugged. "Nope, but I bet a dollar to a dime that the killer does."

ELEVEN

Once Wolfe had processed the Broken Bridge crime scene, Beth climbed into a truck and they went in a procession of vehicles to the meat-processing plant. The crime scene had been much like the first, apart from the black bloodstain on the sidewalk from the poor man just walking his dog. No clues to the killer's identity, and from the CCTV footage, he was just like before, covered from head to foot and wearing gloves. It surprised her to find the local doctor waiting outside. She stood to one side with Styles as Wolfe and his team examined the bodies. It was freezing inside but the smell wasn't too bad. Wolfe and the local doctor talked together for a time over each body. When he was done, she looked at him expectantly. "Find anything of value?"

"Nope." Wolfe frowned. "It's the same ammo as we discovered. I'll run tests to see if it's from the same gun. There are no wasted shots. All the victims received fatal wounds. I figure, he wanted this one to be fast. One thing you might consider is if someone comes by the store regular around the same time each night. If so, you'll know this killer is stalking his victims, or making sure he hits the stores at a low-customer time."

Impressed, Beth nodded. "We'll look into that. Thanks."

She turned to Styles. "Is there anything else or are we done here?"

"I'm good." Styles rubbed the scar on his chin. "Wolfe has a point. That might prove a motive. If he has been stalking his victims, he's not an opportunistic killer, is he?"

Beth shook her head. "No, and if we can prove that, we'll open up a whole new can of worms."

She led the way outside to where Sheriff Weston leaned against his truck staring at his phone. "Sheriff, we have a job for you. We need you to find out if anyone regularly walked by the convenience store around the time of the murders."

"Yeah, well, I know that already. My deputy was first on scene because he patrols regular between eight and twelve on Friday nights. His report is in the files I gave you. Seeing that we have miners in town, we take turns over the weekends, patrolling from the saloons to the local motel. Some nights it can get a little rowdy and a police presence calms everyone down."

It was as if the planets were falling into alignment. Beth nodded. "Thanks. Can you drive us back to the choppers? Contact us if Cassidy shows up in your county. We'll be staying out at Roaring Creek for a time, but we won't get there until after dark. If anything changes, we'll let you know. Are you okay to leave now?"

"Sure. Not a problem." Sheriff Weston touched the brim of his hat.

They headed back to the chopper and Beth waited until they lifted into the air before she discussed the case. She understood the case and flying the chopper took a toll on Styles. It had been a very long day and it wasn't over yet. "Okay, what have we got so far? The killer plans his kills. As we thought, the cash he steals has nothing to do with his motive." She waited, hoping Styles' insight that she'd come to admire would lead him to the same conclusion as she'd made.

"Nope, he enjoys killing, that's for darn sure. I figure you're right: he's using the robberies as a cover to abduct his victims. It's slick and fast, he leaves no witnesses, and is high on his kills by the time he gets to her. The store kills are his meal, and the girl is the dessert."

TWELVE

Wolf Valley, Mischief

Dark shadows bathed the blacktop as the bus's brakes squealed and came to a stop. The doors whooshed open, and Layla Cooper stepped down into total darkness. She stood for a second as the bus lumbered away in its own pool of light as if sucking the darkness behind it. In this part of town, sidewalks didn't exist and she used the flashlight on her phone to find her way along the blacktop. She had no fear of being hit by a vehicle. At this time of night, most people were safely home in bed. Layla didn't have a choice but to take the bus. Her mom needed the truck for work, and Layla attended Mischief College. She worked at the diner until ten each night and then caught the last bus from town. It was a half-mile walk to the home she shared with her mother. Her father had cleared out years ago after working in the mines most of his life. Determined to finish college and make a life for herself, Layla worked nights and weekends to pay for her tuition. Her mother's nine-to-five job in the general store didn't pay for luxuries, but they got by. When she graduated, hopefully they'd leave this dead-end town and she'd be earning enough money to support them both.

The chilled temperature outside made her wish for the cozy interior of the bus. Although it had that weird smell all buses have, of body odor, smelly feet, bad breath, and sometimes dog, it was better than walking and she wished it traveled another half-mile before turning back to the depot. She hunched her back, watching the road ahead of her in the small pool of light, fully aware of the wildlife that roamed the area at night looking for their supper. A cold wind buffeted her, swirling her coat around her legs, and the branches in the trees alongside the blacktop creaked and whined. It would be easy to get hysterical at this time of night, when owls dropped from the sky and came close enough to pull on her hair. She took a few deep breaths of the cold night air and doggedly placed one foot in front of the other.

The sound of a vehicle surprised her, and she stepped cautiously into the long mud-streaked grass beside the blacktop to allow it to pass. She turned and looked into brilliant blue-white orbs of light. She blinked rapidly, trying to remove the red spots in her eyes. The vehicle slowed and came to a stop beside her. Still dazzled by the light, she peered at the driver. The hairs on the back of her neck prickled as his window buzzed down. Instinctively, she took two steps back and almost fell into the ditch.

"Hey, little lady, mind your step there." The man's arm rested on the frame of the open window and his teeth flashed in the dark interior. "I don't want to fish you out of that ditch. It's muddy and wet."

Layla recognized the vehicle but not the man inside. She shrugged as nonchalantly as possible. "I'm not planning on falling into the ditch anytime soon, but thanks for your concern." She turned to go, moving away at a fast pace, but the vehicle kept right alongside of her.

"You know it's not safe for you to be walking these back-roads at night?" The man hung out the window, smiling at her. "It's my civic duty to take you home to your mom. Get in the vehicle." He smiled. "If you're worried, I might try and jump your bones, ride in the back. I know you girls figure that's all us men are after." He shook his head. "Not me. I'm one of the good guys. You know that, right?"

It was a long walk home and she did recognize him now. She could see him properly. Layla stared at the dark road ahead and then climbed into the back of the vehicle. "I live about half a mile along. The house is down a dirt road on the left. There's a white mailbox at this end of the road."

"Okay." The vehicle drove off and the man hummed to tunes on the radio. "You know that old warehouse down the road aways?"

Frowning, Layla nodded. "Yeah, it's been vacant for years."

"I had a call from someone who said they'd seen my missing dog heading inside." He smiled at her in the rearview mirror. "Mind if I take a look inside?"

Layla bit on her bottom lip. She guessed it was a reasonable request. He hadn't needed to stop and offer her a ride. She'd remain in the vehicle and wait. "Sure. I'm guessing that's why you came out this way."

The vehicle swung into the driveway of the old warehouse, illuminating it in a halo of light. The once pristine concrete slab-built driveway had grass sprouting between its cracks. Gray neglected wooden panels on the sides of the old warehouse hung open to form gaps. Layla peered out of the window. The roof of rusted corrugated sheets flapped in the wind, rattling like the cars of a locomotive running over a bridge. Outside, brush had grown waist high, green tufts of new growth fighting for survival between the dead brown vegetation. The old sliding door was open halfway, the metal wheels at the top of the door so rusted they'd never move again.

The man climbed out and whistled a few times and using his flashlight ducked inside. Moments later, he stuck his head out and beckoned her. Layla just stared at him.

"I can see him. He's caught in some wire. He looks weak. I'll need you to hold the flashlight so I can free him." He turned and said something to the dog.

Reluctantly, Layla left her phone and backpack in the back seat and went to assist him. Inside she peered around, following the arc of his flashlight. She could see nothing. An icy chill shivered down her spine and she took a step backward. "Where's the dog?"

"Just over there." He held out the flashlight. "Here take this. In that corner. Can't you see him?"

It was creepy inside the massive open space, with vines and spiders hanging down all over. Hesitantly she took a few steps inside, moving the flashlight around. "I can't see him."

Something whipped around her neck and tightened. She dropped the flashlight, clawing at her throat. She couldn't breathe and the darkness was spinning around her. She tripped and fell face down on something soft, not a mattress, maybe an exercise rug. Air came back into her lungs for just a second as he flipped her over onto her back. The cord tightened again, and she clawed at her neck, trying to force her fingers under the tightening band. Darkness came again but she clung to the edge of consciousness.

"You're not dying yet, little lady." His breath was hot on her cheek, but his face was shadowed from the lights of the vehicle.

Layla tried to push him away and fight back, but each time he tightened the noose just enough to make the blackness come. The headlights caught his smile just as she blacked out again, waking as her clothes were torn from her body. She gathered all her strength and rolled away, but he thrust her hard on her back and punched her in the face.

"See what happens to silly girls who walk home alone in the

dark at night? Look at me. Yeah, that's right. I want my face reflected in your eyes." He tightened the noose again. "You asked for this, didn't you? What did you think would happen?"

Head throbbing, Layla tried to turn her face away. Pinned under him, there was no escape. She opened her mouth to take another breath and the noose tightened again.

"The thing is, this cord is like a light switch." He grinned down at her. "I can turn your life on and off with it. One second, you think the ordeal is over and I release my grip and there you are again, gasping like a landed fish. Next second, your tongue comes out and your face goes blue."

Arms heavy and weak from lack of oxygen, Layla closed her eyes. She couldn't look into his self-satisfied face any longer. He was enjoying her pain and she just wanted it to be over.

"I said look at me." He yanked her head to face him. "I'm your worst nightmare and you're not gonna miss a thing."

THIRTEEN

TUESDAY

Roaring Creek

Styles woke disorientated. A warm body curled against his back and hot breath brushed his neck, sending goosebumps over his flesh. He groaned inwardly and wiped a hand down his face. He recalled going to the saloon with Beth and the local sheriff to pass the time playing pool. He'd had a few drinks and then what had happened? Replaying the night in his mind swiftly, he couldn't recall meeting anyone interesting enough to take back to the motel. His mind slid to Beth—nah, she wasn't a one-night stand kind of gal. So who? He swallowed hard, trying to remember the faces of the people in the saloon but recalled only Beth, the sheriff, and a couple of deputies. He'd had nights at TJ's Bar and Grill in Rattlesnake Creek when he'd stumbled home, a little worse for wear, but since Beth had arrived he'd walked the line. The director had meant him to be an example to her, and overindulging wasn't part of the bargain, although she had been accepting drinks for wins at pool, and like every other darn thing, she was very good at pool.

A wet tongue licked his ear, followed by a blast of doggy

breath. Relieved, Styles grinned. "Is that you, Bear? What are you doing on my bed?"

The dog barked and pounced on him, licking him all over. He gently pushed him away. "Okay, okay. I'll need to shower and dress and then I'll take you out for a walk. What's the time?" He picked up his watch from the bedside table. It was five after six.

After taking a shower, Styles bundled up in warm clothes, and headed outside. He walked toward a wooded area out back of the motel. Icy wind cut into his cheeks and hurt his lungs with every breath. It was spring and the melt had come earlier than normal, but that meant nothing. Snow could come again just as easily as rain. He stared at the sky. A few clouds gathered on the horizon, but apart from that, it was clear and ice blue. The sapphire color would come as the sun rose higher and bring some much-needed warmth to the day. As Bear sniffed around the trees, the case battered against his mind. He needed to offer some idea of a potential suspect. The man's image had been blasted all over the media, and apart from a few crank calls, nothing of interest had been reported. No one saw a man in a long coat wearing a cowboy hat because just about every man in town wore the same clothes. It was cold in the mountains and balaclavas were favored by many. Finding this guy was becoming a nightmare.

Nothing had come in after extensive searches for Cassidy Wilder. The local highways had been searched using teams of locals, and choppers. They'd found zip. He looked up as footsteps crunched on the gravel to see Beth running toward him, blonde hair flying. She often ran early in the morning and sometimes he went with her. She had stamina most women only dreamed of and he'd pushed her to the limit during their workout sessions. It was as if when she dug deep, she found another reservoir of energy that she could release in a frenzy. She'd knocked him on his butt a few times in the beginning and found it highly amusing, but now he noticed when the change came over her and lifted his game. He smiled as she came toward him. "Morning. Do you recall what time the restaurant here opens? I sure need a cup of strong coffee this morning. I can't drink that powdered stuff they leave in the rooms."

"I have the fixings for coffee in my room." She pushed a rogue strand of hair behind one ear and grinned. "I never leave home without my plunger. Give me five to take a shower."

Styles breathed a sigh of relief and filled the air around him with steam. "Thanks."

They were sitting in Beth's room sipping a steaming hot brew when his phone buzzed. "Agent Styles." He put the call on speaker.

"This is Sheriff Tucker out of River's Edge. One of the locals spotted what he figured is a body not far from the highway. I'm on scene now. It looks like the missing girl from Roaring Creek, Cassidy Wilder. Sheriff Bowman gave me your number."

Shooting a glance at Beth, Styles grimaced. "I'll need the coordinates. Make sure no one, and I mean no one, goes near the body. I'll have the medical examiner there ASAP. It's going to take an hour or so for all of us to get there, so secure the crime scene. We'll be coming by chopper. Is there landing space close by?"

"Yeah. Miles." Tucker cleared his throat. *"I found a casing alongside the highway. I bagged it."* He drew a ragged breath. *"The girl is pretty messed up, beaten and a gunshot wound to the back of the head, same as the others."*

A murder scene was overwhelming and it broke many. He sighed. In fact, he wished he didn't have to go and see the body either. "I'm sorry you had to see that but it's all part of the job, isn't it?"

"Yeah, I guess so." Tucker blew out a long breath. *"I'll send you those coordinates now."* He disconnected.

Moments later the message arrived with the details. He forwarded them to Beth and Wolfe. "I'll go and do a preflight check on the chopper. I'm glad we found a place to refuel before we left last night."

"I'll contact Wolfe." Beth gave him a long look. "You need to eat. You look exhausted." She frowned. "Do you often binge drink like that?"

Styles drained his coffee cup, wishing it were ten gallons, and carefully shook his head. "Nope, not since the problems with my ex. I kinda went with the flow last night but I didn't overindulge to that extent. I stopped at ten, just like you... well, I think I did." He shrugged. "You didn't do so bad yourself."

"That's because I poured most of my drinks into the planter. Not yours, by the way. I do have some ethics." Beth chuckled. "Do you have a hangover? I have Tylenol."

He shook his head. "Nope, I'm good, but you're right, I do need to eat. I'll meet you in the restaurant in fifteen minutes. Order for me. It will save time. Oh..." He stood and handed her his room key. "Can you feed Bear for me?"

"Sure." Beth stroked the dog's head, in its usual place resting on her thigh. "Wolfe, Bear, restaurant. Got it."

Styles pulled on his jacket and gloves and headed to the chopper. It was strange not having Bear by his side, but part of him was happy his dog trusted his partner, and apart from him, Bear trusted nobody.

FOURTEEN

Running at dawn in freezing temperatures wasn't Beth's idea of fun but she needed the bite of the cold air in her lungs to keep her dark side at bay. After spending a backslapping, noisy evening with the boys in the local saloon, she'd returned to the motel and chased down the case in Mischief. The more she read the case files, the angrier she became. All the normal protocol parameters had been ignored. There were no first-on-scene reports, witnesses, or a basic timeline of events. In each case, the crime scene had been recorded with only two or three photographs. The medical examination of the bodies had been sketchy. She could hardly describe them as autopsies. The temperature of the bodies hadn't been taken on retrieval and the time of death estimated between the time the girls went missing and when their bodies were found. As there hadn't been many murders in Mischief over the years, she might put this down to the sheriff's lack of experience, but after scanning the files from the basic crimes that had occurred over the last few years, it seemed that the stealing of a horse or cow was more important than the murder of a young woman. The case reeked of interference. Someone high up in the food chain was leaning on the sheriff to prevent them from revealing the killer. Perhaps the killer was one of the local councilman's sons?

Running both hands through her hair, Beth sighed and sipped the coffee the server had brought her the moment she'd sat down. Covering up crimes of the rich and powerful wasn't new, but it made those responsible as guilty as the perpetrator. Beth might well be a serial killer, but she'd never been corrupt. She followed a set of rules and stuck to them. The people she took down must be untouchable by law enforcement or have evaded justice. She must witness a crime or kill the perpetrator to prevent one happening before her eyes. Some might say her choice to put herself in the role of victim was irresponsible, but FBI agents and others went undercover all the time and put themselves in life-threatening situations. Her job was highly dangerous on a daily basis. Putting her body on the line for justice and killing in self-defense was something she could live with, and it made her different from all the rest of her kind.

She had no choice but to wait until the killer the media was now referring to as the Night Creeper, struck again in Mischief. The murder would come through the office as it was local, and she'd mention it to Styles and try and convince him that they needed to ask Wolfe to look at the body for similarities between cases. It was her only hope to walk into the rat's nest, and lay baits to catch the killer. It had to be someone close to the investigation, either omitting or ignoring reports. She'd find him and the last person he'd see would be the Tarot Killer.

Dragged from her thoughts, she looked up from her laptop when the bell over the door to the restaurant tinkled and Styles blew in on a blast of freezing air. The room was empty. The round wooden tables, each with a menu, sat waiting for customers. She figured most people made their way to breakfast later or ordered room service, because there were vehicles outside the other rooms. She closed her laptop and waited for

Styles to remove his coat, scarf, and gloves before he sat down. "Are we ready to go? Is the weather okay?"

"Yeah, it's all good." Styles looked at the menu. "What did you order?"

Beth tapped her finger on the menu. "The Miner's Special. Sausage, eggs, breakfast potatoes, mushrooms, and grilled tomatoes." She raised both eyebrows. "Orange juice and a gallon of coffee."

"Perfect." Styles yawned violently and covered his mouth. "Oh, sorry. Even the cold hasn't lifted the cobwebs yet. I feel like I was drugged last night. How did we get back here?"

Raising an eyebrow, Beth stared at him. "We walked. Maybe you were more exhausted than you imagined. Add alcohol and the body just shuts down. I suggest an early night tonight. I figure once we've processed the crime scene and Wolfe has taken the body, we need to head home. I have the facial-recognition software running and it may have identified someone by now." She shrugged. "If it offers us a few suggestions, we can make a list of potential suspects, and it will give us a starting point."

"I've been thinking too." Styles looked away to smile at the server who poured his coffee. "Leave the pot and keep it coming, please."

"Hard night, huh?" The server puffed up her hair and gave him a wink before turning away.

"Do I look that bad?" Styles removed his hat, dropped it on the seat beside him, and ran both hands through his hair.

Beth blew out a breath and shook her head slowly. "No. She was probably thinking how good you looked. Now, can we forget about her and talk about what you'd been thinking about the case, Styles? You do recall the murders we're investigating, right?"

"I recall them just fine." Styles' eyes twinkled with amusement. "So you think I look good, huh?"

Annoyed, Beth leaned forward and gave him her dark-side glare. "The case?"

"Oh, here comes the bad cop." Styles held up his hands in surrender. "Sure, sure. I do listen to everything you say and what you've said before about serial killers having a comfort zone. I figure he lives right here in town. This is his central position and the communities around here are his comfort zone. I gave it a lot of thought this morning, considering who would naturally move between towns in this county. Like, what do they all have in common?"

Nodding, Beth considered the question as the server returned with the huge meals. "Well, they're all mining towns. They all have saloons, stores, and the like."

"Yeah, but Roaring Creek is the main hub and forms the main supply chain, right?" Styles cut into a sausage, chewed, and sighed. "So if our guy moves between the towns frequently, he wouldn't be noticed, he'd be part of the scenery."

Thinking it through, Beth sipped her coffee. "Yeah, the mining camps would need a constant supply of everything. Then there's the mail, newspapers, milk, etcetera. I figure the bakery in Roaring Creek supplies most of the county. It's huge. I noticed it when we flew in. It has its name on the roof."

"Exactly, so maybe we need to start by hunting down people who run deliveries to convenience stores." Styles waved his fork at her and then continued to eat.

Nodding, Beth ate slowly. She never rushed her food. "Yeah, that would give him the layout of each store, the positions of the cameras, if any. Then if he's in and out of there frequently, any DNA he accidentally left behind would be covered by his usual visits."

"Trying to discover which place he plans to hit next will be a problem. He might expand his circle. Mischief is a massive county, with many small mining communities all over."

Agreeing, Beth smiled at him. "That's going to be difficult, but we'll try and think like he does and work it out. We'll need a watchlist of suspects and to find out where they go and when. We can interview them and work it out or maybe it's time for me to go undercover again? It would mean staying in the town for a few days, and hoping I get his attention as a possible target."

"The problem with that idea is that he kills all the witnesses and then abducts the woman. You'd need to take him down before he gets off his first shot. I know you're darn good, but in a volatile situation like that, anything could happen." Styles shook his head. "There's no way I'm risking lives to take down this guy. We do this one by the book. Right?"

She smiled at him. "Your book or my book?"

FIFTEEN

River's Edge

Wolfe circled the crime scene in a wide perimeter before dropping it down into scrubland not far from the FBI chopper. The entire area looked remote, with only a small patch of woods at the northern end of the field. The soil had been plowed recently but the closest ranch house he'd noticed was over a mile away. Opposite the field, the mountain range rose up dark against the morning sky. The body was situated about ten to twelve yards from the highway. Face down with arms and legs spread out, the young woman carried a backpack. Had she run away to escape or had her killer wanted her to run so he could use her for target practice? In his time as medical examiner, he'd seen many examples of the latter.

Agents Katz and Styles had secured the area and stood on the blacktop as Styles recorded the scene using his phone camera. He motioned his assistant, Colt Webber, to follow him, and after collecting his forensic kit from the chopper, walked over to them. "What have we got? Is she presumably the missing woman from the Roaring Creek convenience store?"

"It's hard to tell." Styles met his gaze. "She has a gunshot wound to the back of the head that exited through her face. The clothes she is wearing are the same as in the CCTV footage." He pointed to an area marked with chalk. "Here is where the sheriff found the bullet casing. Just the one. No footprints. This guy is super slick. He didn't as much as place the tip of his boot into the dirt."

Wolfe turned to Webber. "Record the scene. Take note of any footprints along the way." He turned to Styles. "First on scene?"

"A local but he observed only from his vehicle at sunup." Styles waved toward the cruiser parked alongside the highway. "Sheriff Tucker was first on scene at six this morning. Tucker walked out, checked it was a body, and walked back. He called Sheriff Bowman, who gave him my number. We came and secured the scene. To preserve evidence, we came in from the north. I dropped my bird down in the field, and we walked twenty yards to the body. We returned to the bird, and I dropped her over yonder, where it's drier."

Nodding, Wolfe turned three-sixty degrees slowly. "This place is desolate. The killer knows the area. Not a soul would have been past to see him kill this woman." He rubbed his chin. "How many vehicles have been by since you arrived?"

"Zero." Beth looked up at him, her eyes flashing with annoyance. "We need something to go on. We've seen this guy and still we can't put a name to him or come close to knowing who the heck he is."

Taking gloves and a face mask from his kit, he understood Beth's frustration, but he did at least have something for her. "First up, we have a positive DNA match on Arizona Carson. Looking over the previous cases, I'm assuming he keeps the women overnight, and from the physical evidence, bruising, and swelling, I'd say he tortures them for many hours. The rape of the previous victim was particularly brutal. He used a condom.

There are bruises all over the body made by large hands." He held out his hand. "My size." He looked from one to the other. "The strange thing is, I found absolutely no trace evidence or DNA on the body of Arizona Carson. I queried the doctor at Roaring Creek General and asked if Arizona's body had been washed, and the answer was no, which I found very interesting as y'all know someone who has been raped and brutalized usually has trace evidence all over. Not necessarily human DNA if the killer was careful, but dirt, fibers, and suchlike. So I tested the body for various cleansers and discovered she'd been bathed all over, including her hair, in PCR Clean. It must have been diluted because she has no chemical burns, but it would have burned the skin and eyes."

"PCR Clean?" Beth stared at him in disbelief. "They wouldn't bathe her in that at the hospital before burial. I carry a small, diluted quantity myself to avoid cross-contamination at crime scenes, but using it on a body, no way."

"What did you discover?" Styles tipped back his Stetson and raised his eyebrows in question.

Wolfe's eyes narrowed. "This is where it gets interesting. They do use that chemical at the hospital for general cleaning of the morgue, but after grilling the orderly and bringing down hell and brimstone on the staff, they all emphatically assured me it's never used on a corpse." He glanced over at the body lying in the dirt. "I'll get her back to the morgue in Black Rock Falls, and if she's been bathed in PCR Clean, you might be able to tie it to the killer."

"This also means he must have a secluded place he takes them to, where he can bathe them." Beth scanned the horizon. She turned bleak eyes on Wolfe. "I know just what he's doing. I can almost see inside his warped mind."

"How so?" Styles stood hands on hips staring at her.

"He's already shown them what he's capable of doing by killing all the witnesses in the convenience store." Beth folded her arms across her chest and stared into the distance. "The women are already traumatized and terrified, but he spared their lives. I figure he makes a bargain with them. If they do whatever he tells them to do without complaint, he'll let them go in the morning. Heck, he even allows them to shower but insists they use the PCR Clean, and it would sting like hell even diluted. He drives them out to the middle of nowhere and lets them go. His twisted mind tells him he's keeping his word." She turned her troubled gaze on his face. "What he didn't promise is that he wouldn't kill them."

Finding Beth's insight remarkable, Wolfe turned toward the body. "Well, if y'all follow me, I'll see if there's any other glaring evidence you can use." He made his way along the plow furrows to the body.

"I'm done here." Webber pushed his phone into his pocket and pulled on examination gloves.

Wolfe took in the position of the body. He'd seen many victims shot in the back or head while running and they all seemed to fall the same way. A head shot was instant, but the legs kept moving before the body fell down face-first. He walked back and forth, examining the blood and brain-matter spatter on the soil. The girl's head was turned to one side, the bullet passing at an angle through her skull. She had lived for a minute before dying, enough to turn her face away as she fell. He turned and looked at the others. "She wasn't expecting to be shot and was making a beeline for the woods. I figure she heard him racking a bullet. Her footprints zigzag before she is hit." He sighed. "There's little I can do here apart from take her liver temperature." He removed the device from his kit and lifted her clothes and went to work. "Okay, I'll get her back to the morgue and work on her today. I have a DNA comparison, so if this is who we suspect, I'll be able to give you an answer by this afternoon." He looked from one to the other. "This is a tough one, but the answers are always there."

"Yeah, I'm running a facial-recognition program back at the office on the shooter." Beth sighed. "I've looped in all the CCTV cameras from everywhere around here. We only have his eyes, but I might get a match or a close match. That's all we need to start the ball rolling."

Wolfe nodded. Having a cybercrime expert was an advantage. "You know, if you need any assistance, Jo Wells and Ty Carter are close by and they have a superb IT whiz kid working with them. It only takes a phone call."

"Yeah, we've been thinking about asking Jo about her thoughts on the profile of this killer, but I believe we've figured him out." Styles cleared his throat. "Not his motive. It's not money, and we don't know why he's killing, but we figure he's using the holdups as a cover to abduct the girls."

The idea made sense, but to find a psychopath they'd need more. Wolfe frowned. "Okay, so the murdering bravado is for the benefit of the women. He's showing off or trying to dominate them." He sighed. "You really need to talk to Jo. She'll be able to help you establish his pattern. We've caught many killers by preempting what they're planning next."

"That sounds like a plan." Styles nodded. "We'll head home and get at it."

Wolfe stared after them. "Good luck."

SIXTEEN

Rattlesnake Creek

It was after one by the time Styles put the chopper down on the top of the FBI building. The intense morning had dragged on. He'd given verbal and written reports to the local sheriffs in each county and suggested they work together. They needed to find suspects and he gave them a list of the killer's possible employment. They'd assumed the Convenience Store Killer, the name the media had given him, lived in Roaring Creek and that place was his home base, but without a name to go on, finding him would be difficult. Locating where he took the women seemed impossible as it could be in any one of three counties. He removed his headset and placed it on the hook and looked at Beth as the chopper blades slowed. She'd been different the past few days. He'd seen the angry flash in her eyes at crime scenes, as if she took each victim's death personally. This time, she seemed preoccupied, drifting off and not speaking for ages, when during their flights she usually never stopped discussing cases. Maybe the long hours were getting to her. Unlike the city, where crime was on the doorstep, here it was often counties away. The traveling, although by chopper, was tiring on top of a difficult investigation. If he asked her if she was tired and wanted a break, she'd tear him a new one. He'd become accustomed, well almost, to know how to phrase things so he didn't upset the status quo. "I need a break. I'm gonna drop my stuff in the office and then go over to Tommy Joe's Bar and Grill. You coming?"

When Beth blinked a few times like an AI robot coming back online, Styles repeated the question.

"Ah, yeah sure." She removed her headset and hurriedly gathered her things. "Sorry. I was miles away. Mind if we walk? I need some fresh air."

Styles pulled their bags out of the back of the chopper and dropped them on the ground. Bear bounced out, sniffing around as if making sure no other dog had dared to invade his space. "Sure."

He headed for the entry, used his retina scan to enter, and headed for his apartment. He dumped his bag inside and used the bathroom and then waited outside by the elevator for her. She came out a few moments later, hair brushed and wearing a different coat. He pressed the button on the elevator and they walked into the car. "You seem distracted. Anything I can help you with?"

"Oh, I have a number of things spinning around inside my head at the moment." She strolled along Main beside him, the cool wind tossing her hair out behind her like a silken scarf. "Nothing specific, just yet."

He buttoned up his coat and then pulled gloves from his pocket. "This is why we have a partner, so we can discuss things. Looking at evidence from different angles often solves a case."

"It's not this case I've been pondering over." Beth stared straight ahead. "I have an alert on my computer that gives me the latest information about serial killers or suspicious deaths in the country." She flicked him a gaze. "I blame Jo Wells. Her books have given me this new interest in psychopaths and how they hide in plain sight, so I've become hungry for information. Any case that suggests psychopathic behavior is of interest to me."

Nodding, Styles shortened his step to walk beside her. "I do much the same when we're not working intense cases. Any information is good information. So what did you find?" He pushed open the door to TJ's and inhaled the aroma of barbecue pork and sighed.

"I'll explain after we've ordered." Beth led the way to the counter and ordered the pork and a slice of cherry pie.

Styles placed his order, joked a little with TJ about flying miles just to eat lunch, and then followed Beth to a table. He removed his coat, gloves, and hat and sat down. "Okay what did you find that's doing your head in? Don't tell me it isn't, because you haven't said two words to me since we left Roaring Creek."

"I'm sorry, it's just my mind's been on this other case." Beth drummed her fingers on the table. "Do you know a county around here called Mischief?"

Leaning back in his chair and stretching out his legs, Styles nodded. "Yeah. Follow the line of the mountain range and you'll run right into it. Why?"

"It may be nothing, but they've been having murders there too." Beth raised her gaze to him. "Girls go missing and end up dumped all over the place. There are many mining towns in that area with small communities all run under the same sheriff's department. If it's not that far from here. I've been wondering if the murders are connected."

Unconvinced, Styles frowned, not wanting to get involved. Right now, he had enough killings in his caseload. "How so?"

"There was a rash of killings over six weeks or so. They stopped and then the ones started around Roaring Creek." Beth smiled as TJ delivered their meals and filled coffee cups. "Thanks, TJ. This looks delicious."

"My pleasure." TJ added silverware and headed back to serve another customer.

"Now we're on scene and prominent. Our guy will likely slow down some or move to a different location." Beth sipped her coffee and lifted her fork. "I figure if the crimes are connected, the next kill will be somewhere around Mischief. If it is, I figure we need to take a look at the body."

Sighing as he enjoyed his first bite of the pork, he nodded. "Okay, that makes sense. What headway has the local sheriff made in the case?"

"Nothing of interest. The police work is sketchy. It's as if they don't have the experience to handle murders. They have a serial killer in their county and the sheriff is trying to work the case with two deputies. I could say they're incompetent, but maybe some would say we are too, considering that we don't have a clue who is killing the women hereabouts either." Beth dabbed at her mouth with a paper napkin.

Barking a laugh, Styles shook his head slowly. "We've been on the case for one day, Beth. I figure we've moved mountains in a very short time. How far has the sheriff got in his investigation? Does he have any suspects?"

"Yeah, he's interviewed a few suspects, but all of them seem to have alibis at the time of the murders." Beth stared at him from across the table, her intent expression boring into him. "This is what interests me. It's as if we're chasing the same ghost. If they find another body in the next few days, I figure it's worth taking a look."

Impressed by the way she looked outside the box, Styles nodded. "That works for me."

SEVENTEEN

Impressed with her ingenuity, Beth smiled inwardly. She'd managed to set the groundwork to get into the rat's nest that was the Mischief Sheriff's Department. Styles wasn't an easy nut to crack. She'd expected him to question her a little closer about her reasons to want to go to Mischief. As she waited for her dessert to arrive, she observed him, wondering if his silence meant he was running her plan through his mind, evaluating her reasons, but then he didn't think like she did. His thought processes were normal, whereas it had been necessary for her to be aware of everyone around her. She needed to dissect people's thoughts and actions to survive, and she did these calculations in nanoseconds. When he looked up at her, she smiled at him. His eyes held no hint of concern. He was just enjoying his pie. "Have you had any more thoughts about me looking for your sister?"

"Nope." Styles pushed his plate away and reached for his coffee. "It's a big step to take, and I'm not quite ready for it yet. I'll let you know when I am."

Nodding, Beth sipped her coffee. "I hope that facial-recognition software has picked up someone, or better still, a few people. I know the local sheriffs are searching for suspects by linking people to different occupations, but that idea is hit and miss. We have a general idea of his height, weight, and build. If we can add an occupation or even a hobby that takes him to the towns on the days of the murders, we'll have him." She shrugged. "Or I'll risk it and go undercover. We could both go into the convenience store, as in one at a time, and linger. He's not going to draw down on both of us before we'll be able to take him down because we'll be expecting it. The moment he walks into the store, we'll be on him."

"Let's try the conventional approach first." Styles dug into his pie and sighed. A look of absolute bliss crossed his face. "First, we need suspects, interviews, and hopefully we'll make an arrest before we need to risk our lives."

They left TJ's Bar and Grill and followed Bear along the sidewalk, his mouth grinning around a large bone and his tail wagging back and forth. They were just about to cross the road to go to the office when a woman came screaming out of the general store. "What is it?"

"Call the sheriff." She pointed wildly behind her. "There's a man in there. He has my little girl and says he'll kill her if the clerk doesn't empty the cash register."

Time was of the essence and Beth grabbed a passerby. "Call 911. Tell the sheriff there's a gunman in the general store and the FBI is on scene."

"Yes, ma'am." The stranger pulled out his phone.

"Stay here. We'll get your daughter." Styles looked at the woman and then turned to Beth. "Take the back. I'll go in the front. I'll give you time to enter, and then it's showtime. When you hear the store bell, come out." He pulled his weapon. "Bear. Stay." He took off at a run.

Beth ran after him, pulling her weapon from the shoulder holster. She dashed down the alleyway. The back door of the general store stood wide open, and ahead she could make out a

typical storage room. It was empty and she dashed inside.
Something caught her across the throat and her legs shot out
from under her. Her weapon spun across the floor. Gasping for
air, she tried to get to her feet, but the floor was covered in
liquid detergent. She slipped and turned to see a man staring
down at her with an evil grin on his face. In one hand, he
carried a baseball bat. He stood outside the slick of slippery
soap and swung at her, but she ducked away, unable to avoid a
vicious jab to her ribs that sent her sliding across the room.

Scrambling on hands and knees, she looked around for
anything to use as a weapon. With the ground so slippery, standing
and fighting hand-to-hand would be useless. Her gun had slid
under a bank of metal shelves and was out of reach. She slithered
slowly to one side to peer into the store, hoping to see Styles and
warn him. The man holding a gun to a small girl's head was clearly
visible. The child was crying fitfully, tears streaming down its
chubby cheeks. The store bell rang as the door opened and Beth
held her breath. Styles would be expecting her to back him up.

"FBI. Drop the gun and put down the kid." Styles sounded
calm as usual. "My weapon will take your head clean off your
shoulders. I don't give second chances."

"I'll shoot the kid, and everyone will blame you." The man
laughed. "You don't figure I'm alone, do you?" He indicated
with his chin toward the back room. "Your girlfriend is in big
trouble. She's on her knees where she belongs." His face
screwed up. "I want you to know how it feels to lose someone.
You figure you're the law in town, beating up on innocent folk.
Someone needs to take you down."

"She's not my girlfriend." Styles shrugged nonchalantly. "If
you take her out, the bureau will just send me another one. The
FBI has plenty of agents." He barked a laugh. "She's a pain in
my butt, and I'll be glad to see the back of her."

"We'll see about that." The man waved the clerk forward.

"Stand here in front of me and hold the kid. Move and I'll kill both of you. He ain't going to shoot me, with the kid and you between us." He laughed. "Your girlfriend might not be so lucky. She's already down and she ain't leaving here alive. My friend will mess her up real bad."

"She's not my girlfriend." Styles was edging closer. "She's an FBI agent, same as me. Right now, you and your buddy are in deep shit. Put down your weapon and we'll talk about what your problem is with me. So far, what's happened here, I can forget about."

Beth stared at the man. "You heard him. Stop now and we'll discuss your problem with Agent Styles."

"I'll have me some fun first." The man swung the bat at her, again catching her across the back.

Gritting her teeth, Beth grabbed the legs of a set of shelves stacked with cans of fruit and vegetables and pulled herself closer. Her attacker was not risking slipping in the liquid soap and had one hand wrapped around a post for support. The best he could do was prod her legs as she moved. Getting into a sitting position, she grabbed the shelves and pulled to her feet. "Now what do you plan to do, huh?" She shook her head. "The soap idea was pretty lame."

When he moved to look at his friend, she noticed a pistol stuck in the back of his pants. The situation had suddenly gotten serious. Without a second thought, she grabbed a can of peas, took aim, and hit him full on the back of the head. With a grunt, he hit the floor like a sack of potatoes. Not wasting any time, she grabbed his legs and slid him toward her in the soap. She took his weapon, checked the load, and pushed it into her holster. Using the shelves to keep her balance, she maneuvered to the edge of the soap and stepped onto industrial carpet. She wiped her feet and drew the weapon. Needing to get into Styles' line of sight, she moved across the doorway into the store. He'd seen her. Although his eyes hadn't moved, he'd blinked twice.

Heart thundering, she pressed her back against the wall and nodded to him. The next moment Styles moved closer, engaging the perpetrator in conversation, and she edged silently behind the counter, weapon held out in front of her with both hands. The clerk's attention was fixed on Styles and only the little girl noticed Beth and let out a wail. She'd gotten within a foot of the perpetrator, holding her weapon steady, but didn't dare say a word. His gun was still aimed at the child.

"My partner has her weapon aimed at your head. Your friend is down." Styles moved into the open and Beth could see the massive barrel of his gun. "Put down your weapon. Now!"

If Styles fired, his bullet would go through the clerk and the man and likely Beth as well, but she didn't move. Beth looked at the little girl and smiled. Keeping her voice low and calm, she aimed the gun at the man's head. "I can't miss at this range. Put down your weapon or I'll kill you before you get off a shot."

"Don't threaten me, woman." The man's finger dropped to the trigger.

Confident, Beth fired and shot the pistol out of his hand. The bullet traveled through the man's hand and ricocheted, missing Styles by six inches and exploding a sack of flour. As the man screamed and fell to his knees clutching his hand, she grabbed the child and pushed her into the arms of a middle-aged man pressed against the wall beside a display of fish hooks, before turning back to assist Styles.

A siren wailed in the distance. Beth rushed forward but Styles already had the perpetrator face down on the floor and had secured him with zip ties. She sat the shaken clerk down in a chair behind the counter. "Are you okay?"

"Yeah." The clerk sighed. "My ears are ringing, something bad." He pushed a finger in his ear and looked at her. "You don't look so good."

"No, you don't." Styles frowned. "What happened? You're soaked through, bruised, and have something dripping off of your hair. You smell good though." He raised both eyebrows leaned forward, sniffed, and smiled. "Cherry blossom."

His comments on her being disposable and being a pain in his butt had hurt her feelings, but she just shrugged it off. Acting nonchalant usually worked when co-workers made unpleasant comments about her and she'd heard many, but usually when her back was turned. She shouldn't care. Psychopaths didn't care about anything—but *she* did. It would be better if he didn't know his comments had stung. She lifted her chin. "There's a guy out cold in the back. He knocked me over when I ran through the door. I slipped on some soap and dropped my gun. It went under the shelves. I couldn't get up and he attacked me with a baseball bat. I threw a can of peas at him and knocked him out and then came out to help you." She looked up at him. "I'll watch this guy if you can secure the other one."

"Okay." Styles headed out the back of the store.

"What's happening here?" Sheriff Cash Ryder came through the door, gun drawn and making the bell shake erratically. He stared at Beth openmouthed. "What the heck happened to you?"

Beth indicated to the guy on the floor. "He held a gun on that little girl over there and wanted to hurt me in an attempt to get even with Styles. How he knew we'd be walking by I have no idea."

"Sheriff, and ah... ma'am." The man holding the little girl came forward. "There was a woman with them. She locked this kid's mother in the storage room. She had a gun. They were all talking before you arrived. They saw you walk into TJ's and lay in wait. That woman who ran out the door, she's one of them." He hoisted the little girl onto one hip and looked at Beth. "Can I let her mother out of the storeroom now?"

Beth nodded. "Yes, please do, and don't go anywhere. The sheriff will need to take a statement."

"I know this guy." Ryder peered at the man groaning on the floor. "He's just been released from jail. He beat his wife real bad. Styles got her out of the county, and he went to jail for a year. It runs in the family. His brother did time for beating his wife and kids." He glanced around. "I'm guessing the brother is the other guy?"

Beth nodded. "Yeah, the other guy attacked me with a baseball bat. I knocked him out with a can of peas. Styles is restraining him before he regains consciousness." She indicated to the man at her feet. "I shot the gun from his hand, so he might have broken fingers. Best you call Nate. Duty of care and all that."

It surprised Beth, but she actually liked Dr. Nate Mace. He had a very calming manner and helped out in cases when Ryder needed him.

"Okay." Ryder reached for his phone.

"You'll need to call the paramedics to pick up a body." Styles came from the storeroom. He gave Beth a long look. "You've killed him, or he drowned in a pool of soap. Nate will be able to determine the cause of death. If he has soap in his lungs, it's definitive." He held out her gun. "Here, take your gun. I've taken photographs of the scene. Once you're cleaned up, we'll need photographs of your injuries. I'll take some of you now, as well."

Aghast, Beth stared at him. She couldn't believe her ears. There was no way she'd meant to kill the stranger. Had her dark side slipped out and taken control without her knowing? Troubled, she ran the scenario through her mind. Everything had happened so fast. Had what Styles had said about her being replaceable triggered something from her past? Causing her to black out and hit her attacker more than once? No, surely not... *maybe* not. He'd made her mad but not mad enough to kill him.

No, it wasn't possible. She shook her head and glared at Styles. "Dead? He can't be dead. I only clipped him on the back of the head with a can of peas. He was breathing when I left him."

When Styles nodded slowly, her stomach dropped. All she needed right now was an investigation. Being in the spotlight would mean the psychopath in Mischief would just keep on killing young girls. She swallowed hard and looked at him. "Are you suspending me?"

"Nope." Styles shook his head. "I could hear you fighting for your life, Beth. Whatever happened here was self-defense. We'll need to establish cause of death, is all. It's protocol and you know that." He took a few photos of her and smiled. "Can you make it home okay? Or do you want me to walk you across the road?"

Suddenly weary and sore, Beth shook her head. "I'll be fine, but ask Nate if he'd mind taking the photos of me when he's done here. I'll go and get cleaned up." She gave him a long look. "Him being my doctor and all, I'd prefer him to be taking the shots, if you don't mind?"

"Sure, I'll ask him. He'll need to check you out anyway for the report. Can you take Bear with you? I'll help Ryder mop up here and have someone from county come and collect this guy." Styles frowned. "You'll need to be in the office to allow Nate access to the building." His gaze flicked over her and concern filled his eyes. "Are you sure you're okay?"

Hurting all over, Beth nodded. She'd never given in to pain or shown her suffering to anyone. It's how she'd survived years in abusive foster care. It was a weakness she refused to accept, but recently something in her world had shifted. The psychopath side of her shouldn't experience feelings, but since working with Styles, the remoteness she'd experienced after seeing her father murder her mom had eased. In fact, she actually liked the people she worked with, and this included everyone at TJ's. This, *liking people*, had never happened before. She understood her condition was vastly different from others and she'd been able to control her dark side for years. What had happened? Did she actually care what Styles had said about her being disposable? Maybe she had. He was, after all, the only hero she'd ever had. Pushing his words to the back of her mind, she straightened, flicked her sodden hair over her shoulders, and wiped her hands on her ruined coat. She glared at him. "Oh, I'm just peachy, Styles. How couldn't I enjoy being beaten with a baseball bat and then rolled in cherry blossom soap? Don't take all day. We still have a killer to catch." She headed out the door.

EIGHTEEN

Three hours later, Styles walked into the office. The smell of fresh coffee filled the room and Bear climbed out of his basket to greet him, tail wagging and his mouth stretched in a doggy smile. He removed his hat, coat, and gloves and stared at Beth. She was at her desk and he noticed a list of names on the whiteboard. She didn't as much as look up when he went to the kitchenette to pour a cup of coffee. He looked at her over one shoulder, noting her rigid back. He blew out a breath. She controlled her emotions really well now, much better than when she first arrived, but she seemed upset. He poured her a cup of coffee, added the fixings, and took the cup to her desk. "Sorry I took so long. The perp needed X-rays before we sent him to County." He looked her over. "Did Nate pass you fit for duty?"

"He did, and FYI, you do more damage to me when we work out in the mornings." Beth didn't look up. "He took the photographs and said he'll go to the hospital and open up the perp's chest and see if he died of drowning. If he didn't, X-rays will determine if I crushed his skull."

Nodding, Styles leaned against her desk. "Beth."

"What?" She looked up at him eyes flashing.

Okay. Styles cleared his throat. "Is it something I've said? I figured we had a darn good working relationship. So spill it. What's wrong?"

"Well..." Beth leaned back in her chair staring at him. "If you'd told me I was a pain in the butt and you wanted to replace me, I'd have asked the director to reassign me. You don't have to put up with me, Styles. I can work anywhere. It's not like I have any friends or family to worry about, is it?"

Ouch! Realization dawned on him and he grinned. "Oh, back there?" He indicated over one shoulder with his thumb and shook his head. "I was just trash-talking, is all. I didn't want the perp to believe you had value to me." He chewed on his bottom lip trying not to laugh. "You believed that?"

"Well, you sure convinced me." Beth shook her head. "I don't think it's funny. Why are you laughing?"

Styles sobered, not sure if she was joking with him. From her expression, she was serious. He heaved a sigh. Beth sure was a contradiction. Had he glimpsed vulnerability beneath her tough cop exterior? If she needed security, he could give her that and the guys would back him up. They all liked her just fine. It must have been hard on her after such a traumatic childhood to be dragged from a stable position in DC and then dumped into the Wild West. "I'm sorry, Beth. You do have friends here. I'm your friend. TJ, Cash, Wez, and Nate are all friends." He cleared his throat and walked back to his desk. "I admit, I didn't want you around when you first arrived. I liked being alone, but we work together just fine. If you want to stay here, I'll fight to keep you as my partner. I can see no reason why the director would want to move you again. He's ecstatic with our results."

"Okay." Beth frowned. "It's just when people say things behind my back, they usually mean it. I know I'm not the easiest person to work with. I like my space and I work at different angles to most agents."

So, she'd come up against hostility on the job too. Styles took any kind of bullying at work very seriously. He met her gaze. "If ever I have something to say, Beth, I'll say it to your face. You know that I'm a straight-up guy. Right?"

"Yeah, well, I've trusted you with my life and you haven't let me down yet." She reached for her coffee and met his gaze. A small smiled curled her lips. "I like that you're honest with me, Styles, and I don't have faith in too many people."

Relaxing, he nodded. "I'll always have your back. Now, I can see you've been busy. What have you got for me?"

"The facial recognition came back with ten hits. I cross-referenced them with all forms of identification and added race and sex into the mix. We know this is a white guy. We can see his skin color around the balaclava." Beth sipped her coffee and then placed the cup on her desk and stood. She went to the printer and collected four images. "I cross-referenced the names with people who worked in three main areas—the mines—as in transient workers who moved from one place to the next. Delivery drivers. Milk, bread, mail, and other various deliveries. Medical and drugstore supplies was one that Nate mentioned."

Impressed, Styles nodded. "Ah, yeah, the PCR Clean link. You figure a delivery driver would have access to it?"

"Oh, it's used in many places for cleaning." She shrugged. "You might recall that I have some. I use it if I'm moving from one case to another. In my vehicle, for instance, so I don't track DNA from one case to the next. It's not difficult to come by."

Styles walked beside her to the whiteboard. "So how many potential suspects are we talking about?"

"I've narrowed it down to four delivery drivers all with the same height and build." Beth pinned images to the whiteboard and then picked up a pen. "Austin Buck. Delivers newspapers, magazines,

tobacco goods, etcetera, to convenience stores across four towns."
She looked at Styles. "This is Wyatt Cody. He owns his own online
supply service here in Rattlesnake Creek, drives himself and
supplies mining camps and local stores with a variety of goods."

Rubbing the scar on his chin absently, Styles examined the
images. "So you are set on believing the killer is a delivery
driver?"

"It's the best we have to go on right now." Beth turned to
look at him. "These four guys all move around the local areas
and so would be the most likely suspects. Apart from actually
getting names for you, I was able to hack into their work schedules. These guys all had the opportunity to commit the convenience store hits and abduct both of the most recent victims."

Unconvinced, Styles shook his head. "They'll need to have
been in the vicinity at the times of the four holdups for anyone
to look seriously at them for murder." He sighed and pointed to
the other two photographs. "What about these guys?"

"Same as the others, different jobs, is all. Billy Straus
delivers medical supplies and pharmacy orders, mainly to the
mines." Beth made notes on the whiteboard. "Then we have
Clay Maverick. He delivers milk all over four counties." She
turned to look at him. "All fit the weight and height, were in the
area when the murders occurred, and came up as close matches
in the facial-recognition results."

Styles ran what she had said through his mind and held up
a hand. "Just wind this back some. Did you say you'd *hacked*
into their private systems to discover their schedules?"

"It's what I do." Beth raised one eyebrow and shrugged.
"Don't come all legal eagle over me, Styles. You walk a fine edge
between right and wrong to get things done and save lives all
the time. I'm no different. It's not like we're taking these guys to
court, is it? Well, not at this point in time." She smiled at him.
"Go with me with this one so we can move things along a little
faster. We could wait a few days for a judge to issue a warrant

and risk him hitting another convenience store or use the information from hacking the system. The end result is the same." She turned to look at him. "Hacking a work schedule isn't something we'll need to present in court. If necessary, we can obtain that information from witnesses at the places the goods were delivered. Don't sweat the small stuff, Styles."

Holding up one finger, Styles met her gaze. "Is this something you did in cybercrime? I figured it was something different, more like cryptocurrency scams and the like."

"Yeah, all the time. They needed me to discover information fast, like accessing CCTV cameras all over." Beth shrugged. "I hacked personal CCTV cameras, nanny cams, for instance. The idea is to bring down criminals in any way possible. I use everything at my disposal to do my job."

His way of working a case had just flown out of the window. Slightly baffled, Styles nodded. "Okay, so I'm guessing we'll be interviewing these four guys. Do you have home addresses? It's been a long day, but we need to catch this guy."

"He won't hit again so soon. We have a little time." Beth rolled her shoulders. "I'll work out where they'll be and when they'll do their drop-offs tomorrow. It would be better to catch them off guard at work, and it's less lightly they'll be carrying. Don't you agree?"

Emptying his cup, Styles nodded. The confident, slightly arrogant Beth was firmly back in place. "Yeah, I do. Did you run a background check on these guys yet?"

"Not yet. I've been kind of busy." Beth returned to her desk. She gave him a long look and then shrugged. "Anyhow, I figured I'd leave something for you to do before we head to TJ's for dinner."

NINETEEN

Mischief

It's funny but I've always had the urge to video crime scenes from a distance and then play them back in fast-forward. It's easy enough these days with micro cameras to place one or two just so, and nobody ever notices them. The everyday Joe in the street can purchase technology today a spy ten years ago could only dream of. Think about the smartphone and what it's capable of doing now. How it can control just about everything inside your home and what it will be capable of doing going forward. For heaven's sake, I can take a call on my wristwatch, and see if someone is at my front door. Five years ago that would have been science fiction. Now it's usual.

I digress. It's always the same when any law enforcement department is notified about a murder victim. Some passerby starts a hullabaloo and calls 911. The local patrol drops by and tramples all over the scene. Later, more cops arrive and trample all over the scene. The forensic team, if there is one, is next, and like ants they go back and forth, moving evidence from one place to the other. Next, an ambulance arrives and the body is ceremoniously carried out by men with grim faces. All act concerned, but do they really care or is it just another corpse dumped in an abandoned building?

The moment someone found the girl the deputies started complaining about being called out late at night. No one is really interested in seeing a dead body. Most of them just want to get the job done and get back home to bed. I know they wouldn't raise a finger to identify the body tonight. Once they were done, they'd go on home and leave her in the morgue until morning. Once a doctor has pronounced her dead, as if that is needed, and the mortician has made her look presentable for the parents, they'll pick straws to decide who will go and speak to the next of kin.

As the sheriff and deputies come out of the building, the men yawn and scratch, pulling gloves from their hands and tossing them onto the ground. Most look angry, not for the life lost but because the paperwork is piling up. I like to keep them busy because not one of them appreciates my work or recognizes the skill it took for me to lure the girl into the building. At the time, she made my heart race, and the rush of excitement when I killed her was intoxicating. To them, she's just another dead girl, but to me... well now... she's just another dead girl.

When I return home, I'll watch them in the video, running fast as I speed up the playback. I'll laugh at seeing their jerky movements but it's never enough. The thrill is long gone and I crave more. It's like trying to hold the finest wine in my hands. I want to catch it, savor it, but it runs through my fingers, leaving me with just a memory of the smell and taste. Watching them process the scene is always the same, like an anticlimax to a wonderful night. After a murder, the cleanup crew is nothing more than a garbage truck coming by to collect a bin overflowing with bottles and streamers left over from a great party.

TWENTY

WEDNESDAY

Rattlesnake Creek

Exhausted after a long day, Beth had parted company with Styles after dinner and headed to her apartment. She'd made a mental list of what to do the following day. The need to solve the case was eating at her. The moment she discovered another murder had been committed in Mischief, her dark side would be harder to control. Sometimes, her charismatic psychopathic serial killer persona would sneak right up on her and take over. She wouldn't kill anyone, that part of her she could control. To Styles, she'd likely appear to be overfriendly, but in truth, the Tarot Killer wasn't friendly. She manipulated people and the last person she ever wanted to control was Styles. Okay, she'd sown a few seeds about the Mischief murders, but in doing so, it actually brought him into the Tarot Killer's investigation. Of course, he couldn't be involved in murder, but by escorting her there, it gave her a valid reason to snoop. If she could prove there was a bad apple in the Mischief Sheriff's Department, it would lead to the Night Creeper. From there, with Styles safely in a local motel, she'd deal with him personally.

This morning, the moment she set foot in the office, she'd pushed away all thoughts of the Night Creeper and concentrated on the convenience store murders. She'd easily hacked the local businesses' computers and found the schedules for deliveries, cross-referenced them with the names of her suspects, and then made a list of their delivery routes. The list was practical but not immediate, and she wondered if Styles would agree to her proposed interview schedule. He'd had his nose stuck in his laptop since they'd arrived at eight this morning. She saved the list to her phone and looked up at him. "Unfortunately, the only way I'm able to coordinate the deliveries so we can talk to all of them today is after three. As it happens, they'll all be stopping by Roaring Creek at various times this afternoon. Some have multiple deliveries around town, so we should be able to catch them." She pushed a strand of hair behind one ear. "Or we take the chopper and dash between towns."

"After three suits me fine." He sighed. "I can't find any priors of interest on any of them. So nothing there to go on."

Sipping her coffee, Beth eyed him over the rim. "Hmm. That's a shame. If one was abusive, it would make our lives easier."

"Maybe, but I do have something interesting." Styles looked up at her from his laptop. "After we talked about similar cases and the current spate of murders in Mischief, I placed a request for information on the Night Creeper murders. I haven't received any files yet, but a dispatch arrived about a body of a girl found in an abandoned warehouse out at Wolf Valley this morning. I asked for more info, and they sent me the case file. I figure he's hit again, just like you said he would."

Icy fingers walked down Beth's spine and the Tarot Killer rushed to the surface ready to burst out of her to seek justice. *Dammit.* She sucked in a few deep breaths, grabbed her cup, and walked to the kitchenette for a refill, keeping her back turned away from Styles. "When was this?"

"A man walking his dog found her—well, the dog found her —at five after six this morning." Styles' chair creaked as he stood and joined her. "You amaze me."

Oh, that's all she needed to feed her psychopath's ego. Unable to push the Tarot Killer back into her box, she turned and gave Styles a brilliant smile. The full charismatic persona was in control, like one of those awful colleagues at the office party who after overindulging start to flirt with everyone. She noticed his pupils dilate. A sure sign she'd taken him by surprise. She chuckled. "Do I? That's such a nice thing to say, Styles. Why do you prefer *Styles*? Dax is such a lovely name."

"Ah... long story." Styles poured his coffee and leaned against the counter. His ears had turned pink. "I went on vacation to Australia and made a few friends. They're nice people, but when I told the locals my name, they all laughed. Dax is slang for pants. Some of them started calling me Levi as a joke, so since then it's been Styles." He cleared his throat. "You amaze me, the way you have the ability to forecast a perp's next move. The Night Creeper isn't even our case, but after just skimming the media releases you profiled him. I don't figure you know you do this all the time on the fly."

Trying desperately to push down the Tarot Killer and save the situation, she busied herself looking for cookies she didn't want to eat. Heck, Beth Katz rarely gave compliments. She compared herself to a tree: strong and protective; whereas the Tarot Killer was a rose: it looked pretty, smelled wonderful, but could cut a person to shreds. She searched her mind for something to say. "I do seem to be able to analyze a situation and make predictions. It's good of you to recognize my skill. I appreciate it. I guess it's working with computers all the time. My brain works a little differently to some." *If only you knew just how differently.*

"I've noticed." Styles stirred his coffee slowly, his eyes fixed on her. "What are you searching for?"

She found the cookie jar and thrust it into his hands. "Cookies. It's just me doing my thing. I knew you'd be needing a snack about now."

"Okay, so has being stuck with me through winter made you relax some around me or is this the nurturing Beth I haven't seen before?" Styles carried the cookie jar to his desk and smiled at her, eyebrows raised.

Shaking her head and slamming the door firmly on the Tarot Killer, Beth rolled her eyes. "Nah, it's just your stomach starts to complain around nine every morning. I figure meeting it head-on is a solution." She picked up her cup and headed back to her desk. "So what else have you discovered about this recent murder in Mischief?"

"It's the same MO as all the others." Styles munched on a cookie. "They're saying strangled and dumped, is all. As usual, the report is sketchy."

Leaning back in her chair, Beth sighed. She desperately needed to see the body, but it would need to be Styles' idea. Nothing, no suggestions, should lead back to her, not when she intended to remove the killer from existence. "Hmm, you know as there's been so many murders and they could be linked to our guy. Even though our guy prefers shooting, he might be mixing it up to keep the heat off him."

"We can't rely on the local doctor to give us answers." Styles rubbed the back of his neck. "I'll call Wolfe and ask for his advice. If he looks at the body, we'd know once and for all if the cases are linked." He picked up his phone and put it on speaker. "Ah, Shane, it's Dax Styles. There's a homicide over at Mischief. It could possibly be an extension of the Convenience Store Killer's comfort zone." He gave Wolfe the details.

"That many murders and cowboys handling the causes of death." Wolfe blew out a long breath. *"Give me the number of*

the Mischief sheriff. I'll call him personally. I'll need to examine this body and the crime scene before the evidence is lost."

"Sure, I'll message you his details." Styles smiled at Beth. "We'd like to be there. When are you heading out?"

"I can be in the air in half an hour with my team. Just a second." Wolfe issued orders to someone. *"I know Mischief. We helped out in the wildfires a couple of years back. They have a helipad on top of the hospital. I'll send you the coordinates. I'll speak to the hospital and message you with my ETA. We'll need transport. Wolf Valley is a ways away from the city. Can you organize something?"*

"Yeah, sure." Styles flicked a glance at Beth. "Catch you later." He disconnected.

"Grab your things and I'll get the bird ready." Styles pushed to his feet. "We'll check out the murder. We'll be back in time to interview our suspects."

A thrill of excitement ran through Beth and she stood. "Okay, but it won't be enough time to look into the case files at the sheriff's department. I'd like to see what they have, wouldn't you? If mistakes have been made in the causes of death, we need to know."

"Yeah, we do, but if it's not the same man, we can't lose ground on the Convenience Store Killer case." Styles stared into space. "We'll do the interviews as planned and then head back there. It's fifteen minutes away by chopper. We'll need time to look into their case files and speak to the sheriff and his men. He glanced at his watch. "Can you arrange a couple of rentals? I'll be at least forty-five minutes. I'll need to refuel. We'll come back and do the interviews."

Beth made a few notes. "And how do you plan to proceed if we find anything interesting in Mischief?"

"I guess we go back." Styles stared into space for a beat. "It would be easier to stay overnight or maybe a couple of days, depending on what we find."

Perfect. Beth bit back a smile. "Not a problem." She turned back to her laptop.

TWENTY-ONE

Wolf Valley, Mischief

Interested for personal reasons more than anything else, Beth scanned the city of Mischief. As the Tarot Killer, she'd need to move around easily and fast. Luckily, Mischief's town plan was set out in a grid and had a number of suburbs, set around successful mining operations. The state was incredibly rich in a large variety of resources, from precious metals to gemstones and minerals. Mines littered the landscape. As they approached, Styles picked out the ghost towns, places that had once been prosperous gold-mining towns, with significant historic value. Her interest was in the layout and distances between murder scenes. She needed to know the time she'd require for traveling if she set out alone to hunt down a killer. She'd thought long and hard about the case and the only conclusion for so many mistakes was either gross incompetence by the local sheriff's department or a dirty cop. How dirty was the question. Covering up for a perp was one thing, but if she successfully identified the Night Creeper as one of the local law enforcement officers or someone working closely with the sheriff's department, he'd have protection and it would be difficult to stop him.

If it was a dirty cop, then it would be hard proving his guilt because if he was on the job and covering up or conveniently mislaying evidence, it would be enough to keep him out of jail. She'd need to know everything about him before she made her move. Being that close to an investigation, he'd be able to destroy or contaminate evidence and would be right there making decisions on the case, twisting it away from him. Beth never took the taking of a life for granted. She'd evaluate each case very carefully before risking her life to take him down. He'd need to prove himself worthy to be immortalized as one of the Tarot Killer's victims.

Beth always considered her own motives for taking down unstoppable monsters, and being judge, jury, and executioner. It didn't mean she placed herself above the law. In fact, on the right side of the law, cops shot and killed perpetrators on a regular basis and rarely the morality of their actions was mentioned. She weighed up the person's guilt and needed proof before she acted, rather than relying on a split-second gut or kneejerk reaction she'd seen many a time in the field. A dirty cop was bad enough, but a serial killer cop murdering for plea-sure disgusted her. Taking out sadistic murderers didn't thrill her, it made her high on adrenaline, maybe, but in truth, the thrill she received was from outwitting them. Beth only killed people who deserved to die and had escaped justice. Driven by her need to seek revenge for their victims, her rigid code of conduct was self-inflicted torture at times, but it kept her dark side from running amok.

As they circled the city, the small towns, really suburbs of Mischief, seemed like small hubs of industrial areas rather than the ranches she'd seen around Rattlesnake Creek or Black Rock Falls. None were too far away and she easily recognized Wolf Valley, Buffalo Pass, Mortonville, and Last Stop from her phone's maps app. There were more suburbs, but she calculated from the case files the bodies had been dumped within these areas, which made it quite clear to Beth that the Night Creeper lived in the heart of Mischief, and his comfort zone was between the towns of Wolf Valley, Buffalo Pass, Mortonville, and Last Stop.

Most of the time in the air, Styles had been occupied with baseball. Spring training, whatever that was, had begun and Styles was fully immersed. When not talking about cases, fishing, or Bear, his topic of conversation had been about ice hockey all winter and now baseball. She'd always had other things on her mind to consider following sports and had never considered a sporting interest in her future, but to act normal and fit in with her friends, she'd decided to discover more about the games. She now nodded at the right times when the discussions moved to sports. She'd actually gotten into hockey by the time the season ended and wondered if her attraction was the violence. She imagined that taking out her aggression by hitting a puck would be much like hitting a ball in the nets.

As they dropped onto Mischief General's helipad, landing neatly beside the ME's chopper, she turned to him and indicated with her chin toward Wolfe. The ME was walking up and down, phone pressed to one ear and waving his arm. His daughter Emily and his assistant, Colt Webber, were calmly extracting his equipment from the chopper. "What's up with him?"

"I guess we're gonna find out soon enough." Styles climbed out and called Bear to his side. "He looks pretty mad."

"What do you mean your deputies processed the crime scene?" Wolfe stared at the ground. "I gave explicit instructions to preserve the scene, leave the body in situ, and I'd be there ASAP." He paused a beat, listening. "We're on top of the hospital right now. I'm assuming y'all have the rentals Agent

Katz arranged waiting for us close by? We have equipment to take to the crime scene and the body of the victim is coming with me to Black Rock Falls for autopsy. I've reason to believe this case may tie in with our current investigation." He glanced up at Beth, his expression etched in stone and shook his head. "As a state medical examiner I have jurisdiction. I was appointed by the attorney general, so pull your men off the crime scene—now." He disconnected and shook his head slowly. "Our visit may be in vain. The local deputies have already contaminated the scene. The vehicles are waiting out front. We ask for Joey Barnhill at the front counter for the keys." He gave Beth a quizzical stare. "How did you get rentals delivered?"

Smiling, Beth pulled on her gloves. "Mentioning the FBI works like a charm sometimes." She rubbed her arms. "Is it always so cold and windy here? Do we ever get any warm weather?"

"In summer it warms up some, but right now it's an advantage." Wolfe led the way to the entrance. "It will keep the body chilled and preserve the evidence."

They collected the keys, and Beth tossed them to Styles. "You drive. I'll do a background check on the local law enforcement. Look for two white Nissans. I guess it's those two." She pointed to the vehicles parked at the curb.

"Why? Have you discovered anything about the local law enforcement I should know about?" Styles pressed the fob and led the way to a white Nissan Rogue and opened the back door for Bear.

Dropping their gear into the back seat, Beth shrugged. "I'm not sure. While I was waiting for you this morning, I hacked their files. Although they seem to be following procedure, the evidence collecting is less than adequate. If we get the chance, I'd like to get into the office to speak with them. Maybe it's just bad leadership?"

"Maybe." Styles climbed behind the wheel. "If they've messed up before, it will be in their records."

Beth took out her tablet and went to work. "Okay, we have Sheriff Lance Walker, Deputy Dryer, and Deputy Boone. Sheriff Walker was voted in six years ago. Dryer joined him at that time, and Deputy Boone a year ago. Boone was a deputy in Bozeman for six months prior to coming here and is the sheriff's nephew. He moved here after his mother passed. That's it. If they did do anything, the sheriff never mentioned it on their records." She blew out a breath. "I guess voting in a sheriff doesn't mean he's good at his job, does it?"

"Nope." Styles turned the Nissan and followed Wolfe. "Maybe nobody else put their hand up for the job. It doesn't pay that well, does it?"

Pushing her tablet into the backpack she'd filled with essentials, she shrugged. "I have no idea. I've never aspired to be a sheriff. I like the freedom to move around through the states with no restrictions. If we have a lead in Alaska, we can go there. A sheriff is stuck inside the county boundaries unless they get to cooperate with neighboring law enforcement. Plus we're trained for our work. A sheriff has basic requirements and has to pass a public safety officer standards and training course. I wonder if any of them know the basic procedure for processing a crime scene."

"Maybe not." Styles lifted one shoulder. "That would account for what's happening here. I can remember my first murder scene, and it sticks with me forever, but I had the training to work the scene. I'd also seen plenty of dead bodies in my time. It might be just a case of the blind leading the blind."

Checking her watch every five minutes or so to make a mental note of the time it took to travel between different suburbs, Beth took in the dilapidated area they had just driven through. The area the body had been found was situated in an old industrial area. Two or three of the buildings had been gutted with fire. The rest stood empty, cold reminders of prosperity from a bygone era. With the glass long gone from the windowpanes, the buildings stood like a line of skulls, staring into nothingness. Grass grew through the cracked concrete sidewalk and weeds had overtaken the gaping open doorways. She turned to Styles. "What happened here?"

"There used to be railway spurs all through these places years ago, and when they closed, the lifeblood of the manufacturing was cut off. They couldn't move their goods or get regular supplies, and so parts of the town died. It's not unusual. It's happening all over." Styles was keeping back some ways from Wolfe's vehicle and his head was moving back and forth as he scanned the local area. "This is a perfect place to commit murder. No one around, nobody to hear the screaming."

Already noticing the advantages of the area, Beth nodded. "Yeah, they'd know the area and select a building where they could hide a vehicle without being seen." She glanced around. "So many would be perfect. A little recon of the area to clear a space and all he'd need to worry about was getting the victim into his vehicle." She looked at him. "Without autopsy reports we have no idea the extent of the victim's injuries. It seems to me they found a body, noticed the ligature marks on the neck and bruises on the thighs, and just marked down the cause of death in all these cases as a rape and strangulation."

"You figure a doctor would do that without an examination?" Styles pulled up behind Wolfe's vehicle.

Blowing out a sigh, Beth shook her head. "Beats me." She moved her gaze along the three sheriff's department cruisers alongside the sidewalk. "I guess we're going to find out."

TWENTY-TWO

Styles climbed from the Nissan and let Bear out, ordering him to sit and wait as he followed Wolfe's team into the old building. It was dark inside and no more than an empty shell, filled with patches of grass and broken concrete flooring. He respected Wolfe, and in a crime scene situation, he'd stay back and allow him to do his thing, but seeing the cool, calm man annoyed was something unfamiliar. He was like a drill sergeant the way he barked orders at the sheriff and his deputies. Wolfe wanted answers and he wanted them now.

"You three stand over there. My assistant will be collecting DNA, hair, and saliva samples from all of you. This is protocol and not a choice for law enforcement at a crime scene when contamination is suspected. I want fingerprints as well." He turned to Webber. "In your own time, Colt." He swung around and looked at Styles. "I figure you should examine the body with me, and we'll see if it fits your other case. I have powerful flashlights with me." He turned to his daughter. "Emily, grab some flashlights out of our kit." He waited for everyone to turn on the beams and headed toward the body, forensic kit in one hand.

Pulling on a face mask, Styles glanced at Beth. "Watch your step. There are broken bricks all over."

"My eyesight is twenty-twenty and in the dark I see like a cat." Beth flicked him a glance. "But thanks for caring."

The girl was face down, her head turned to one side, eyes staring. Torn clothes littered the surrounding ground, and from what he could see, beside her the grass and weeds had been flattened. Styles frowned. Something was out of place, and he crouched down to peer at the ground, moving his flashlight back and forth.

"She's been moved." Beth bent to examine the body. "The ground is filthy and her back is clean."

Styles nodded. "Yeah, and by the flattened weeds, she was lying on something when he attacked her. When he was done, he rolled her off and took whatever they were lying on." Incredulous, he shook his head. "Well, this is a first. A killer who brings a blanket with him to rape and murder so he doesn't hurt his knees."

"It's thick, maybe three inches by the imprint in the ground, and look over here." Wolfe moved his flashlight around, stopping at two small patches of disturbed soil about a yard apart. "I'd wager that's the tips of cowboy boots." He looked at Styles. "Help me lay out a body bag. We'll need to roll her over and I want to keep her back clean just in case there are any fibers or trace evidence I can use to determine what she was lying on." He moved his flashlight around and shook his head slowly. "Hmm, if I didn't know better, I'd say this is the outline of an exercise mat. Emily has one and rolls it out on the grass at home, and it leaves a similar mark when she's done."

"You saying he's bringing an exercise mat to a murder?" Beth gaped at him. "You're joking, right?"

"Unless it just happened to be here, all nice and clean." Wolfe looked at her. "If a vagrant was sleeping here, the mat wouldn't be very clean and likely had been dumped here a time ago. Seems to me, it's looking like the killer planned this murder."

Styles rubbed the scar on his chin. "Unless it's kids sneaking away to have sex and it got out of hand. Teenagers do all kinds of crazy stuff when the hormones are raging." He bent to assist Wolfe with rolling over the body.

"Maybe one time." Beth shook her head. "But we know these murders are happening all over Mischief. This isn't kids. It's an organized serial killer." She sighed. "Look at her. She's young." She turned back to Styles. "Did the sheriff mention anything about a missing girl?"

Styles shook his head. "Nope but this happened overnight, maybe she hasn't been missed yet."

"What's that mark under the right breast?" Beth moved her flashlight over the body. "A cigarette burn?"

"Possible." Wolfe bent closer. "I'll get a closer look back at the lab."

"Ligature marks on neck, consistent with the use of a cord, not hands. This is very different from your case in a number of ways." Wolfe frowned as he spread the remaining threads of clothes to insert a thermometer into the victim's liver. "The cause of death was described as strangulation, and rape was mentioned, with the other young women found murdered here in Mischief. Is that correct?" He glanced up at Styles.

Clearing his throat, Styles looked at the battered body of the girl and swallowed hard. The notion that his sister might have suffered the same fate made his stomach clench. "They were all teenagers but there's little information in the reports. A local doctor or mortician dealt with the bodies. No official autopsies were performed on any of them." He cleared his throat. "The overall opinion was they were raped and strangled."

"I'll need to get her into my examination room, but I can't see any evidence of rape." Wolfe looked from one to the other.

"Y'all know how significant a failed rape is I assume?" His voice was just above a whisper.

"Yeah." Beth moved closer and Styles could hardly hear her. It was obvious she didn't want to be overheard by the sheriff or his deputies. "The killer couldn't perform and used it as an excuse to murder her. In his mind, killing her would hide his shame. The kidnapping and attacking stimulates him, but he can't get satisfaction unless he kills them."

Styles scratched his head and frowned. "You saying he blames these girls for his problems? This is his motive for killing them?"

"If I discover the others weren't raped after he ripped off their clothes and bruised their thighs, yeah, I'd say it's conclusive." Wolfe shook his head. "The last victim was when?"

"I think, almost a week ago. Her name was Jody Hooper." Beth pulled out her phone and scrolled through her files. "I don't have much info but there's a notice about her funeral. I found it. It's tomorrow. Right now they're conducting viewings for family and friends at a local funeral parlor."

"Okay." Wolfe straightened. "We'll take this victim to the hospital morgue and put her on ice and then get over to the funeral parlor. There's no way I'll allow Jody Hooper to be buried before I've examined her. This could be crucial evidence." He looked at Emily. "Scan around for any fragments of clothes, a cord, or similar used in the strangulation. Bag them and meet us out front. We'll get the body into the back of the Nissan, and when you're done, we'll head straight to the hospital." He looked at Styles. "Give me a hand to carry the body and then locate the mortician. I'll meet you outside the hospital and we'll go from there."

Styles bent to lift one end of the body bag. "Gotcha."

After watching Wolfe drive away with his team, Styles looked at Beth. "This isn't part of our case. Wolfe will probably call in Carter and Jo to deal with it. We're handling enough work right now."

"Call me inquisitive, but after seeing what's going on here, don't you figure we owe it to that murdered girl to take a look while we're here?" Beth stood hands on hips staring at him. She indicated with her chin toward the sheriff and deputies. "These murders have been practically ignored. I, for one, want to examine their murder books. If everything is in order, fine, but Carter and Jo will need a rundown of the case, right?"

Seeing her point, Styles nodded. "I'll need to clear it with the director, but if he agrees, we'll head home after visiting the funeral parlor and then swing by Black Rock Falls in the morning to attend the autopsy. Once we get Wolfe's findings, we'll head back here and go through their files. It would save another team time if we do the groundwork. We'll give it a day or so unless we get a breakthrough in our case." He sighed. "I hate grunt work, but if that were my sister, I'd want to know someone cared enough to go the extra mile. I'll give him a call." He checked his watch. "We have time before we meet Wolfe to go grab a coffee at the diner opposite the sheriff's office and hunt down a place to stay for a couple of nights."

"Sounds like a plan." Beth smiled. "How's our budget?"

Styles smiled. "Very healthy, so find somewhere nice and not some seedy motel. I hear they have one decent hotel here in town, with a restaurant that does a good steak."

"Don't forget, we'll need to be back in Rattlesnake Creek by three to interview our suspects." Beth walked to the Nissan. "I wouldn't mention anything to the sheriff about coming back tomorrow to look through his files. If he is incompetent, I'd prefer catching him by surprise."

Laughing, Styles waved Bear into the truck. "Me too."

TWENTY-THREE

Funeral parlors gave Beth the creeps. The morticians always seemed to be the same, as if pressed from the same mold. They had a way about them and a smell that made her skin crawl. She often wondered how a person could want to be a mortician. She understood these people were very important in the way of things and needed in society, but although she dealt with death all the time, the thought of adding cosmetics to dead flesh to make a body presentable for burial reminded her too much of past cases she'd rather forget. She glanced at Styles as they approached the building and cleared her throat. "I hate this bit."

"Okay, I'll give you something amusing from my distant past to take your mind off it." He pulled up behind Wolfe's truck and smiled at her. "When I was an MP and off duty, which wasn't often because I was on call just about twenty-four/seven, if someone called, I'd answer the phone in a creepy voice and say, 'Happy Field Crematorium, how can I help you in your hour of need?' The person calling usually disconnected real fast. They'd call back again a few minutes later or never, and I'd act like nothing was up." He shrugged. "It was a nasty prank, I know, but I was young and reckless."

Laughing, Beth nodded. "There are two sides to you, Styles. I'm not sure about the regimented hard-ass, but I'm starting to like the bad-boy side of you. I did a few crazy things in my youth too and usually got myself into trouble."

"I figure as long as you don't hurt anyone, it's fine." He gave her a long searching look. "You didn't hurt anyone did you, Beth?"

If only you knew. Beth shook her head. "Only their ego." She indicated toward Wolfe on the sidewalk. "Wolfe is waiting for us. He has that look again. I know he was in the military and I can see it's never far from his mind. He wants things done by the book and when they're not, he gets a little riled."

"More like, he wants to find the truth for victims, much like us." Styles shrugged. "When people make mistakes, killers go free. That's what's upsetting him right now. He's a caring man. He wants the truth, is all, and he'll find it. He's like a dog with a bone. He'll never give up."

The funeral parlor smelled of flowers in the foyer, but the arrangements weren't real. The overpowering floral perfume came from a dispenser on the wall that sprayed out a mist to dispel odors. It made Beth nauseous because it only overlaid the smell of chemicals used to preserve bodies. The stale air seemed to close in around her, suffocating her with each step along the passageways and into the viewing room. She glanced around. No one was there apart from the open casket and a pale face resting on a pink silk cushion, long brown hair arranged around her face to cover her neck.

"I'll need to examine the body of Jody Hooper." Wolfe was talking in hushed tones to the mortician. "In your back room. The body will need to be removed from the casket, undressed, and placed on a gurney for examination." He held up a hand at the man's protests. "Either that or I'll take the body back to Black Rock Falls."

"Very well." The mortician, wearing round spectacles on the end of his nose, peered at him like a small frightened animal. "My assistant is away today. I'll need help to lift the body."

"That's not a problem." Wolfe indicated to everyone. "I have a team with me. Leave it to me and we'll have her back in her coffin before you know it."

"What is the purpose of the examination?" The mortician peered at Wolfe over his spectacles. "I'm afraid she's been embalmed. There won't be any evidence for you to find on her body."

"Just leave the details to me." Wolfe pushed the casket toward the doorway. "Which way?"

"Through the double doors at the end of the passageway." The timid man pointed a shaking finger.

"Who signed the death certificate?" Wolfe turned to look at him. "I'll need a name and contact details. Do you have a copy by any chance?"

"I'll have one on file." The mortician pushed his glasses up onto his nose. "The details will be on the certificate. I'll print one for you." He hurried from the room.

It was difficult to be there while Wolfe proceeded with his examination. Beside him, Colt Webber took photographs for evidence, but the internal examination was recorded on a laptop via a small camera, before and after a dye was introduced into the cavities to highlight any damage. Wolfe wasn't giving a running commentary and was way too busy to take questions. To link the cases, Beth needed to find a similar burn mark on the victim and moved closer. She scanned the body and found the small burn mark, clearly with a distinct marking of a Celtic rune. She waited for Wolfe to finish his examination and then pointed it out. "Look another burn mark. Do you figure this is a signature?"

"Yeah, I noticed that, and Webber has taken images." Wolfe went to his kit and pulled out instruments. "As this victim is being buried, I'll need to take this as evidence." He went about removing the small area of skin. "I'll compare this to the mark we found on the other victim. I can see this one clearly has a mark. It's maybe from a ring or similar. Something like this could break a case wide open." He looked at Beth. "I hope there are images of the other victims we can use for comparison. I'll get my team onto it as soon as we get back to the office."

It didn't take too long at all for Wolfe to finish, and the body was redressed and placed back into the casket. Emily Wolfe rearranged the victim's hair and gave her a little pat on the arm before nodding to Webber to take the body back to the viewing room. That gentle kindness surprised Beth. She'd have imagined after the victim was through the process, they'd be just another case, but then maybe that was her psychopath side not understanding the way of things.

Although Beth often experienced strong emotions and understood that the presumed complete lack of empathy in psychopaths all the experts professed was flawed, over the years she'd come to understand many things about herself and others like her. It was strong emotions that triggered their behavior in the first instance. The same drive that pushed them to kill repeatedly. What made her different was her understanding about why it happened—how the trigger drove the person to kill.

For years, she'd compartmentalized the bad things in her life. She'd locked away seeing her father murder her mother, the years of abuse in foster care, and placed them where they couldn't control her emotions. Normal people do this all the time. Someone is nasty to them, so they lock the memory of what happened away and forget it. It's a way of coping with bad things in life. The problem with a psychopath is their brain is slightly different and the fail-safe everyone else has that stops them acting on impulse is missing. So when their emotional trigger happens, all those boxes carrying all those bad memories open up and flood the mind. It's like a powerful drug and it had taken Beth a long time to bring the impulses to fight back under a modicum of control. The problem was, if she didn't direct her anger toward stopping the unstoppable monsters, she'd lose control. She could become a "shoot first and ask questions later" type of special agent, by placing herself in impossible and dangerous situations. That action could be considered to be on the right side of the law. Many would see her as a hero, but how long would that last? No, she'd keep to her own code of doing things, using self-defense as her proof or seeing a crime committed before she acted as the Tarot Killer.

"Beth." Styles touched her arm. "You okay?"

Dragging her mind back to the case, she nodded. "Just thinking, is all."

"No rape." Wolfe removed his gloves and mask and tossed them into the garbage and then washed his hands. "She has bruises and burn marks all over her from where her clothes were torn, same as the other victim. I'm not seeing defensive wounds on either victim either, and there are multiple ligature marks, so he used the cord to subdue rather than kill. The scratches on the neck are from the victim clawing at the cord. The bruises on the thighs would suggest rape but it didn't happen in this case. I'll do a more conclusive examination on the other victim, but the fact he wants to rape them and doesn't is significant." He looked at Beth and Styles. "This isn't the same killer as the Convenience Store Killer. His victims were savagely raped, and this man is looking impotent. If you decide to continue with this case, I suggest you consult with Jo Wells. She'll be able to give you an insight into this killer's motive, especially if we can tie in the burn marks as well."

Beth nodded. "I'm seeing gross incompetence by the local

sheriff's office here. It's something we need to call in. I'd appreciate it if we keep this information to ourselves right now."

"Y'all thinking there's been a cover-up?" Wolfe's eyes narrowed. "Involving the local doctors as well?"

"I figure it's something we need to look into." Styles let out a long sigh. "I checked out the files and seems to me the sheriff called in someone different every time they found a body. That in itself is unusual. In homicide you need comparisons to make a case and I'm not seeing that here."

"This is something I can explore." Wolfe's brows knitted together in a frown. "If any of the local doctors are skirting the rules, I'll report them. It's part of my job. I'll need copies of everything you have so I can compare the information on every victim."

"I'll upload everything onto the server." Styles smiled. "We have a few files Beth pulled from the sheriff's department computers. I've cleared our involvement with the director. We'll be dropping by for another visit first thing tomorrow to go through the sheriff's murder books and see what else he has hidden away in evidence."

"That's a ton of work"—Emily looked from one to the other —"running two cases back-to-back. What if the Convenience Store Killer strikes again while you're here?"

Not wanting her plans disrupted, Beth shrugged. "We're interviewing suspects this afternoon, but apart from some sketchy facial-recognition hits on eye shape, we have zip on the killer. That case is our priority, but as both killers have just struck, it's unlikely they'll kill again soon. I figure we can work both of them for a day or so. If it looks like a cover-up on this case, then we'll call in another team to take over. Right now, it's a gut feeling, is all."

"Okay." Styles checked his watch. "We need to go. I'll follow up with the sheriff and see if he has any reports on missing girls, so we can get an ID on the latest victim. If he has anything, I'll upload the details. We'll swing by first thing and attend the autopsy on the other victim. I want to know what you discover about the burn mark."

"Okay." Wolfe picked up his forensic kit. "Autopsy is at ten."

TWENTY-FOUR

Roaring Creek

In the air and heading to Roaring Creek, Beth checked her phone for the local map of the area. "We can walk to where they're dropping by with deliveries for the first two. The second and third are mining camps and we'll need transport. I called Sheriff Bowman and he'll have a cruiser we can use standing by." She scrolled through her phone. "Just a rundown on the suspects to refresh our memories. Austin Buck delivers newspapers, magazines, tobacco goods, etcetera, to stores in all four towns. The delivery this afternoon is to the local gas station. The manager there is Ann Jones. Next, Clay Maverick delivers dairy products to the diner. The contact there is Elizabeth McGill. Both these businesses are expecting us, so there won't be a problem."

"Okay and where to after that?" Styles flicked her a glance.

Beth scrolled through her notes. "No contact for the next one, Wyatt Cody. I hacked his delivery schedule. Cody, as I mentioned before, owns his own online supply service. He supplies mining camps and local stores with a variety of goods.

So we head out to the Lost Gold mining camp about two miles out of town. He's due there around four and as luck would have it Billy Straus is due at the same camp at four-thirty. He handles medical supplies and delivers pharmacy orders mainly to the mines."

Ten minutes later, they dropped down on top of Roaring Creek General and after being buffeted by the howling wind, headed down the stairs and out into the sunshine. She checked the map on her phone. "The local gas station is along Main on the right."

"We're early." Styles checked his watch. "Isn't that a delivery van parked in the alleyway?"

Beth increased her pace. "Yeah, maybe he's early."

They waited patiently for the driver to unload his goods and close his van doors before approaching him. He was the right size for the shooter and she'd seen this man on the CCTV footage in the store before the shooting. She waited for Styles to take the lead and took out a notebook and pen.

"Austin Buck?" Styles held up his cred pack. "Agents Styles and Katz. Do you mind if we ask you a few questions?"

"No, but I can't be too long. I'm on a schedule." Buck folded his arms across his chest and leaned against the back of his van. "What can I do for you? If it's about illegal tobacco products, I don't touch any of that stuff. All my deliveries are legit."

"I believe you were in town the night the convenience store was robbed." Styles stood relaxed, his expression unreadable.

"Yeah, I had a stopover." He shrugged. "We're only allowed to drive a certain number of hours. I was over my limit, so took a room at the motel."

"Did you go to the convenience store during your time here?" Styles narrowed his gaze. "As in, were you in the vicinity of the convenience store anytime after dark?"

"Yeah, well, you know I was, right?" Buck gave him a direct

stare. "They've got CCTV cameras. So what's this really all about?"

Beth looked up from taking notes. "What did you see that night? The night of the shooting."

"I'm not sure." Buck shrugged. "I went in for a soda and some snacks, is all. You know, to eat watching TV?"

"Did you see anyone hanging around the store or along the sidewalk, parked outside and sitting in a vehicle, that you can recall?" Styles was staring as if looking straight through him.

"Nope. There was a girl walking toward the store as I came out, she was really pretty and had long hair. Too young for me though." Buck checked his watch. "There were people in the store. Vehicles parked outside. I don't recall how many. I just grabbed my stuff and walked back to my van. I was tired. It had been a long day."

Beth exchanged a glance with Styles. "What time was this?"

"Around nine, I guess." Buck looked from one to the other. "That's all I have. I heard about the shootings on the news the next morning. I guess I'm lucky to be alive, huh?"

"Yeah, seems that way." Styles handed him a card. "If anything else comes to mind, give me a call. Thanks for your time." He turned to go and glanced at Beth. "It's not him."

Not understanding, Beth stared at him. "How do you know?"

"Half of his right index finger is missing." He raised both eyebrows. "When he removed his gloves just before, I noticed. The shooter was right-handed and used that finger to pull the trigger."

The wind whipped Beth's hair into her eyes as they headed for the diner. As she stepped inside, she gathered it up and secured it with a band from around her wrist. She'd let it down from the ponytail to get the stink of the funeral parlor out of it. That smell could sure cling. She approached the counter and smiled at the woman waiting to serve them. She glanced at Styles. "We're early, want coffee?"

"Might as well." He smiled at the woman behind the counter. "You'd be Elizabeth McGill?"

"That's me. I'm guessing you're the FBI agents come to speak with Clay Maverick?" She smiled back. "I've known Clay for a long time. He lives here in town and has been delivering small goods to us for a few years now. I've never had a problem with him. What's he done?"

"We don't believe he's done anything, ma'am." Styles shook his head. "We're interviewing anyone who was around town the night of the shooting, is all. We're looking for witnesses. Were you here at that time? Did you see anyone hanging around the convenience store?"

"I was here at the time." Elizabeth McGill indicated behind her. "I live out back and didn't hear anything. It's a ways away from here and with the TV on I don't hear much of what goes on outside."

Beth ordered coffee and two slices of pie. She'd suddenly gotten her appetite back after the funeral parlor and had missed lunch. "That's fine. We'll wait for Clay to arrive. It's just routine questions, nothing for him to worry about." She waited for the pie and coffee, and they carried their meal to a table in the window. "Hmm, the nice guy. Now that sets off alarm bells right away."

"We'll see." Styles dug into his pie and smiled at her. "How did you know I wanted a slice of pie?"

Shaking her head, Beth shrugged and looked him straight in the eye. "Really? You have to ask me? When don't you want a slice of pie?"

"True." Styles ate slowly. "Nice, but not as good as TJ's and those pies we bought from Aunt Betty's Café out at Black Rock Falls. Man, I've never eaten a cherry pie so good."

Beth sipped her coffee and peered at him over the rim.

"Next time we find a body, maybe you can ask Wolfe to bring one with him."

"What?" Styles spluttered his coffee, grabbing a wad of paper napkins to press to his mouth. "Oh, Beth, you'll be the death of me. I can imagine the conversation. *Wolfe, can you get here ASAP. We have a homicide, and can I get a slice of cherry pie with that?* Can you imagine his reaction?"

Beth savored a forkful of pie and chuckled. "It was just a suggestion. We're heading there in the morning. You want pie, we'll grab some before we leave. It's only a few minutes out of our day."

"I'll bring a cooler." Styles drained his cup and looked at her. "Heads up, someone is heading our way." He stood and faced the man approaching them, instantly recognizing him as Clay Maverick. Beth had chosen suspects who all fit the general description of the shooter.

"Liz mentioned you wanted to speak to me?" Maverick pushed up the brim of his cowboy hat and looked from one to the other. "What's up? It's not usual to have the FBI in town."

"Two mass murders in six months and we'll come running." Styles waved him to a seat. "Why don't you sit down so we can have a chat?"

Beth placed her fork on her plate and pushed it away. She took out her notebook. "Liz mentioned you live in town. You know about the shootings. Have you seen any strangers hanging around lately?"

"Nope." Clay Maverick scratched his cheek and leaned casually back in his chair. "You figure, if there's a gunman taking out people in town, anyone is going to spill their guts about him?" He looked slowly from one to the other. "Most of us are carrying but we don't intend to kill no one. It's a dog-eat-dog world out there. When I'm out doing deliveries, I never know who might decide to pull me over and steal my cargo."

"There's a big demand for dairy products around here,

huh?" Styles snorted. "Maybe cigarettes and beer, but cheese and yogurt, maybe not so much." He stared him down. "You live around town, so you go to the convenience store how many times a week would you say?"

"I dunno, couple of times, maybe three." Maverick shrugged. "I went by the night of the shooting and saw the bodies everywhere. I didn't see the girl they said was abducted but I did pass a truck heading north."

Beth lifted her pen. "What make of truck? Color?"

"I don't recall." Maverick smiled at her. "I was thinking about ice cream. What flavor I wanted. Do you like ice cream? You look like a chocolate chip girl to me."

The way he smoothly took over the conversation, guiding it away from the questioning, made Beth smile. Oh, he was good. "Do I? Well, you'll never know, will you? What time was this?"

"Are FBI female agents so hard to get along with?" Maverick looked at Styles.

"Just answer the questions, Mr. Maverick, and then we can be on our way." Styles cleared his throat. "What time was this?"

"A little after nine." Maverick shrugged. "I wasn't the only one there. People were running around waving guns and screaming orders. The cops arrived and sent everyone home."

"Did anyone go inside to check on the victims?" Styles leaned forward, pressing his clasped hands on the table.

"Nope." Maverick gave him a long look. "There was blood all over, and a woman was lying near the door. She was dead. Her eyes were just staring. The others had head shots. No one was walking out of there alive."

Beth eyed him critically. "You don't seem too upset about witnessing a mass murder. Have you served in the military?"

"Me? Heavens no." Maverick barked a laugh. "I hunt. Blood doesn't bother me. I didn't know any of the people, so it was kind of like watching a horror movie, like from outside."

"Try to think back to the truck you saw driving away."

Styles looked at him. "What type? You know it's a truck, so what type?"

"Hmm, could have been a Ram. It had a covered bed, windows were tinted. It was dark, as in not white or silver. That's all I've got." Maverick looked from one to the other. "Can I go now? Liz has a slice of chocolate cake with my name on it out back."

Beth leaned forward. "One thing." She smiled. "Are you married or do you live alone?"

"I haven't left home yet." Maverick shrugged. "Pretty bad, huh? Living with parents at my age, but around here, we often stay put until we have a place of our own."

"Yeah. I've noticed." Styles handed him a card. "If anything else comes to mind about that night, give me a call."

Beth watched him walk away and turned to Styles. "Possible. He fits the profile and he has all his fingers."

TWENTY-FIVE

It had started to rain as they headed for the sheriff's department. The cold drops splashed Beth's cheeks as the wind picked up, sending the rain almost horizontal. As they walked, the temperature dropped so fast clouds of steam came out of her nose with every breath. The rain turned to ice, and sleet peppered them in icy shards. They ran the last few yards to the entrance and fell inside, glad to be out of the cold. She bypassed the front desk and led the way to Sheriff Bowman's office and knocked on the door. "We've come for the vehicle. One thing, did you take the names of the crowd members who gathered at the murder scene?"

"Nope." Bowman handed her a set of keys. "It wasn't necessary to question a bunch of traumatized townsfolk. I knew all of them. They live close by. If they'd seen anything, they'd have told me. It's a close-knit community."

Shaking her head, Beth looked at him incredulous. "And yet a gunman, probably the same gunman, hit the same place twice and not a soul witnessed anything?" She raised both eyebrows. "Is this the case or are people afraid to say anything around here?"

"Afraid?" Bowman looked perplexed. "Why would they be afraid? If someone threatened them with a weapon, they'd defend themselves."

"Yet people died in the convenience store." Styles narrowed his gaze. "Nobody attempted to take down the gunman, did they?"

"I guess not everyone was carrying." Bowman shrugged. "I don't have an answer for you."

"Okay." Styles nodded. "Thanks for the vehicle. We'll have it back in a couple of hours."

"The vehicle is the department's SUV and is parked right outside. If we're gone for the day, leave it at the hospital parking lot and the keys at the counter." Bowman frowned. "Watch your backs at the mining camp. Those roughnecks don't take too kindly to law enforcement."

Pulling up her collar against the sleet, Beth glanced at Styles as they headed out into the cold. "Oh, this day just gets better by the second." She handed him the keys. "You drive. I'll navigate."

After adding the address of the mining camp to the GPS, they headed out of town. The GPS sent them along a highway for a time and then onto dirt roads heading into the mountains and then down toward a valley. The scenery had been destroyed. Large bare patches of soil and mounds of rubble littered the once picturesque mountain landscape. It was a hive of activity. Men in hard hats, rubber boots, and slickers moved around intent on their work. The noise was deafening. Beth shook her head. Noise and land pollution wasn't something she appreciated. "Oh, this is terrible."

"I never took you for a nature lover, being a city girl and all." Styles maneuvered the truck around a wet, uneven rut in the track. "Ah, yeah, but you paint landscapes, so I guess you appreciate beautiful scenery." He sighed. "Don't worry, there's plenty

more to see around Rattlesnake Creek. The town has boundaries to preserve the area from mining."

She shook her head, gaping at the gush of dirty water
spilling from a soil-rinsing machine and into a once pristine
stream. Heavy machinery sat beside mounds of dirt, spilling
fumes into the air. The entire scene horrified her. How could
this mess ever be returned back to its natural state? "I figured
this was a gold mine, like underground."

"Nah, these days most of the miners go over old timers'
claims." Styles stared at the sky. "Miners collect their overburden, the piles of waste from the mines, and process it. There are
usually gold fragments left behind, as in millions of dollars of
gold, and they extract it from the waste. It's not the tailings.
That's waste that has been processed using mercury, which is
too dangerous to work." He smiled at her. "This might look bad
to you, but the old timers left toxic waste and did nothing to
clean up afterward. These miners at least have to return the site
to its original condition."

Snorting, Beth looked at him. "What, mounds of what did
you call them? Ah yes, *overburden* and toxic dumps. That
sounds like a solid plan. Maybe it needs to be looked into by the
Forest Service, and get them to insist they plant trees and shrubs
and smooth down the mounds of rubble."

"Put it to the next council meeting." Styles smiled at her.
"You'll have support. Although miners are the town's lifeblood,
no one wants the environment damaged." He looked ahead.
"Ah, there's the office. I'll stop there and ask where deliveries
are dropped." He pulled up alongside the front door and
climbed out. "You might as well wait here. Pointless both of us
getting wet."

He was back in a few seconds, and they headed down a
wide dirt road covered in gravel. She turned to him. "Did you
ask about the suspects?"

"Nope, just about the deliveries." Styles kept his attention on the road. "They don't need to know why we're here."

They drove to the back of what looked like a cookhouse and beside it was a small store, a place when the miners could purchase a few necessities. Beth noticed it opened early in the morning and at six at night. "So the miners sleep and eat here?"

"Yeah." Styles pulled up beside one of two delivery vans. "There are many different types of companies. Some are owned by partners, or a group of guys all put in cash to buy a lease and work it, split the profits. Others work for a company. There are many different gold mines all through this area. The gems are usually mined by companies. They're underground and danger-ous. The miners need to know what they're doing down in the mines." He indicated to the vans backed up to an opening in the building. "I figure those vans belong to our suspects. They beat us to it, and it looks like they're almost finished unloading. I hope we can detain them both for questioning."

Beth reached for the door handle. "That's what I use my badge for and it usually works. Not many people will leave if the FBI needs to talk to them." She looked at him. "I figure we split up and take the men away from each other for questioning."

"That will sure save time." Styles pulled up his collar and turned to Bear. "Wait here, Bear. It's freezing and wet outside."

Beth pulled the hood of her jacket over her head and ducked out of the truck, running for the open roller door in the back of the building and skirting the vans. Inside, a group of men eyed her with surprise. She took out her cred pack and held it up for them to see it. "Special Agent Beth Katz. I'm here with Agent Styles and we'd like a word with Wyatt Cody and Billy Straus. She scanned the men. Looking for any signs of apprehension.

"I'm Cody." A slim but muscular young man strolled toward her, his gaze moved up and down her in a blatant appraisal before a small smile twitched the sides of his lips. "A woman FBI agent in this neck of the woods. Go figure."

Beth stood her ground and mirrored his actions. It was good to see his expression change. Her reaction wasn't what he'd expected, and she had turned from being the hunted to the hunter. She wondered how he felt being appraised like a prize bull. Maybe he had the delusional idea that a frank appraisal was a compliment, when in her mind it was an insult. She lifted her chin. "Is there somewhere out of the wind we can talk?"

"Sure, the canteen is out front of the cookhouse. They serve meals and coffee all day. Most of the guys here work odd hours. It depends on the conditions." Cody indicated toward a door a few yards into the back of the area. "Through there."

Hanging back, she glanced at Styles, who nodded. "We'll follow you." Behind her she could hear Styles speaking to the other driver.

As they walked into a room with tables and chairs and a long counter with various food items and pastries set behind glass display cabinets, she followed Cody to a separate table with coffee machines, cups, and fixings.

"Like I said, coffee runs twenty-four/seven here." Cody poured a cup of coffee and smiled at her. "How do you take yours?"

"Cream and sugar, thanks." She pulled off her gloves and reached inside her jacket for her notebook and pen.

When the coffee was ready, she followed Cody to a table a few yards away, near a woodstove. It was toasty inside, and Beth removed her coat and hung it over the back of the chair. She sat down and stared at him. "Okay, we're trying to establish a time-line for the stop and rob out at Roaring Creek Sunday last and the previous one out at Broken Bridge on Friday." She gave him a direct stare, watching his reaction. "You move between towns, and we have reason to believe you were in the areas at the times of the shootings."

"It's likely." Cody leaned back in his seat, coffee in one hand, one boot resting casually on the opposite knee. "I run my own delivery business but I'm the whole deal. I do everything, so I take extra orders when they come in. It's good for business. So, yeah, so what if I was in the local area at the time? So were many other people. What is it you want from me, Agent Katz?"

Beth looked him over. Confident and relaxed. Yet many people being confronted by an FBI agent would be on edge. All the men they'd interviewed appeared to be nonchalant. Maybe it was the relaxed way of life in the mountains? She stared at him, hoping he'd wilt in front of her eyes, but he just smiled at her. Perhaps staring at him was regarded as a come-on? As the questions slipped back into her mind, she cleared her throat. Maybe let him believe he had the upper hand. "We're chasing down witnesses, as you were in town around the times of both incidents, the chances are high that you saw something. We have CCTV footage of you in one of the stores." That statement was a lie to some extent. If he wasn't the killer, it was pure fabrication, but if he was, well, they did have a video of the murders.

"I don't recall anything unusual happening in either place." Cody sipped his coffee and stared at the ceiling as if thinking hard. "Hmm, in Broken Bridge, when I came out of the store, I did see the man with the dog. The dog was barking, if I recall. I figure that's the man the killer shot when he was leaving." He dropped his gaze back to her. "I didn't witness the shooting. I was long gone by then."

Beth wanted more information and it was like pulling teeth from this man. "When you were in the store, do you recall seeing a girl or anyone else inside?"

"The kidnapped girl they found murdered?" Cody sipped his drink. "Yeah, she went in just before me and went to the back of the store. There were other people but I don't recall anyone in particular."

Acting casual, Beth made a few notes and lifted her gaze to him. "What vehicles did you see outside the store?"

"I parked beside a Ram, but I don't recall the others or how many." He shrugged. "I wasn't thinking about cars just about getting home to watch football."

There was that Ram vehicle again. She wrote fast and then looked at him. "What about Sunday night out at Roaring Creek?"

"I dropped by to grab a to-go cup of coffee for the road." He shrugged and, dropping his boot from his knee, placed the cup on the table. "I saw the guy at the desk, is all. I don't recall seeing anyone in the store and I don't recall what vehicles were parked outside. I was tired and just wanted to get home." He opened his hands wide. "I wish I could help but I have nothing."

Beth nodded. "Are you married?"

"Oh, that's a loaded question!" Cody barked a laugh. "Are you interested?"

Shaking her head, Beth caught Styles' gaze on her from across the room. "No. I just wondered if you had an alibi for either of those nights. A wife or partner would do."

"No wife, just my mom." He sighed. "You could ask her, but she's usually in bed by nine." He gave her a long look. "You obviously have my address, so go and ask her. Be my guest."

"Okay, that's all I need." Beth folded her notebook and placed it inside her pocket. "Thank you for your cooperation." She stood, picked up her cup, and headed toward Styles' table. Behind her, she heard the scrape of a chair as Cody left.

"There isn't anything else I can tell you." The fourth suspect, Billy Straus shrugged. "I was sick and someone else took over the deliveries. I didn't ask who it was. They just stepped in. I wasn't in Roaring Creek or Broken Bridge on either of those days."

"Is there anyone who can verify your whereabouts on those days?" Styles stared at him.

"My mom was sick too and my aunt dropped by with some chicken soup." Straus shrugged. "You could ask her, I guess."

"Give me her name and number." Styles pushed his notebook toward him. He waited for the man to comply and then nodded. "Okay, thanks. That's all for this time."

Beth looked at Styles. "Cody was overconfident but gave some information. He lives with his mom, so we can check out his alibi. Although she goes to bed at nine, she might have heard him or knew if he didn't go home that night." She sighed. "It's not even close to valid circumstantial evidence on any of our suspects. There could have been countless men around the convenience stores at the times of the murders. We can't haul people in because they were in the vicinity. The only solid was the Ram truck. The thing is, I see that type of truck driving around all over, and we can't haul every driver in for questioning. We're chasing shadows."

"Just a minute." Styles stood and went to the coffee machine and poured a coffee before returning. "Okay, I've got nothing either. That guy was nervous and was sick over the times of the last shootings. I don't think we need worry about him. In fact, as the other three cooperated and we're not any closer to catching this guy, we have only one option."

Beth rolled her eyes. "And that is?"

"We try and anticipate where he's going to strike next." Styles sipped his coffee. "He has a comfort zone. The local sheriffs can stake out the convenience stores."

Shaking her head, Beth stared at him. "The convenience store was just that... convenient. Now he knows the FBI is on the case, he could strike at any store in any place. What would you do, Styles? Follow a pattern or would you be smart enough to mix things up a bit?"

"Yeah, I'd mix things up." He frowned. "So where do we go from here? We haven't the manpower to watch every store in town."

This had been in the front of Beth's mind all day. She had no idea how to prevent another shooting. They were random and happened in seconds. The chances of being there when the shooting went down would be infinitesimal. "It's an impossible task unless we had an army and then the shooter wouldn't hit a place, would he? No one is that stupid. Our only chance is to figure out either where he takes the woman after the shootings or where he intends to kill her. He has chosen places along the county border."

"So you figure we do nothing, allow more innocent people to die and then try and get to him before he murders another woman?" Styles shook his head. "You're batshit crazy."

Seeing his confusion, Beth shook her head. If he wanted a show of empathy, she could do that, although in truth, her detachment kept her dark side under control, but she couldn't use that as an excuse. "I'm not saying we do nothing, Styles, I'm saying we're only two people and we can't possibly cover four counties in the hope we might hit the lottery. It's an impossible task." She sighed. "Of course I don't want him killing again. Do you honestly believe I'd stand around and do nothing if I could stop him? I want to catch him before he kills again, but we both know the chances of that are remote."

"Yeah, they are." Styles ran a hand through his hair. "It will be like looking for a needle in a haystack."

Nodding, Beth swallowed hard. "This guy is going to keep doing this, you need to face facts that we can't stop him until we work out who he is or where he intends to strike next. We can send out a media release so people are aware of the danger and take precautions, but that's all. I can try something. I'll run a probability algorithm. I'll feed in all the information on the places he executed his abducted victims and get the probabilities. When he abducts another woman, we can use the chopper and be there before he has the chance to kill her. From what we've seen, part of his fantasy is to let them go and then shoot them. So he needs an open secluded area close to the county border and one he hasn't used before, close to a road." She turned her coffee cup around in her fingers. "Yes, people could die. I want to avoid that happening as much as you do, but if you plan on catching this guy, this is our only chance."

TWENTY-SIX

THURSDAY, WEEK TWO

Black Rock Falls

The following morning, Styles headed the chopper toward Black Rock Falls. Leaving a case hanging played on his mind. Overnight he'd mulled over Beth's conclusions on the Convenience Store Killer case and reluctantly agreed to concentrate on the Night Creeper case for a day or two. In truth, they had no way of catching the Convenience Store Killer in the act or preventing another mass shooting. The previous evening Beth had set to work, and they'd left her computer running her specially designed software to give them a better chance of anticipating his next move. It was a shot in the dark, but it was all they had right now. He'd called all the local sheriffs and instructed them to send out media releases to warn the local residents a gunman was a threat to their communities. There was always a chance, if the shooter struck again, one of the townsfolk would step in and take out the gunman. It had happened before when lives were threatened. Styles' pride at being able to protect people had taken a bashing with this case. Feeling useless in this type of situation wasn't part of his character and it was intolerable. He forced his mind away from the probable senseless deaths of more innocent people and back to the Night Creeper case. Beth's concern of a cover-up by someone in the sheriff's department left a bad taste in his mouth, but from what he'd seen so far, it was the only solid explanation for the Night Creeper's continued reign of terror around Mischief.

He landed and powered down the chopper. As he gathered his things he noticed Beth had only removed her headset and was staring straight ahead, shoulders rigid. He frowned and looked at her. "Ready?"

"Is it something I said?" Beth turned in her seat to look at him. "You spent hours hitting balls last night and this morning you've not said a word to me about what's troubling you. We need to communicate if we're planning on solving either of our cases."

Styles had always played his cards close to the vest. He'd revealed more to Beth about his private life than he had to anyone, mainly, he believed, to help her face her own demons. He understood people, mainly from dealing with soldiers freshly back from tours of duty, with their heads scrambled and unable to cope. Talking about problems rather than holding them inside did help. He'd made a huge mistake when his mentally sick wife exerted coercive control over him before trying to kill him. He'd known something was terribly wrong and because he loved her so much had tried to handle the situation himself. He looked at Beth. Her eyes held the same steady expression as always. He'd seen anger and concern in those eyes, but he wondered if she'd ever loved anyone or could love anyone after being abused in foster care. "I'm sorry. Sometimes I just have to let out my personal demons, Beth. I'm angry with myself for not being able to stop the shooter. It's a failure to me and I don't take failure too well. I can see your point. We can't be everywhere at once, and I can't save the world."

"We'll catch him." Beth cleared her throat. "There's nothing we can do until we outsmart him. We will outsmart him. He's just one man and has never been up against people like us before." She shrugged. "Put that case out of your mind for now. The local sheriffs are dealing with it, and we need all our attention on the Night Creeper. After the autopsy findings, it will be interesting to see what we find in the murder books and case files." She glanced at him. "I'd personally like to know, in this digital age, why the heck he isn't uploading all his cases to his server. He has one, and apart from local misdemeanors, there's nothing there at all. The Night Creeper murders mention only someone died and a very sketchy report from the hospital or local doctors and morticians. It's the weirdest setup I've ever seen."

Climbing from the chopper and letting Bear out, Styles smiled at her. "I can't imagine how Sheriff Walker is going to cope with you hauling him over the coals. He chuckled. "I figure it's going to make my day." He clicked his fingers for Bear to follow them and pulled open the heavy metal door to the entrance.

As they descended the stairs and went into the elevator that took them down to the mortuary and examination rooms in the medical examiner's office, he glanced at Beth. "You sure you don't want to call in Jo Wells to assist in the Convenience Store Killer case? She might be able to discover something about this maniac that we've missed."

"Not yet." Beth folded her arms across her chest. "I don't have any information to give her. Just bringing her in now will make us look incompetent."

Nodding, Styles waited for the elevator doors to open. The familiar smell of the examination rooms wafted toward them. The place was surgically clean. White tiles from floor to ceiling gleamed without one speck of dust anywhere and the smell of decaying flesh had been masked to some extent by floral disinfectants and air freshener plug-ins in power outlets in strategic areas. Strangely enough, Wolfe never carried the odor of death. How he managed to avoid the stench Styles didn't know. He figured he must live in the shower. As they walked along the passageway to Wolfe's office, the door opened and two people, accompanied by a bloodhound, walked out with Wolfe. His attention drifted over the petite beautiful woman, and he blinked. He recognized her and the huge guy at her side after seeing them in the local newspaper. They made quite the couple, like the handsome football player and the stunning cheerleader prom king and queen. What a mistake anyone would make if they believed these two were a pushover, as this was Sheriff Jenna Alton and her husband, Deputy Dave Kane, two of the most respected law enforcement officers in these parts. Even their dog, Duke, was a legend in his own right after digging out Kane from a mudslide and saving his life.

When Wolfe came toward them and made introductions, he could actually feel Beth stiffen beside him. He glanced at her and she seemed to be making all the normal responses. He shook hands and smiled. "I've heard so much about you and your team. Very impressive."

"It's nice to meet you at last." Jenna turned to Beth and she frowned. "Have we met? You look familiar."

"No, I arrived from DC last fall." Beth smiled and offered her hand. "I did spend a short time in Helena but I'm sure I'd remember meeting you. I mean, you're in books and all."

"Ah, well, I hope we'll have time to chat soon." Jenna smiled.

"Great to meet you." Kane's handshake was firm and his smile reached his eyes.

Styles nodded. "Maybe we'll get together over a case one of these days? We can't allow Carter and Jo to have all the fun."

"We'll be sure to call if we need you." Jenna looked at

Wolfe. "Thanks, Shane. We'll wait for your report. Don't forget to try and make it to the cookout this Sunday."

"I'll do my best." Wolfe smiled at her. "I have three cases on the run at the moment." As Jenna and Kane walked away, he waved a hand toward the examination rooms. "Leave Bear in my office. There's food, water, and a dog bed in there. Grab scrubs, masks, and gloves from the alcove. I'm ready to start. I have only Webber assisting today. Em is taking a class."

Styles hung back until Wolfe had walked into the examination room with a red light glowing outside and followed Beth to the alcove. As they removed their coats, gloves, and hats, he looked at her. "You didn't look too impressed meeting the local sheriff. Is there something I should know?"

"Not impressed?" Beth pulled on scrubs and grinned at him. "I was impressed. What you were seeing was dumbstruck with awe. You know, like meeting a favorite movie star? It's hard to act casual, when I've been trained to the highest level and I'm expected to know how to solve cases, right?" She pulled on a mask and then gloves. "Then I'm expected to compete, with literally no formal training, against an elected sheriff and deputy who can run rings around me with their eyes shut. They don't just solve crimes, they do it to such an extent someone put their cases into a bestselling series of books. I mean, come on, Styles. That doesn't make you awestruck?"

Never having been awestruck by anyone, Styles shrugged. "I know Kane has a military background. Ty Carter mentioned it in passing. Plus they have an impressive team around them. One of their deputies worked as a gold shield detective in LA, then they have Carter and Jo and Wolfe and his team." He snapped on gloves. "We do just fine and we've solved cases just as notorious. Give it time, our cases will make it into a true crime series as well."

"Oh, I'm not sure I'd want the publicity. They'd dig into my past and use it against me for sure." Beth's brow furrowed into a frown. "Right now, they have targets on their backs. Serial killers are already coming here. There are so many who would see these vast areas of forest as a perfect place to hunt. Just how many would want to be the first to take them out? For them it would be the ultimate trophy."

Intrigued by the way she thought, Styles glanced at the examination room door and figured he had another minute to talk to her before Wolfe came looking for them. "Maybe, but they have experience now and that's everything when dealing with psychopaths, right?"

"Getting married was their first mistake... family, well that's two." Beth turned to look at him. "You know as well as I do that psychopaths are smart and they take vulnerabilities and use them to their advantage. It's like staking out a live goat to catch a bear. If they set their sights on taking down one of them, they'll use what works best. Trust me, people they love will make the best goats."

TWENTY-SEVEN

Still reeling from coming face-to-face with Jenna Alton, Beth followed Styles into the examination room. She'd taken down a serial killer more than once in Black Rock Falls, but to keep her Tarot Killer identity a secret she'd had no choice but to make up an explanation on the fly. Styles was so perceptive and picked up the slightest change in her body language. Part of her wished she could come clean and tell him, but Styles was a law-abiding man and she couldn't risk the chance of him turning her in. She sensed he believed she'd spun him a yarn by the way he lifted one eyebrow when she'd given her excuses. How could she tell him that Jenna had seen her, as herself, not hours after she'd dispatched an unstoppable serial killer. The one in question would have been in the wind long before Jenna and her team had gotten to him. Out of options, she had to act. It had been self-defense; he'd tried to kill her and she'd turned the tables on him. She had no witnesses, and she never planned to have any either. Not that it mattered. Deep down inside, her conscience was clear, just as it would be if she killed someone firing on her in an FBI shootout. One side of the line is murder, and the other is ruled as a justified shooting.

"Y'all ready?" Wolfe looked from one to the other. "In your absence, I took X-rays, blood samples, and swabs of all areas of interest." He indicated to the array of screens on the wall. "I've established the ID of the victim as Layla Cooper out of Wolf Valley. We had her mom by earlier to identify her. She reported her missing first thing this morning. As most folks do, she'd called everyone, driven around the roads. Just in case she'd missed the bus home, the sheriff was notified. He called the local bus station. The driver recalls dropping her at her usual stop. She takes the bus regular. He didn't recall seeing anyone in the local vicinity at the time."

"You've just about done all our work for us." Styles stared at Wolfe. "Do you know where she was last seen?"

"I sure do." Wolfe pulled up a map on the screen and they all moved closer. "Bus stop is here. She usually walks from here to her home." He moved his finger across the map. "This is the old industrial area where we found the body. It's a mile or so away in the opposite direction. There's no reason she'd head out there. The bus driver insisted she got down from the bus alone and he saw no one waiting for her, and no vehicles in the immediate area."

Beth moved her attention to the X-rays and pointed to the neck. "She has a broken hyoid bone, so is that conclusive of strangulation?"

"In layman's terms, yeah." Wolfe looked at her. "*Asphyxiation* is the term I'd use, by means of a cord." He moved back to the body and flipped back the sheet.

"As I assumed when we examined the body in situ, the killer used a cord to immobilize but not kill his victim." Wolfe indicated to the circles of ligature marks crisscrossing the neck. "As she fought to remove the cord, it was tightened enough to render her unconscious, and then with her subdued, he attempted to rape her." He indicated to the bruises to her thighs. "I can see why a local doctor or a mortician seeing this bruising would assume rape took place. In the instance of Jody Hooper, the victim we examined at the funeral parlor yesterday, a swab was taken by a local doctor, but without a full rape kit diagnosis, we had no positive proof of rape. It was an assumption. We now know that no rape took place." He looked from one to the other. "I'll conduct the same examination now." He collected his instruments and went to work.

Watching the screen rather than the process, Beth waited for the dye to be introduced into the cavities to allow tears and damage to show out very clearly on the scope. She shook her head. The vaginal cavity was undamaged. The hymen was clearly intact, confirming the victim was a virgin. "At least, it will give the parents some peace to know she wasn't raped."

"I can't imagine the horror of losing a child." Wolfe removed the instruments and set them back on the aluminum tray. "Attempted rape in both victims. The others are inconclusive because I can't trust the examination reports. This is not the same guy as in Roaring River. He multiple-raped his victims. I don't believe this guy is capable, as in, he becomes impotent during the attack, or is impotent and hopes a violent situation will stimulate him."

"Maybe he has a religious upbringing and it works as a barrier." Styles glanced at Beth. "You know, he hears his father's or priest's voice in his ear telling him sex outside of marriage is a sin?"

Knowing how this type of sadistic psychopath worked, Beth shrugged nonchalantly. "I don't think so. He's impotent, that's a given, and he blames the victims. He wants to make them suffer like he is suffering mentally. This is why he doesn't strangle them completely. He likes to see their eyes, the fear. He wants them to fight back in the hope they'll stimulate him. It was probably a fantasy at one time, the kidnap and rape. It's violence and dominance he feeds on, but he needs an excuse to validate his behavior. In his mind, she failed him and deserves to die. He won't stop. He lives for violence."

"I've covered the cause of death." Wolfe looked from one to the other. "Time of death is between when she was let down from the bus and when the dog found her at five after six this morning. The body hadn't been moved, apart from being rolled from the mat, so she wasn't attacked somewhere else and dumped there. I found no ligature marks on her wrists or ankles, and no head injuries or other injuries that might suggest an abduction."

"So she got into his vehicle of her own free will?" Styles raised both eyebrows. "That sounds a little far-fetched."

Blowing out a sigh, Beth shook her head. "Not if someone drove up beside her and aimed a gun at her. She'd get into the vehicle. The problem with everyone carrying a weapon, this could happen at any time." She shrugged. "We have to assume she either knew her killer, or he held a weapon on her to make her comply." She looked at Wolfe. "Anything else? Fiber or latent DNA, drugs in her system, anything we can use?"

"Nope." Wolfe indicated to Webber to remove the body. "What I found were traces of isopropyl alcohol. It had been sprayed all over the body." He leaned against the counter. "How many people carry it around? I can tell you hundreds, if not thousands, use the spray to clean their hands, shopping carts, and the like to kill germs. Unfortunately, it breaks down DNA as well. I'm surprised the Convenience Store Killer didn't use it as it's easily available and would do much the same job as PCR Clean."

Beth nodded. She preferred the other method. It was one hundred percent. She couldn't risk any less. "So this killer is fully aware of DNA and trace DNA, the same as the Convenience Store Killer?" She looked up at the screen. "I see you have a comparison between the burn marks found on the Night Creeper's victims. They look the same to me."

"Yeah, I examined them microscopically, and they're identical and they also match one other from another victim." Wolfe remove his mask and gloves and tossed them into the garbage. "The third image isn't conclusive, but it's too close to ignore. This killer is branding his victims. It's a brand of a rune. I looked up the symbol and it represents *nauthiz,* or the letter N. It has various translations, some in magic, others in language, but the one I found interesting was that it represents coming in touch with a person's nasty, uncontrollable side."

A chill ran down Beth's spine, as that made a lot of sense. This killer was out of control, binging on young girls with apparent abandon, and someone was covering his back. If it was someone in the sheriff's department, she'd take them down because as sure as the sun came up each morning, the cover-ups would go deep and they'd never get enough evidence for a conviction. She glanced at Styles. "This is all very interesting. I figure it's time to search the hardcopy files at the Mischief Sheriff's Department and see what we can find."

"Y'all planning on pursuing this case, when it's not connected to your current one?" Wolfe frowned. "It seems like you're making a ton of work for yourselves, and people are dying. You can't possibly be in two places at the same time."

"Right now, we have nothing but dead girls and a brand connecting them, no suspects." Styles slowly removed his gloves and mask, balled them up, and then tossed them across the room as if aiming for a basketball hoop. "We're on scene and will check out the files. If we find anything that hints at a cover-up, which we suspect, we'll hand it over to another team."

Beth cleared her throat. "We can't go to the director with assumptions. He wants proof before he sends in a team. As it stands, we're stepping on toes, as the local sheriff hasn't requested assistance. We're here in the guise of trying to link this case with the one in Roaring Creek." She sighed. "So far, he's cooperated, but we don't know how long that will last. He isn't expecting a visit from us this afternoon. The director might, as it's a serial killer situation, send in a team anyway. He has the authority in multiple murders." She pulled off her gloves, leaving her mask until she reached the corridor. Once outside she turned back to Wolfe. "Thanks for your assistance. You've been a great help." She stripped off the scrubs and dressed.

"I'll have the reports of both victims on the server this afternoon." Wolfe waited for them to dress. "You should have the previous victim out of Roaring Creek on the server by this afternoon as well." He smiled as he led the way back to his office. "I'm here anytime you need to discuss a case. Don't hesitate to call."

Nodding, Beth rubbed Bear's ears as he bounded out to greet them. "Thank you."

TWENTY-EIGHT

As Bear needed to stretch his legs, they took him to the park. As the smell wafting along the sidewalk from Aunt Betty's Café was calling to Styles, he crossed over the blacktop and looked at Beth. "I'm starving and it's going to be a long afternoon. This place is supposed to be very good, and going on the pie we ordered, we must give it a try while we're in town. What do you say?"

"Sure." Beth followed him inside. "It sure smells good."

Inside, they stared at the specials board and both ordered chili, fresh-baked apple pie, and coffee. The service was fast, and the server offered Bear a plate of leftover meat. Styles accepted the offer and nudged Beth. "This is a remarkable place. I didn't believe anywhere as good as TJ's existed in these backwoods towns."

"It's hardly a backwoods town anymore." Beth ate slowly, her eyes flicking back and forth, ever alert. "It's a massive tourist destination. People come here to be terrified. Others visit the ski resort or go hunting. I hear they have white-water rapids as well."

Styles chuckled. "That's what I like about you, Beth. You've always done your research on places we visit."

"It's my analytical mind, I guess." Beth sipped her coffee. "I need all the information just in case it's important."

After finishing their meal, they headed back to the ME's office and Styles flashed his card to gain access to the elevator to the rooftop. Moments later they were on their way to Mischief. They hadn't called ahead, and walked in the sleety conditions to the sheriff's department and went to the front counter and asked to see him. When Sheriff Lance Walker came out of his office, his surprised expression said volumes. Styles greeted him with a smile. "Sorry to barge in without notice but we're still on the convenience store shootings and abduction-murder case out at Roaring Creek. We figure there might be a connection. Our guy might be dropping by here to abduct girls. He seems to get a kick out of it. Do you mind if we look over your case files and see if they connect?"

"I guess not." Walker moved his shoulders as if his shirt were suddenly too tight and indicated with his thumb to the back room. "The deputies work in there. All the murder books are there too. I'm old-school. I like files that can't be hacked and are easy to find, so you'll need to go through them. You can copy anything you need. The scanner is down the hall on the right."

"How many deputies do you have?" Beth took out her notebook and looked at him, pen raised.

"Just the two, Deputy Branch Dryer and Deputy Dirk Boone. They're on a break right now, so I'm sure they'll give you their full cooperation."

"Dryer and Boone." Beth smiled. "Got it. Are they married?"

"Ah, no." The sheriff raised both eyebrows and looked at her. "You hankering after a husband?"

"You never know." Beth gave a wave of her hand and headed along the corridor to the open door.

Styles stared after her and turned to the sheriff. "Thanks for your help. We appreciate it."

Wondering what the heck Beth had planned now, Styles made his way to the next office. Inside, he found her smiling and chatting with the deputies like they were old friends. He walked inside and waited for her to stop talking and nodded as Beth made the introductions. He cleared his throat. "We'll need to look at the murder books for the Night Creeper case."

"Sure." Dryer tossed him a set of keys. "Knock yourself out but my house keys are on that keyring. I'll need them back." He indicated to a table with two chairs opposite. "You can use that desk. There's coffee in the copy room."

Styles took the keys, opened a filing cabinet, and handed the keys to Beth. "Let's get at it."

"We're staying overnight." Beth ignored him and perched on one of the desks. She pulled her long blonde hair from its restraints. "Is there any nightlife around here? This town is much bigger than Rattlesnake Creek and it's been ages since I went out."

Surprised, as Beth refused so many dates with the locals in Rattlesnake Creek, preferring her own company most times, Styles occupied himself looking for files. Whatever plan she had was going into motion and he was obviously out of the loop.

"I go to the Dancing Lady Saloon, is all." Dryer gave her a lazy smile. "I spend some time there before I head out on patrol and usually drop by when I've finished. It's a nice place to relax, play some pool. The music is good. Live bands or karaoke some nights."

"Sounds nice." Beth stood and moved the bunch of keys from one hand to the next. "Have the patrols increased since the murders?"

"Nope." Deputy Boone shrugged. "The chance we have of catching that guy is a million to one. He doesn't have any kind of pattern. We drive all over, checking old places and all through town, and he still manages to kill some poor girl. All our suspects have alibis." He waved a hand toward the filing cabinets. "It's all in there. We don't know if it's one guy or a whole bunch. If you can find a clue, let us know because we have zip."

Open file in hand, Styles looked from one to the other. "Who makes the decision about autopsies?"

"The sheriff most times." Dryer leaned back in his chair. "We use the local doctor or whoever is on call at the hospital. Weekends the funeral parlor deals with dead bodies. Most are natural causes. We don't have too many murders around these parts. The recent ones, we figure, were committed by someone from out of town. One of those serial killers we hear about running wild in your part of the state."

"We feel the same way." Beth opened all the filing cabinets and then looked at Dryer. "I know you're on your lunch break, but I'd really like a sandwich. It's cold and wet outside. Could you possibly give me a ride to the local diner?"

"Well, I sure can. Toss me my keys and I'll drive you. My cruiser is just outside." Dryer gave her a lopsided smile as if all his birthdays had come at once and caught the keys she threw to him. "Come right this way." He stood and waved her out the door.

Perplexed, Styles stared after her. *What the heck was Beth up to now?*

TWENTY-NINE

Beth listened to the smooth-talking man beside her in the cruiser. She'd had her suspicions about him from the moment she'd laid eyes on him. He fit her profile of the Night Creeper and then she'd noticed a few small scratches on his wrists, in the place a woman would grab him in an effort to pull on his hands if he was trying to throttle her. At first, she'd planned to watch him and then she'd seen his set of keys. Her dark side had surfaced in such a rush she'd fought hard to contain it. The moment the bunch of keys hit her palm her attention riveted on a small metal stick hanging from the keyring. She'd turned it over casually in her hand, and on one end she'd found the same rune, carved into the metal, she'd seen burned into the victims' flesh. She turned her head to stare at him. Right beside her was the Night Creeper. She'd needed an excuse to get him alone and discover which cruiser was his ride. What better excuse than to go and get some takeout? "It must be lonely patrolling out here all alone at night. We noticed many of the streets are like ghost towns. All the old industrial buildings are sitting empty."

"I like being alone sometimes." Dryer turned and smiled at

her. "It gives me time to think. I always volunteer for the night patrols. I like them."

As they pulled in front of the diner, everything fell in place for Beth. She smelled the stink of cigarettes on his breath. He no doubt carried a Zippo, perfect for heating the branding tool on his keyring. He used his vehicle for picking up girls. They'd get into a sheriff's department cruiser and think they were safe. If he messed up and evidence came to light, he'd destroy it. It was just about a perfect plan until she'd come along. As they reached the diner, she looked at him. "Don't get out. I'll only be a minute and it's cold out here." She smiled. "Can I get you anything?"

"No thanks, I've just eaten." He leaned back, grinning at her. "Take your time."

Inside the diner, Beth searched her pockets for the tracker device she'd made a habit of carrying for a time. Knowing where a killer was located at any time made her job easy. Now all she had to do was trigger him and see what happened. She wouldn't allow another innocent girl to be slaughtered but she had many tricks in her arsenal to catch a killer. After collecting a couple of packets of sandwiches, she walked out of the diner, dropped a bunch of paper napkins beside the cruiser, and while bending to grab them, slipped the tracker neatly under the passenger door. She climbed inside. "I'm so clumsy."

"You're not what I expected for an FBI agent." Dryer tipped back his hat and smiled, looking her over. "You look and talk like a city girl. Come out with me tonight, and we'll take the city out of you and replace it with some country."

Beth giggled like a schoolgirl. Oh my, he'd fallen right into her trap. She understood men like him. Dominant and aggressive when they didn't get their own way. Women triggered them by refusing them or making them look insignificant. Ridiculing them in front of friends was also a trigger. Which one should she use? This guy was already on full throttle and it wouldn't take much to push him over the edge, and right now he wouldn't have another victim lined up. He'd just grab any woman to prove a point. "I'll need to ask Styles just how long he plans on working today." She kept her voice husky and a little breathless. "He's my superior and can be so hard on me at times."

"Ah, that's not fair." Dryer pulled up outside the sheriff's department. "Maybe you should ask him. It will be a night to remember, I promise. We can go back to my place after a few drinks."

Amazed by the way Dryer was falling perfectly into line for her, she headed back to the office. Once inside, she met Styles' disapproving glare. He knew she had something planned and, Styles being Styles, he didn't like being out of the loop. She placed the sandwiches on the desk and, lowering her voice so not to be overheard, bent to speak to him. "Would you believe Dryer hit on me in the cruiser? I was just being the good cop and trying to extract information."

"What did he say?" Styles opened a paper sack and looked inside.

"He asked me out and I said I'd ask you when we'll be finished here." Beth sighed. "It wasn't that, but he was very suggestive."

"How so?" Styles' eyes narrowed. "You might have misinterpreted his meaning."

Beth rolled her eyes. "I don't think so. He said we could have a few drinks and go back to his place and 'he'd like to take the city girl out of me and replace it with country.'" She looked at him and shrugged. "We need these guys' cooperation, so I didn't react. I kept my cool, but saying nothing is as good as agreeing, isn't it? Now what do I do? I don't feel comfortable around him, but I don't want to make a scene."

"Why did you ask the sheriff if they were married?" Styles gave her a long searching look. "Maybe he mentioned it to Dryer?"

Rolling her eyes, Beth shook her head. "I needed to know if they lived alone, as in having people to give them alibis." She frowned. "That's still no excuse for hitting on me like that, is it? I need to work here, Styles, and don't need this type of attention."

"Leave it to me." Styles stood so violently that his chair tipped over and he walked out of the office and returned with the sheriff. He looked from one man to the next. "Agent Katz is a federal officer and deserves respect. Deputy Dryer made comments to the effect he could take the city girl out of her and replace it with country. That is sexual harassment. Is this the kind of behavior you allow in your office, Sheriff?"

Bang, there it was, the trigger. Humiliation did it every time and Beth could see Dryer change in front of her. She'd seen it in her own reflection many times. The look he gave her was terrifying, as if in a flick of a switch she'd seen his true self. The sadistic serial killer was ready to bring his endgame and he didn't care who he murdered this time, but she'd be his first preference. There was no doubt this was the Night Creeper and he'd try and strike tonight, but this time, the Tarot Killer would be right behind him.

THIRTY

Styles took in the angry man glaring at him and shook his head. "Don't you figure, when Agent Katz asked me what time we'd be through here, that I'd ask her why?" He flicked a glance at the sheriff. "She's currently on multiple cases and has no downtime unless I agree to it." He glanced at Dryer. "She didn't want to give me the details, but I insisted. Just because a female agent is trying to get along with you, it doesn't give you the right to hit on her."

"She asked me about the nightlife." Dryer's eyes blazed with anger. "That was a 'come and get me' invitation."

Styles shook his head slowly. "Not from where I'm standing. I've been working alongside her for over six months now and I've never seen her act inappropriately at any time."

"Okay." Dryer glared at Beth. "I apologize for being a nice guy and offering you a drink. My bad. Trust me, it will never happen again. You're not my type anyway."

"That's enough, Dryer." Sheriff Walker tipped his head toward the door. "Go and help out at the counter. Boone, make sure the agents get everything they need."

Wanting to get Beth alone, Styles shook his head. "No need,

we have everything we need. There's not too much here. We'll take a break and then finish up and get out of your hair."

"Okay." The sheriff looked at Boone. "There are some unpaid parking tickets at the counter. Chase down the offenders and put the fear of God into them." He looked at Styles. "I'll leave you to it." He turned and left, shutting the door behind him.

Blowing out a long sigh, Styles turned to Beth. "Okay, what's going on?"

"I found pages missing in three of the reports written by Dryer." Beth pulled out files and handed them to him. "See, the murder books all have pages missing. The evidence mentioned in this murder isn't in the evidence locker. These are all errors or cover-ups by Dryer." She shrugged. "He did hit on me, that's the truth, but honestly, I could handle him. I just needed them out of the office so we could work alone. It's all I could think of." She looked at him. "I know his type. Act friendly and giggle at the right time, get him alone, and he'll ask me out."

Shaking his head, Styles looked at her. "Are men so transparent?"

"Some are. He's a player. He likes to be in charge, so I took a chance to see if he'd take the bait." She waved a hand around the office. "No CCTV. You keep watch and I'll search their computers and desks to see if they have anything hidden."

Unable to believe his ears, Styles stared at her. "You can't search the office without a warrant. Anything you find will be inadmissible."

"We can't get a warrant without probable cause and what's the point if there's nothing here to find?" Beth stood, hands on hips, and looked at him. "If we know there's evidence of case tampering, and give the files as our probable cause, we'll have him. I need to get inside his computer and his personal stuff and see if he's keeping anything from the crimes."

Clearing his throat, Styles leaned one hip against a desk. "Taking souvenirs from the crimes? Why would he do that?"

"Maybe he's keeping them for whoever he's tampering the evidence for. It could be a relative or close friend." Beth munched on a sandwich.

Thinking a beat, Styles stared at her. She had her innocent look about her right now. He'd seen so many faces of Beth Katz. She was like a revolving door of emotions, and he never quite knew which mood to expect. Although, she'd found evidence someone had tampered with the files. "You figure someone here, most likely Dryer, knows the killer?"

"Yeah." Beth nodded. "Something like that."

Not convinced, Styles flicked through the murder books. "How do we know it's Dryer? Any one of them could have tampered with the files. They all have access. Just because Dryer wrote the report doesn't necessarily mean it was him. If Boone was involved, for instance, he could have removed evidence as well."

"The point is, one of them tampered with evidence." She picked up an evidence book from the desk and waved it in the air. "This is evidence." She shrugged. "Who did it remains to be proved, but we need to know how many people have access to the filing cabinets for a start."

Styles stared at the filing cabinets and then back to her. "The filing cabinet I was working from had Boone's murder books. They must have a filing cabinet each. I didn't see any alterations or pages missing. We could scan Dryer's files for prints. He's not going to be wearing gloves in the office. It's our best chance. Scan the pages either side of the missing ones for prints. If it comes back it's only him, we'll need to write that up in our report. We're only here for a look-see. We have a case to solve, and this will need to be handed over to someone else."

"Okay." Beth smiled at him. "I'm guessing you have your digital fingerprint scanner tucked away in a pocket somewhere?

I'll collect all of his files and you can scan them. I'll work on my laptop and when you're done I'll search for a match. The deputies' and sheriff's fingerprints are already on the server. They were uploaded by Wolfe yesterday."

He set to work, meticulously scanning every page surrounding each of the local murder cases and uploading them to the server. He needed fingerprints and the actual files. It was long, tedious, slow work, checking every page and going back a spell just in case the tampering went way back. It didn't take Beth long to find a match for the prints, and they scanned any suspicious pages and a few on either side in Dryer's murder books. The prints all belonged to Dryer. As Beth suspected, he was the one tampering with the files. When she moved to Dryer's computer, Styles leaned over her shoulder. Amazed how fast she had bypassed his password. "Find anything?"

"Not yet but he's been sending crime scene photographs to another device. It may be a home computer or a stick drive. These ones taken at the hospital and mortician's are the ones we found before coming here. They were all taken by someone's phone. We'll need to find out if any are missing. There may be more evidence pointing to the killer he didn't put into the files." Beth glanced up. "This is evidence suggesting tampering and has his fingers all over it." She bent and went through the drawers in his desk. "Nothing of interest here. I'd love to do a forensic sweep of his vehicle."

Concerned she was overstepping the boundaries of law and basic human rights, Styles shook his head. "Not yet. We hand over what we have to the director and see if he wants us to proceed." He sighed. "If you recall this was a look-see just to follow a hunch. We've gathered evidence. Don't lose sight of the fact the Convenience Store Killer is our main objective. We don't have too much more time to spend chasing down a cop who covers up evidence with a mass murderer running riot in the next county." He checked his watch. "It's almost five. We need to put all this back as we found it and get checked into the hotel."

"Do they have cabs in this town?" Beth was closing down Dryer's computer. "It's still pelting with sleet and we need to get our bags from the chopper."

They heard voices outside and Styles added the files to the cabinet just as Dryer and Boone walked inside. He smiled at them. "We're all done here for today, but we'll be back in the morning. Thanks for your help. Do they have cabs in this town?"

"Yeah." Boone frowned. "There's a cab stand outside the hotel. You can get one from there in the morning, but I'll call you a cab for now." He reached for his phone and made the call. A short time later, he nodded to them. "It will be outside in five minutes or so. They don't get busy most nights until the saloons close."

Styles waited for Beth to pull on her coat and gather the information they'd collected over the day. He'd copied everything to the server, but Beth had made hardcopies as well.

"Are we going to speak tomorrow to everyone who handled the bodies?" Beth followed him outside, pulling on her gloves.

Styles nodded. "I have all the information on my phone. I'll make a list tonight and we'll work through it in the morning. We really need our own transport, but we'll just have to walk or use a cab to get around. It would be easier if it stopped raining." A cab crawled to a halt alongside the curb. "That's our ride, let's go."

THIRTY-ONE

The hotel had been built during the gold rush and likely hadn't been aired out since then. Beth's room was a good size, with a reasonably modern bathroom, obviously an addition from the original, but it had a clawfoot tub with a shower overhead. The basin in the vanity resembled a flower, with petals curling over the sides, and the mirror had brown spots all through. At least it had good lighting and Beth took her time in the tub before heading down to meet Styles in the restaurant. Amused to see the doors resembling those on a Wild West saloon, she pushed through and met Styles at the counter without Bear. She'd made a point of dressing nice and had brought two large suitcases with her, much to his dismay, but she needed to make sure she could cover any situation and explained that a city girl needed changes of clothes in strange towns. In truth, she had one suit-case filled with her special effects gear, various disguises, and costumes. She had no idea if or when she'd get the chance to follow Dryer. Catching a cab to a murder was usually out of the question, but she'd use whatever means of transport she had at hand. Knowing where Dryer was at any given time would be an advantage if he struck again soon.

"Our table is ready." Styles smiled at her. "Now, I know why you brought all the luggage. Am I allowed to say you look spectacular without being sexist?"

Beth laughed. "Yes, and thank you. I won't take offense if you say I look good." She sighed. "People confuse me sometimes."

"How so?" He took the offered seat and faced her across the table as the server handed them menus and wandered away.

Beth met his gaze over the menu and cleared her throat. "Men act in two opposite ways with me: either they hit on me or tiptoe around me. You're my friend as well as work partner and I respect you, so please speak your mind to me. You won't offend me. I don't figure you could if you tried." She smiled at him. "So loosen up. We're friends, and we've shared confidences."

"I'm good with that." Styles folded his menu. "Although, I don't have to tell you how good you look, Beth. Every eye turned toward you the moment you walked in. You know you have a magnetism that's very attractive."

Beth scanned the menu, placed it aside, and looked at him. "Thanks, but I'm like you. We're both damaged goods, and bad things take time to heal, don't they? I enjoy working with you, Styles, but how you cope with me is still a mystery. I know I can be difficult at times. You honestly do have the patience of a saint."

"Many of the world's best problem solvers are a little eccentric." Styles shrugged. "I can live with that part of you. The rest I'll play by ear." He beckoned the server, and they ordered dinner.

They discussed the cases over their meal, and Beth had finished her second glass of very good wine when Styles' phone buzzed.

"Sheriff Bowman, what can I do for you?" He passed Beth one of his wireless earbuds.

Surprised to find it was a call from Sheriff Bowman out of Roaring Creek, Beth raised both eyebrows and listened with interest.

"There's been another shooting out of River's Edge. Sheriff Tucker is on scene. The store clerk was murdered and we found a purse belonging to a young woman by the name of Cheyenne Dimple. She's missing. She's seventeen, lives close by, drops by most nights for milk and bread around the same time. We've spoken to her mom."

"I'm currently in Mischief and can't fly there tonight. I'll need to refuel." Styles frowned. "Sheriff Tucker will need to process the scene and preserve everything until we can get there in the morning. Have the victim's body taken to a local hospital or mortuary. Is there a place close by the crime scene where I can land the chopper?"

"Yeah, I'll send you the coordinates and Tucker's contact details. Let him know your ETA and he'll meet you and take you to the scene. I'll ask him to arrange transport for you if necessary."

"Okay, thanks." Glancing at Beth across the table, and raising both eyebrows, Styles sighed. He disconnected and looked at Beth. "The case here will need to wait. We might have a chance of saving this girl. We'll need to check out your algorithms and try and determine where he plans to murder her and get there. We'll be leaving at sunup."

After handing back the earbud, Beth finished her wine and leaned back in her chair. "It's just as well the killer isn't an early riser. From Wolfe's report, from the insect invasion on the bodies, the victims weren't shot early. He figures they were found no more than two hours after he shot them, so we can figure he murdered them around eleven or later, not earlier. If we get back to the office by six, we can leave within the hour, if you need to refuel, and we grab our gear. I'm not planning on going after him without wearing a liquid Kevlar vest, that's for darn sure."

"That's a given." Styles nodded and checked his watch. "I suggest an early night. Unless you have other ideas?"

Suddenly elated, Beth rubbed her temples to cover her excitement. A small window of opportunity had just opened up for her to find and prevent Dryer from murdering more girls. She looked at Styles. "Me, no. I have a headache after studying all those files. An early night sounds like heaven."

"Great. I'm beat." Styles motioned to the server for the bill. "I'll sleep like the dead tonight."

THIRTY-TWO

Making plans to take out Dryer as they rode the elevator to their rooms, Beth glanced at the room service attendant with her cart piled high with towels. "Do you mind if I grab a couple of extra towels?"

"Go right ahead." The woman handed a pile to her. "I'm finished for the night as soon as I take my cart back." She smiled. "It's been a long day."

As Beth moved closer, she unclipped the master room card from the woman's belt and held it under the towels. The sleight of hand was part of years of training. She'd attended night classes in magic for many years. All the skills she'd acquired were practiced regularly to give her the edge she needed to succeed. She could remove a man's watch or his wallet or slip one of her tarot cards into his pocket and he'd never know. Picking locks, learning the art of using botanicals and poisons to her advantage, and spending many years in classes honing her skills in special effects makeup were only a small part of her knowledge. The FBI valued her skills as an undercover agent and how she could transform into a man or a young woman in her teens, but she'd only ever revealed a part of her skills to them. She kept in shape and being naturally fine boned, even at thirty, with the right silicone overlays, face tape, makeup, and wigs, she could pass as just about anyone. She had fat suits and muscle suits to enhance her slim frame, and clothes completed the illusion. Her skill at falling into any character was a gift she'd picked up along the way. Her psychopath side of her brain was indeed a great help when it came to portraying someone. If she hadn't been an FBI agent, she'd have loved being onstage. The problem was, in a fight scene she might just get carried away, and that couldn't happen. She smiled to herself. Not at any time had anyone noticed she wasn't the person she portrayed. Not even Styles when he knew about her disguise.

When they reached their floor, she gave Styles a wave, opened her door, and slipped inside. The moment the door clicked shut behind her, she kicked off her shoes and checked the tracker app on her phone. Good, Dryer was at the saloon, his favorite place to drown his sorrows. He would likely spend some time there and then drive around town until he found someone to take out his anger on, but she couldn't allow that to happen. She'd discovered he left to complete his patrol around ten each night. She checked her watch and then went to her bag. This time, she'd become a barfly and attempt to draw him into a quiet area of the saloon. As he'd been triggered, he would likely speak to her and make plans to meet her somewhere. He wouldn't be stupid enough to be seen with one of his victims, even in trigger mode.

She dropped her suitcase on the bed and pulled out everything she needed from her bag of tricks. She had many silicone shapes she could use to change her appearance. A different nose, pitted skin, and a short black wig would work well with dark brown contacts. A set of over-white teeth pushed out her top lip and lipstick added to the pout. In less than half an hour she'd changed her face and slipped into a bra that gave her huge breasts. She selected her clothes with care. In this town, she'd wear jeans, a tight sweater, high heels, plenty of silver bangles, and long dangly silver earrings. She pulled on thin leather gloves and removed a tarot card from its protective cover before placing it in her pocket. She'd chosen poison as her weapon of choice. Spilling a small amount of her drink over Dryer would be risky but essential. The poison would absorb through his skin at a slow rate, killing him in twelve hours or maybe more. By that time, she'd be back in Rattlesnake Creek with Styles. It was the perfect plan. All she had to do was get out of the hotel and back in without being seen.

She glanced at her selection of coats. Nothing would do for what she needed, and getting soaked through wasn't an option. Slowly opening the door, she peered outside. A service elevator was at the end of the passageway. To avoid being seen, she'd ride it down and find the staff entrance. It was a few hours before the place closed for the evening and the likelihood of someone leaving a coat hanging to dry at the entrance was a good possibility. She rode down, glad when the elevator zoomed past all the floors and stopped in the basement. Her heart pounded when the doors opened and voices came from some-where close by. She peeked around the door to see two men heading for double doors pushing trollies piled high with dishes. An illuminated exit sign shone like a beacon, and she dashed toward it. On one side was a door with the sign STAFF ONLY.

She used the card, it clicked open, and inside was just what she expected. A row of hangers by the door with wet shoes and boots underneath. Another wall held a row of lockers with combination locks and in the middle a table with a few dirty coffee cups and an ashtray. She ignored the lockers and ran her hands over the coats, finding a long, hooded raincoat, still damp from the weather. She took it down and slipped it on, pulling the hood over her head and down to her eyes. Dressed like this, she'd take a cab to the saloon and no one would recognize her. She went back out into the passageway and took the exit into an alleyway. A few moments later she climbed into a cab and, using her best Southern drawl, gave instructions to the driver to take her to the Dancing Lady Saloon. On arrival, she paid in cash and went inside, removing her coat and shaking it before heading for the bar. She scanned the room, spotting Dryer at the pool table. He wasn't playing, just leaning against the wall watching the game. As if he'd sensed her arrival, he looked at her and she pushed back her shoulders, sending him a wide smile before turning and ordering a drink. "Bourbon, straight up."

"Gotcha." The barman poured the drink and placed it on a coaster. He pushed a dish of nuts toward her and smiled. "You new around here?"

Beth smiled. "Just passing through." She sighed with relief when someone at the other end of the bar waved at him.

As the bartender walked away, she flipped open the tiny vial of cyanide and tipped it into her drink. Capping the container, she dropped it into her pocket, glad she still wore her gloves. Although the leather was no barrier to the poison, the fragment of dust possibly left behind wouldn't cause her a problem. She swirled her drink, watching the dust dissolve into a lethal mixture of instant death if consumed. The smell of cigarette breath wafted over her and goosebumps rose on her flesh. Dryer was right behind her. Had he seen her empty the bottle? Maybe not, she'd shielded her movements, but now it was game on. As he leaned on the bar, she twirled the glass in her fingers.

"You gonna drink that or play with it?" Dryer leaned on the bar grinning at her.

Knowing how to push his buttons, Beth shrugged. "I like to play." She spun around in her seat and smiled at him. "Do you?"

"Are you propositioning a deputy?" Dryer looked her up and down slowly. "Maybe I should arrest you?"

Shrugging, Beth met his gaze. He was chomping at the bit. His next kill so close he was finding it hard to control himself. She caught the flash of triumph in his eyes, just like her own, and kept her voice low and sultry. "I'll go quietly if you promise to use handcuffs."

"Oh, you're good." Dryer looked around slowly and then set his gaze on her. "In the alleyway out back, give me five minutes to bring the cruiser around. I have a place close by."

The time was now, Beth turned and knocked the glass from the bar, spilling it over Dryer's knees. She gasped and stepped away as it smashed on the floor and looked at him. "Oh dear, now you'll have to get out of those wet pants."

"That's the plan." Dryer ignored the wet patches and stood. He looked at the barman. "Broken glass over here."

Moments later the barman came around with a long-handled dustpan and broom and swept it up and then dumped it into the garbage. The evidence had been disposed of and now it was time for her to go. She slipped from the chair, pulled on her coat, and then ran a hand down Dryer's back. In the next second, she'd deposited the tarot card into the back pocket of his Levi's. "Catch you later, deputy." She headed for the exit to the alleyway.

THIRTY-THREE

Believing her job was done, Beth intended to walk around front and catch a cab, a plan that came to an abrupt halt when she noticed Dryer heading her way. Pulling her hood low, she turned and ran in the opposite direction. Sleet lashed her face as she ran, and the wind pushed back her hood. Much more of a soaking and her disguise would be gone. She must get away from him and fled, jumping over rivers of dirty rainwater spilling across the sidewalk and overflowing the drains. It was imperative to avoid conflict and being seen interacting with Dryer aggressively in public. And if he took her in for questioning, the deputy would search her and everything would be lost. As she turned a corner, she reached inside her pocket and dropped the empty vial into a brown swirling mass of water heading for the drain. Evidence successfully disposed of, she picked up her pace and headed down the next alleyway in the hope of doubling back to catch a cab.

The next second, the roar of an engine and a screech of brakes came close as a cruiser came to a halt blocking her way. She looked left and right but no one was out in the freezing sleet at this time of night. The passenger door swung open and she stared at Dryer. Rain splattered his jacket and his cowboy hat was dripping water. The deluge had gathered alongside the curb and rushed past, gurgling and carrying leaves, twigs, and candy wrappers. Beth stumbled forward as if planning on getting inside the cruiser, tripped, and dropped to her knees. She reached under the vehicle and plucked off the tracker, dropping it into the flowing water, and then pretended to gather herself, pulled up her hood, and stared at him. "I've changed my mind. I'm heading home. It was nice meeting you."

"Not so fast." Dryer glared at her. "There's still the matter of soliciting. You can pay my fine or see the judge in the morning. Your choice."

Beth straightened, turned, and ran back down the alleyway. The heels were a problem and she kicked them off and kept going. Rain blasted her face and small shards of ice cut into her cheeks as she increased her speed. She rushed out of the end of the alleyway and turned right, hoping she'd make it back to the cab stand. It would be a long walk back to the hotel from here. Gasping for breath, she searched the dark sidewalk. Not a soul walked around at this time of night. It was as if someone had turned off life in town. The streets were so empty the only sound was the patter of sleet on her hood and the gurgle of water running along the gutter. The next moment, the cruiser came around the block, a searchlight illuminating the sidewalk as Dryer crept along looking for her. There was nowhere to hide and, alarmed, Beth dashed across the road. Dark storefronts pressed together as if seeking shelter, only broken by alleyways at the end of each block.

Unarmed against a serial killer carrying a weapon and a badge, she needed to keep moving. Standing and fighting him, even if he was slowly dying, wasn't an option. She gritted her teeth, determined to outwit him. He wasn't leaving the dry cruiser anytime soon, and she could use that to her advantage by dashing back and forth across the blacktop. He couldn't turn his vehicle fast enough to catch her. If she could make it back to the alleyway, she might just be able to jump into one of the cabs waiting outside the saloon and get away before he made it around the block again. She moved off again at a run, glad for all the times Styles had insisted she hit the gym with him and she'd worked out until she dropped with exhaustion. Her stamina had increased dramatically since she'd started their morning workouts.

Dryer was getting frustrated and as Beth dashed across the road behind his cruiser, he backed up suddenly. Fear gripped her and she dived for the sidewalk and rolled in the gutter. Dripping with water, she turned as he lurched forward and then spun the back of the cruiser toward her intent on mowing her down. Exhausted, with every muscle aching, she dragged herself up as he mounted the sidewalk, tires spinning in the water. He'd lost control and all he wanted to do was kill her. The bloodlust was fogging his brain now. He'd turned into the beast.

Throwing herself to one side, Beth crouched, waiting for his next move. The vehicle's engine roared and the car jerked back, running up the curb to make the turn, heedless of hitting the streetlights in his efforts. Metal ground and screeched as the back wheels of the cruiser spun across the blacktop, sending up a great shower of muddy water. Beth sprung to her feet and as the vehicle reversed ran around the hood and dashed down the alleyway. Running until her lungs burst, she came out opposite the saloon, dashed across the road, and flung herself into a cab. "Oh, thank goodness. I'm so lost. I need to get back to my hotel." She gave him the details.

"Sure." The cab driver gave her only a cursory look and drove away at a sedate pace, wipers flashing back and forth.

Beth ducked down in the back seat as the deputy's cruiser howled around the block and slowed, searching the sidewalk.

As they headed for the other side of town, she relaxed. "Nice town you have here. Shame it's raining."

"You staying here long?" The driver glanced at her in the rearview mirror.

"Just visiting my folks for their fiftieth wedding anniversary. The Doolies." She smiled at him. "Do you know them?"

"Nope, but I did see their picture out front of the hotel." He nodded wisely. "It will be an event."

Beth had seen the poster as well. "It sure will."

The cab stopped out front of the hotel. Beth paid in cash and stepped out just in time to see Styles walking along the sidewalk outside the hotel with Bear. *Dammit!* As the cab drove away, she turned and headed for the alleyway and ran toward the back entrance. She slipped inside, returned the coat, and after dropping the master room card on the table, headed for the door. Looking both ways, she sneaked out into the passageway and took the elevator to her floor. Falling inside her room, she headed straight for the bathroom and ran a hot bath. She stripped off, bundling her wet clothes into a large plastic bag. These would go into the incinerator the moment she returned to Rattlesnake Creek. The silicone, she stripped from her face, wrapped it in toilet paper, and piece by piece flushed it down the toilet.

She sank into the hot bath and washed her hair. Her knees were scraped, but her gloves had protected her hands. She sighed. Having ten pairs of thin leather gloves on hand was a definite advantage. She would need to order more items for her disguise kit soon. Luckily, as the FBI was fully aware she went undercover, there was never a question about her unusual purchases. Ten minutes later, she heard a knock on her door. She stiffened and waited. The next moment her phone buzzed and she dried one hand to grab it and, seeing it was Styles, accepted the call. She put it on speaker. "Yeah?"

"Sorry to bother you, but Bear went ballistic outside before, chasing shadows, I figure." Styles cleared his throat. "Long story short, he's sitting outside your door and won't move. Do you mind opening your door so he can see you?"

Beth moaned. "I'm in the tub. Give me five."

Hauling herself from the tub, she double-bagged her soiled clothes and pushed them into her bag, opened her clothes bag, and pulled out a robe. With this wrapped around her still damp body and her hair wrapped in a towel, she went to the door. "I guess you'd better come inside." She looked at Bear. The dog was wet and raindrops clung to his whiskers. "What's up with you?"

The dog sniffed her and then sat at her feet leaning against her leg. She looked at Styles. He wasn't wet and had changed his clothes before coming to see her. "Has he done this before?"

"Only when he believes I'm in danger." Styles glanced around the room. "I thought you were going straight to bed."

Raising both eyebrows, Beth stared at him. "I decided to soak in a bath. What's up? Do you miss me already? Do you want to come in?"

THIRTY-FOUR

Examining her flushed face, Styles swallowed hard. Beth had this way of looking at him sometimes and he found it difficult to interpret her mood. Was she joking or deadly serious? She'd been the perfect partner during these investigations, working hard without a complaint. Her company at dinner had been nice, almost like an old married couple. He smiled and hoped it was the best reaction. "Ah, I'm fine but thanks for the offer. Bear here was just checking you're okay, is all. He likes you and I guess he wondered where you'd gone. I figured you must be in bed, and then when Bear stopped here and refused to move, I noticed the light under the door. When you didn't answer the door, I figured something might be wrong, so I called. That's what partners and friends do, Beth. They take care of each other."

"Thanks for caring. Won't you change your mind and come in? I'd enjoy your company." Beth removed the towel around her head and shook out her wet hair. "Why don't you call room service and order some hot chocolate with extra marshmallows? We could drink it in front of the fire." She smiled at him and handed him the towel. "Before you do that, dry Bear. He is soaked through. There are more towels on the bed if you need them. I'll duck into the bathroom and get into my PJs and dry my hair. If I leave it like this, it will be tangled in the morning. I figure Bear needs to know we're both safe. He's so used to seeing us together, he probably believes something is up. It must have been stressful for him, leaving him in a strange hotel room all alone."

Surprised, Styles went to the housephone and called room service. It hadn't been more than an hour and a half since they'd eaten dinner, but he added cookies to the order and went about drying Bear. Ten minutes later, she opened the bathroom door, and he watched her dry her long blonde hair until it fell like silk down her back. He stood when room service came to the door and allowed the server to come inside and place the tray on the table. He gave the man a tip and closed the door behind him. He looked at Beth and smiled. "There goes my reputation."

"Your reputation?" Beth raised both eyebrows. "I'm in my PJs with my superior in a hotel room." She laughed. "I don't think that server is going to go running to the sheriff. He doesn't know we're FBI." She took a cup and the plate of cookies and set them on the coffee table in front of the fire and then sat down on the sofa. "I've been busy, running a few abstract scenarios through a software program I created. I'll validate my findings when we get back to Rattlesnake Creek, but I have a feeling the Convenience Store Killer will attempt to murder and dump his current victim out at Broken Bridge. I figure if we search for an area with open spaces alongside a highway, we'll find him. If he follows his usual MO, which seems to be the case as far as we know, we'll be able to get there before he drives by to release the girl."

Sipping hot chocolate, Styles nodded. "How do you figure we disguise the chopper? It would be nice to have a cloak of invisibility, but an FBI chopper kind of sticks out from a mile away. Wide open spaces will mean we'll need to get there in time to catch him in the act. I'll need to drop the bird a mile or so away or he'll see us."

"I can't answer that until I get the results and view a map." Beth shrugged and nibbled on a cookie. "Up to now, he's chosen straight lengths of highway, so he can see anyone coming in both directions, and near a clump of trees. I figure he tells the woman to run for the trees, maybe to make her believe that she can call for help at a house close by or something. He aims as she runs and shoots her. That's his endgame, the cherry on the cake."

Running what he knew of the local area through his mind, Styles nodded. "I do have a camouflage tarp we could drape around the chopper if we get time. I'll bring it with us. The main problem is that many of the open areas running alongside the creek are riddled with mineshafts. The old timers dug underground there. It's not safe to drop a chopper in most areas, and we'll need to find an old mining lease map to check it out. It's overgrown with wheatgrass and people just walking by have fallen down old shafts. He looked at her. "Can you find that information before we leave? It will be one heck of a rush getting there as it is. We'll be working on a hunch and hoping we can stop him. The odds aren't in the favor of the victim right now."

"I can only do my best, Styles." Beth finished her drink and smiled at him. "I'm beat. Bear is fine. Mind if I hit the sack now?"

Styles emptied his cup and smiled at her. "My thoughts exactly. I talked room service into getting our breakfast here by five. Can you be ready to leave by five-thirty? I'll need to do a preflight and it would be easier if you are with me, so we can leave without delay."

"Sure." Beth walked him to the door. "Why don't you have them bring the breakfast in here."

Styles headed for the door. "Okay, sure." He paused and gave her a long searching look. "Sleep well, Beth."

THIRTY-FIVE

FRIDAY, WEEK TWO

Rattlesnake Creek

The rain had stopped in the morning but everything around was damp and cold when they arrived in Rattlesnake Creek. Beth carried her bags to her room, grabbed her liquid Kevlar vest, and dressed in gear suitable for running across rough terrain. They'd decided not to wear their FBI jackets, as appearing as a couple walking a dog would be their best option if noticed. She packed a backpack with everything she'd need for a long hike, checked her weapon, and added more ammo to her pocket. Leaving her door open, she waited to hear Styles head to the office and then dragged her bag of wet clothes to the incinerator and slid them inside. They used the incinerator for their household garbage as well as any contaminated forensic gear, so it wasn't unusual for either of them to activate it at any time. She made her way to the elevator and once inside the office checked her computer and scrolled down the results. Smiling at Styles over one shoulder, she pointed to the screen. "It agrees with me. The probability of him dumping the body out at Broken Bridge is eighty-nine percent. That's good enough for me." She indicated to the screen. "These are the maps of the area. You check them out and I'll get on my laptop and search for the old mining leases."

"The clock is ticking, Beth." Styles searched the map. "Okay, we need an open space, a wooded area, and a long stretch of open highway. There are only three options, but we don't have the time to go to all three."

Beth glanced at him. "Which is the most remote highway, the one not many people would use?"

"Okay. That would be a small place called Randy's Mine. I'm guessing this guy owned the lease way back. Can you find it in the leases?"

Beth did a search and waited for the results. "Yeah, mines all over but not from behind the trees. From the diagram, the lease cut off just before the trees." She overlapped the lease diagram on the map. "There's nothing on the map apart from what could be the remains of a small building." She waited for Styles to look over her shoulder. "What do you think?"

"I figure it's safe to land the chopper there and we'll have the trees for cover." He straightened. "I'll bring my rifle. If he lets the girl escape, I'll be able to take him down from there before he kills her."

Excitement tingled through Beth, she loved the chase to catch a killer, and now her dark side was appeased the need to take out the Convenience Store Killer had calmed to a low hum. All she needed now was the call telling them Deputy Branch Dryer had died in mysterious circumstances and her world would be complete. "Okay, let's make this happen." She looked at him. "So you're a sharpshooter with a rifle? I don't see you shoot very often, well, apart from the practice range."

"I do okay." Styles smiled at her. "I figure I shoot as good as I can fly." He chuckled. "It was a requirement to be an MP, you know."

Gathering up her laptop and pulling on her coat, she

grabbed her backpack and headed for the door. "Just as well. We're going to need all the help we can get."

As they arrived in Broken Bridge and Styles circled the outlying areas, Beth used field glasses to peer at the highway. Styles had taken the chopper high and vehicles below looked like ants. As they approached Randy's Mine the roads were deserted, but far in the distance Beth picked out a vehicle following the highway. "There's someone coming. It's the only vehicle on the highway heading in this direction. The road makes a sweeping bend before it hits the straightaway. This could be our man."

"I see it. He must be fifteen miles away. We have time to drop down in the cover of the trees without detection." Styles' voice came through her headset. "The chances of him seeing us unless he comes into the straightaway before we land is minimal. The trees alongside that part of the highway will block his vision."

Within minutes they'd landed, and Styles was out the chopper and draping the camouflage tarp around it. It was obvious he'd done this a number of times and worked fast. Even when Beth moved away, holding the backpacks, the chopper appeared to have blended into the trees. Only the main rotor blades and tail seemed to hang in midair. "That's a useful thing to have on hand."

"Yeah." Styles came toward her, shrugged into his backpack, and picked up his rifle. "We should be able to get a good view of him from the edge of these woods, but that clump of trees closer to the highway would be our best option for an ambush." He glanced at her. "You're planning on taking him alive, right?" He frowned at her. "Sorry, Beth, but I'm not playing executioner here, even though he deserves it."

She'd expected his reaction, he'd come to understand her to some extent, but working with Styles, she'd be working within the law... well, as close to within the law as possible. Beth gave him a sideways glance. "Even if he's aiming at the girl with intent to kill, you're not planning on using deadly force?" She shrugged. "What part of the book is that rule in? I must have missed it. We have a serial killer hell-bent on murdering an innocent victim. Deadly force is warranted if and when he pulls a weapon on the victim."

"I'll take him down." Styles gave her a long hard stare. "I figure what he's done, killing him is just too darn easy. I want to see him suffer in jail for the rest of his life, in solitary confinement if possible, or out in the general population so he can meet some of the really hardened criminals." He straightened, squaring his shoulders, and his mouth set in a determined line. "This time, it's my call." He met her gaze. "We need to run to that clump of trees. I don't want him seeing us or he'll just drive on by and we'll be stuck here. Stay close behind me." He signaled to Bear and took off at a run.

Beth caught up with him and they bounded through the tall wheatgrass toward the trees. A step ahead of her, Styles appeared to pitch forward and the next second the ground gave way beneath her feet. Her stomach flip-flopped as she plunged down into darkness. With no time to grab anything, she dropped like a stone. Tumbling into a space without light. Vines whipped at her face as she bounced off the wall and hit something furry. She heard a loud moan and the sound of a body hitting the ground. The next second, she hit bottom, but she hadn't landed on dirt. A sharp pain slammed into one shoulder, but something had broken her fall. Winded, she gasped for breath and tried to rise, but where was she? Under her hands, she could feel a body. She'd fallen on Styles and he hadn't said a word.

Panic gripped her, moving could be deadly. They could be on the edge of another mineshaft. The air was hardly breathable, dank and musky with the smell of decay. Beside her, a whine came out of the darkness. Bear was with them, and she reached out one hand and found him trembling beside them. "Stay, Bear. There's a good boy."

Trying to breathe when her lungs ached, Beth moved her hand up Styles' torso, found his neck, and felt for a pulse. Under her fingers, the artery throbbed reassuringly. She slid her hand to his chest and held her breath, waiting until it rose and fell slowly. All good signs, but he could be injured and being plastered on top of him wouldn't be helping. She'd need to roll him onto his side, but if he'd broken his neck, she could kill him. In the pitch black she had no idea of the immediate danger surrounding them. Beside her, Bear edged closer and licked Styles' face. She couldn't see him but she could hear him. The dog was a protector and his handler was down. He'd never leave Styles' side. Beth needed to be firm with him. "Okay, that's enough licking, Bear. I'll take care of him. Stay, for goodness' sake. We might be stuck on a ledge."

Blackness pressed against her like a wall, squeezing the air from her lungs. She needed Styles conscious and moved her hand over his body, found one shoulder, and gave him a shake. He still hadn't moved. "Styles, are you okay?"

No response.

Fear she hadn't known existed gripped her for his safety. It was as if a wall had dropped, exposing her emotions, and the uncertainty confused her. She shook him hard again. "Styles, you must wake up. Open your eyes. Wake up!"

Nothing.

THIRTY-SIX

Heart racing, she pushed her hand through the debris-strewn ground, feeling around for a safe place to move. In the dark she'd become helpless and needed to remove her backpack. Her powerful flashlight was in a side pocket. Moving like a snail, Beth rolled away from Styles and found the flashlight. She gasped as the beam moved around them. They were in a small overgrown tunnel. Dried carcasses of dead animals littered the ground, skin stretched grotesquely over bones, and empty eye sockets stared into nothingness. The walls seemed to close in all around her. As she moved the flashlight around, red eyes peered at her and rats scattered in a rush of tiny feet, running in all directions. It was her worst nightmare. She hated small confined spaces, and dark tunnels filled with rats rated high on her list. Pushing down the rising need to scream, she turned the flashlight on Styles and swallowed hard. His face was sheet white and blood trickled from a cut on his brow. He needed help, and she pulled her phone from the backpack to call search and rescue. They'd arrive in under an hour. She stared in dismay at the screen. "Why, when anything bad happens there's always no darn bars?" She looked at Bear. "It looks like we're on our own."

Beside her, Bear whined and stood, shaking the dust from his coat. He looked fine. Beth put out a hand to him and rubbed his ears. "Are you okay?" It wasn't as if the dog could reply, but just having him there, his intelligent eyes summing up the situation, made her feel better. "Right, I'll need to check Styles and hope he hasn't broken anything. Although how the heck I'm going to get you both out of here is anyone's guess."

She flinched as pain shot through her shoulder and realized she'd fallen on Styles' rifle. It had fallen down one arm and lay half under him. With care, she dragged it away. Being the Tarot Killer had opened up her life to many experiences and knowledge. To take down the worst type of killers, she'd masqueraded as many types of people. This meant becoming someone else in every way possible: the herbalist, the physical therapist, the businesswoman, pole dancer, fortune teller, and sex worker, to name just a few of her personas. The physical therapist, she'd actually studied for, it being a profession she needed to complete a sting undercover operation for the FBI. She'd found the knowledge amazingly useful, not only for herself to recover from injuries sustained on the job but in situations like the one she found herself in right now. She stripped off her leather gloves and, with care, checked Styles' head. He had a lump on the back of his skull, but his neck seemed to be uninjured. She moved over each shoulder, down his arms, and then checked his ribs and moved down his torso. She'd reached his hips when his voice startled her.

"If you're planning on continuing, I'll expect a wedding ring." Styles blew out a long breath.

Relieved, Beth glared at him. "Oh, very funny. Don't move. You're bleeding. I'll get the first aid kit. You were out cold, and I was checking for broken bones, is all."

"I guessed as much." He grinned at her and then winced.

"What the heck happened? Where are we?" He lifted his head and moaned. "Oh, I must have cracked my head and I figure my ribs are bruised."

Handing him the flashlight, Beth cleared her throat. "I tried to call for help but there's no bars down here." She sighed. "You fell down the shaft first, and then Bear and I landed on top of you. I'm not surprised your ribs are bruised. I was concerned you'd broken your neck. You didn't look so good for a time."

"My head hurts at the back. I guess my landing wasn't so good." He looked her over. "You're hurt. What can I do to help?"

Shaking her head, Beth rubbed her shoulder. "I hit the rifle when I landed. It will be bruised, is all. I'm fine." She glanced up the mineshaft. "So much for preventing another murder."

"We'll never get out of here in time to save her." Styles let out a long sigh. "That poor woman is as good as dead now." He shone the light around the confined space. "*If* we ever get out of here."

"First things first. Right now, you're my priority." Beth found the first aid box, pulled on examination gloves, and went about cleaning the laceration. It needed stitching and she pressed a dressing hard against it in an attempt to stop the bleeding. "Don't move. It's difficult seeing what I'm doing as it is, and this cut needs sutures."

"Your bedside manner needs a little adjustment. You're supposed to at least try and make me feel better, Beth." Styles looked at her, but he was his usual calm, collected self. Nothing seemed to worry him.

Blowing out a breath of frustration, Beth flicked him a glance. "We'll I did check on Bear first and he's not complaining." She pressed his chest to keep him still. "Now hold the light steady and stop complaining. Trust me, this is my best bedside manner."

"You're concerned about me, and you never look worried."

Styles put a hand to his head and Beth batted it away. "Are my brains hanging out or something?"

Shaking her head, Beth found a packet of Steri-Strips and stuck them along the cut, doing her best to pull the sides together. She shook her head. "No. You'll be fine if you allow me to fix you up." The distinct echo of a shot rang out high above them and she stared at Styles. "But I don't like her chances."

THIRTY-SEVEN

Broken Bridge

Terrified, Cheyenne Dimple didn't move a muscle. Playing dead was her only chance right now. She'd endured a terrible night with a local delivery driver. She'd watched in horror as he'd shot the clerk and then turned the gun on her. With his promises of release, she'd complied to his demands. Her parents had told her she could do anything she put her mind to, and so she'd kept her mouth shut and endured. The one thing about the entire horrific night was that, apart from the actual shooting, he'd made no attempt to conceal his identity from her. He must know she recognized him. He'd been by the general store delivering items many times she'd been there working. In fact, she had to bite her tongue to prevent using his name a few times. He'd been so nice during her ordeal, as if he had been doing her a great favor by hurting her. She'd realized very fast he wasn't acting normal. This wasn't the man she'd met previously. He was usually quiet without too much to say, but the moment he'd gotten her inside his vehicle he couldn't stop talking.

If she'd had the guts to escape overnight, she'd have tried.

The gun had slipped from his fingers and had lain on the mattress beside him most of the night. If she'd been strong enough, she'd have shot him dead and run away, but if he'd woken, he'd have beaten her again. If she had escaped, she had no idea where he'd taken her. Outside was wilderness and a long slow death of starvation, thirst, or exposure. She couldn't take his truck and had no idea where he kept the keys. Her only hope was that he'd keep his word and set her free come morning. What a fool she'd been. Could anyone be that stupid to fall for his charm? Her mind wandered to her parents. How would they cope when they discovered what had happened to her? Would the church throw her out? Would her friends disown her? No man would want her now.

A remoteness came over her, a floating strange feeling like being on the edge of falling asleep. She blinked, watching ants walking in single file toward her prone body. The line of them stretching out beyond her field of vision. It was strange how one eye seemed to work just fine but the other didn't. He'd shot her in the head, she understood that well enough, but it hadn't hurt at all. The fall, face down on a patch of concrete, left over from when a shed was built there many years ago, hurt more. Her nose throbbed and her chin had scraped along the rough surface. As a pool of blood ran into her line of vision, a strange calmness came over her. She'd been shot in the head and left to die in the middle of a field of wheatgrass. No one would ever find her body, let alone come dashing to save her life.

She couldn't allow him to get away with what he'd done to her. If there was one chance someone would find her, she needed to leave them a message to tell them who had killed her. She waited until the roar of an engine sounded along the highway and disappeared into the distance before attempting to move. The left side of her body was unresponsive, but she lifted her right arm and moving it like a snow angel, wiped away the dirt to clear a space on the concrete slab. She dipped one finger in the blood pooling around her face and painstakingly slowly, wrote his name and added the words *my killer*.

Exhausted, she looked up at the crows, flocking to the trees close by. The horrible sleet and rain had gone, leaving the wheatgrass glistening with raindrops. They danced like diamonds with each gust of wind. She stared into the deep blue sky and watched one single white cloud drift by. Exhaustion gripped her, so profound all she wanted to do was bathe in the rays of the sun and close her eyes. Slowly she drifted away, in peace.

THIRTY-EIGHT

Fighting waves of nausea, Styles pushed into a sitting position as he slipped off his backpack and grabbed a water bottle and his flashlight. "Pass me some Tylenol and can you check my pupils? I won't be able to fly the chopper if I have a concussion."

"Your pupils are reacting normally to light." Beth flicked the flashlight back and forth and then found the pain meds and handed them to him. She squeezed his arm and pushed a lock of hair from his brow. "Sit for a beat. You were unconscious, and it takes time for our brains to switch back on when something weird happens." She rubbed one shoulder and winced.

Realizing he'd looked over at Bear, wagging his tail and jumping on the spot, to check he was okay but hadn't asked about *her* well-being, Styles touched her arm. "Beth, your shoulder is hurting, isn't it? Do you want me to take a look?"

"Nope, I'm fine." Beth grabbed two Tylenol and swallowed them with water. "It just made my fingers numb for a time. I'll get some ice on it when we get home. I'm more worried about you." Her gaze slid over him and she bit her bottom lip. "You took a bad fall. I thought you'd broken your neck. I need to get you out of here." She moved the flashlight around the narrow tunnel. "From what I can see, the shaft we fell down was likely used for ventilation. It doesn't have any ladders or anything and the sides look smooth, so climbing out that way will be impossible."

Looking all around, Styles noticed broken tools and other miners' equipment lying around from a century ago. He could clearly make out parallel lines made of steel peeking through the dirt-covered floor, the metal rusty and blending in with the colors on the ground. "Not necessarily. There's an old track here, so the miners pushed carts along them. We could follow and hope to find a way out, but the mineshaft is the best way to get out of here." He looked at Beth. "I'll try and climb out. I have rope in the chopper I can lower it down so we can haul Bear out and then you."

"Why not just follow the tracks?" Beth pointed her flashlight down the tunnel.

Unsteady, Styles stood slowly and leaned against the wall until the dizziness subsided. He recovered fast in most situations, and they needed to get out of this hole right now. "We might follow it for miles and find it's been sealed at the other end or encounter rockfalls, bears, or anything else. Yeah, we could shoot them, but the noise could cause a cave-in. I'll put on my backpack and try and walk my way up the shaft. I've done similar things before and there's roots growing all over. They'll make good footholds. Worse case, I fall back down, so keep out of the way. I don't figure you'd survive me falling on you from way up there." He looked at her. "Will you be okay down here alone? It's not the best place to be trapped."

"I'll have Bear." She rubbed the dog's ears. "He's an amazing dog. He snuggled up to you and licked your face."

Styles nodded. "Yeah, he is, but it's part of their breeding. They nurture, so will protect those they care about. So you'll be fine. He won't allow anything to happen to you while I'm gone."

"That's good to know." Beth helped him with his backpack. "Why wear the backpack? Won't it get in the way?"

Styles shook his head. "Nope it will help clear the shaft. I'll go up backward, pressing my hands and feet on each side. Let's just hope it works. If I can't make it out, I might get bars closer to the top of the shaft and will call for assistance." He frowned. "Ty Carter would be the closest and most experienced chopper pilot. He'd be able to drop a harness down here and haul us out."

"Okay." Beth's expression was serious. "Take it slow. You still look sick. Maybe you should wait a little longer?"

Smiling to reassure her, Styles hauled himself up the vines hanging down the walls and backed into the shaft. He'd walked up very slippery rock walls similar to this many times. The vines would be an advantage and he edged his way up, one step at a time. His head throbbed and the cut on his forehead dribbled blood into his right eye. Without a free hand to wipe it, he blinked away the thick red screen blocking his vision and pressed on. Muscles burning with overexertion and screaming for him to take a break, he pushed through the pain. Stopping would mean disaster because starting again with muscles cramping would be suicide. It seemed to take forever before light illuminated the walls and he gripped the edge of the shaft. Taking a firm grip of the roots of a dead bush, he swung his legs down and pulled himself onto the grass. He lay on his back for a few moments staring at the sky and sucking in great lungfuls of clean air. Crawling to his feet, he shook out the cramps and bent over the shaft. "I'm going to get the rope. I won't be long."

He stood for a few seconds, staring around. If the woman had been shot close by, he couldn't see her from his position, but he could make out the way they'd come previously by the trampled wheatgrass. To one side of the shaft was a cottonwood tree sitting alongside a dry riverbed. He walked cautiously toward it, checking the ground before him. He could use the tree with a pulley system he carried in the chopper to haul Beth and Bear out of the mine. Without delay, he dumped his backpack and took off back to the chopper.

Carrying everything he needed over one shoulder he made fast time returning to the mineshaft and securing the pulley system. He dropped down the end of the rope. "Okay, Beth. Attach the rope to Bear's harness. He won't want to leave you, so tell him to find me. Okay?"

"Yeah." Beth's voice sounded a long way away as she coaxed Bear toward the shaft. "Come on Bear, good boy. Don't fight me." Beth tugged on the rope. "He's good to go."

Styles flexed his muscles and hauled the dog to the surface. After untying Bear, he dropped the rope down the shaft again. Beth's injured shoulder would be a problem. He wiped the blood from his eyes and grabbed hold of the rope. "Tie it around your waist and walk up the side of the shaft, use the tree roots to pull yourself up. I won't let you fall."

"Okay, I'm ready but you'll need to pull me into the shaft, I can't reach it. I'm not tall enough." Beth sounded concerned. "It's awful dark down here without the flashlight."

Surprised the dark worried her, Styles peered down the hole. "Bend your knees and spring up. Okay, on three—one, two, three, jump." He leaned back and pulled hard, lifting Beth and her backpack into the shaft. The rope slackened as she gripped hold of the vines. He leaned back and hauled in the rope hand over hand. "There you go. Keep climbing. I'll pull you up."

Relief flooded him when her blonde head popped up, covered in cobwebs and leaves. He hauled her over the edge and they both lay in the grass panting with Bear determined to lick them all over. Styles rolled over and untied the rope from around her waist. "Exhausted as we are, we need to go and see if he's killed the woman. That was a shot we heard and we can't leave until we've checked it out."

"We've got no hope of finding her on ground level." Beth sat up slowly, brushing dirt from her hands and looking all around. "I'm sure as heck not risking falling down another mineshaft. I checked the maps and there was no mention of any shafts from the woods to those trees."

Styles got slowly to his feet and rolled up the rope. He took the pulley from the tree and handed it to her, then picked up his backpack. "Unregistered mines, I guess. I agree with you. We'll take up the bird and look for a body. There are no mines alongside the highway. If we see anything, I'll set the chopper down there and we can go and take a look." He pointed to the track in the wheatgrass. "Stay behind me and walk in my steps. Bear, by me." He headed off toward the chopper.

THIRTY-NINE

Eyes gritty from being in the mine, Beth scoured the area alongside the highway. She noticed something close to a dilapidated barn. "I see something. I'm sure it's a body. There, near that old barn. There's a road on the other side. Is it wide enough for you to land?"

"Yeah, as long as I can get the skids down safely on solid ground and that road has a blacktop. I can't see any trees close by or overhead wires. We're good to go." Styles took the chopper down.

The smell of blood came on the breeze as they rushed toward the body. She looked alive, her hair moving in the breeze, and Beth bent to check life signs, but she was gone. Sorrow gripped her and she looked at Styles. "Her name was Cheyenne, such a lovely name, and here she is lying face down in a pool of blood. Dumped like yesterday's garbage. We must stop this maniac."

"There's no signs of anyone else being here." Styles followed the girl's path through the wheatgrass and then turned back. "There's only one track made by her."

Cheyenne had been shot in the back of the head, but from

the outstretched hand, she'd remained alive for a few minutes after the shooting. Beside the hand was a scratch game floating in the blood and marks as if she'd tried to write something. The sight angered Beth. A senseless waste of life they could have prevented if they hadn't fallen down a mineshaft. As Styles came to her side, she pointed to the squiggles on the concrete beside the woman's hand. "Another scratch game, and look here, she's tried to write something. It's a name. It starts with a *W*. Can you make it out?"

"I figure we'll need to get down to her sight level to work it out." Styles kneeled beside the outstretched hand and bent low to peer at the writing. "It's clear from here. It says, 'Wyatt Cody, my killer.'" He took out his phone and snapped pictures from all angles.

Stunned, Beth stared at him. "Wyatt Cody?" She ran his interview through her mind. Had she missed something? The guy had been laid-back and confident, but it was obvious from his demeanor he hadn't taken her seriously. She looked at Styles. "I rarely miss picking up on a serial killer. Cody was all about hitting on me, rather than worrying about being accused of homicide."

"You have mentioned that smooth charismatic types are typical." Styles shrugged. "He was pushing your buttons, is all. Trying to dominate you, most like. This"—he pointed to the victim—"is how he plays his games. What he's done here is pure domination. He lives with his mom, right? I bet she's a dominating woman. I'd say his father is long gone."

Nodding, Beth understood the type just fine. "A dominating, cruel mother could be his trigger, but it would take more than that. He's focusing on young women, so somewhere along the line something traumatic happened involving a young woman to add to his psychosis." She looked at him. "Psychopaths aren't all killers. It takes a number of triggers to push them into destructive behavior."

"We'll worry about the why he acted like this later." Styles pushed up his Stetson and stared into the distance. "Right now, we have to find him and bring him in. Do you still have his work schedule on your phone?"

Trying to keep it together as her dark side rose up needing to seek revenge, Beth sucked in a few deep breaths. This time it must be by the book. Everyone would be watching and she would be the model FBI agent. She pulled out her phone. "Yeah, but first I'll call it in. We need a team out here ASAP."

"I'll call Wolfe. He'll want to view the scene and autopsy the body." Styles pulled out his phone. "I'll call Cash to meet us at the office. We'll bring him up to date. Our killer lives in Rattlesnake Creek and he'll need to make the arrest."

Uneasy, Beth shot him a glance. "Make sure he waits for us before heading to Cody's home. I don't want him to be Cody's next victim." She made the call.

They stood beside the body as cruisers came dashing along the highway. Sheriff Weston would have jurisdiction and it wasn't long before the sheriff's team had the crime scene secured. Moments later Wolfe's chopper landed, and Beth followed Styles to meet him. She nodded to Emily and Webber as they pulled a gurney and body bag from the chopper.

"I've been to the scene of the convenience store shooting and was finishing up there when you called." Wolfe stared at Styles and shook his head. "What happened to you?"

"We fell down a mineshaft. The entire area is covered with them." Styles shrugged. "I'm fine."

"Sit down." Wolfe leaned into the chopper for his medical bag and flipped it open. "My team will record the scene. I have time to examine that laceration and make sure you're fit to fly."

"I'm okay." Styles wiped at his eye. "Nurse Beth fixed me up in the mine. It's all good."

"She did a great job, but when an injury bleeds like that, it needs more than Steri-Strips." Wolfe pulled on examination gloves and filled a syringe. "You won't feel a thing." He went to work.

"Go and see Nate in ten days to take out the sutures. You can get it wet. I'll spray on a barrier to protect it."

It didn't take long for Wolfe to clean and suture the wound. He covered it with spray barrier film and then went about pressing his fingers all over Styles' head and neck.

Beth frowned. "Is he okay? He was out for a while. I fell on him."

"I'm fine." Styles narrowed his gaze at her. "Maybe you should check her shoulder. She's stubborn and will say she's fine."

"Sure." Wolfe checked Styles' eyes and nodded before turning to Beth. "He'll do. You didn't break him." He smiled at her. "There's no one here. Show me your left shoulder." He sighed. "I know it's injured; I could tell before Styles mentioned it."

"I'll go and assist the team." Styles walked away.

Removing her coat and Kevlar vest, she reluctantly stripped to her bra and turned to face him. With surprisingly gentle hands, Wolfe examined her shoulder. She looked at him. "It's nothing."

"Y'all the same." Wolfe met her gaze but there was nothing but kindness in his expression. "In the field y'all want to be heroes. I carry a full complement of drugs because I'm often called in when no medical team is available. I can give you a shot that won't impede your performance but will reduce the swelling in that joint and give relief immediately. I can't force you, but if you're planning on taking down this killer, you'll need to be in shape." He turned to his bag and looked at her over one shoulder. "What's it to be, Beth?"

Nodding, Beth appreciated his concern. He really cared about her well-being. Heck, that was a first. "Yeah, thanks, Shane."

"Y'all know, being alone out there working on homicide most of the time turns people like us into lone wolfs." Wolfe administered the needle, dropped the garbage into a bag, and removed his gloves. "You're part of a family of lawmakers here now, Beth. Carter and Jo are good people and you've met Jenna and Kane from Black Rock Falls. With my team, we are people you can trust with your life to have your back. Styles is a good man and you're not alone anymore." He gave her a long, concerned look. "If you need someone to talk to about anything worrying you, come to see me as a GP. I'll always be able to talk through any concerns you have in absolute secrecy. No matter what you tell me, I won't go behind your back and tell the director. I know what happened to you as a child could start to surface, and when it does, you shouldn't face it alone. You can trust me and Styles. He won't go running to the director with private conversations either. It's not in his makeup, and although I never break my word, I'm bound by my Hippocratic oath. So if you ever need help, we'll be here for you."

Pulling on her clothes, Beth's mind was on overdrive. Wolfe had always seemed to see right through her. Could he see the turmoil going on inside her? No one could ever solve her problems or what she had become inside. She'd been born a psychopath. Her dark side had been triggered at an early age and once that happened there was no going back. She'd read every scrap of information about her condition. The only possible outcome was to direct her anger in a controlled situation. Her actions had never been the result of an uncontrolled frenzy. If it came down to killing to save a victim, it was a choice... an innocent life or the life of a homicidal maniac? It didn't take a judge and jury to decide. Any cop would pull their weapon and shoot in the same circumstances. This action was legal in the state of Montana and in most states. The same as self-defense. Her way of dealing with her dark side was the only option. Or she could go to jail and watch as psychopaths murdered innocents without anyone to stop them. The Tarot Killer was her calling and she'd embrace the challenge.

"Do you need to speak to me about anything, Beth?" Wolfe picked up his forensic kit. "You seem very subdued."

Lifting her chin, Beth shook her head. "I've been trying to recall the night my mom died. I can remember eating dinner and then being in foster care and not knowing why I was there. Everything that happened there is something I'll never forget but it's difficult to talk about because it's so personal." She met his gaze. "If the other stuff does surface, I'll call you. I figure it must be real bad and I'll need help coping."

"Can I ask what happened in foster care?" Wolfe frowned. "You were moved around. Did you run away?"

Memories came rushing back and Beth shuddered. "Yeah, all the time." She searched his face and made a decision to trust him. "I was raped, many times, so many times. That I remember. What happened the night my mom was murdered is a blank. The foster care I wish I could forget. It messes with my head sometimes. I have problems forming relationships, although Styles has been really kind to me. He understands me, more than most men I've met."

"He's a good man." Wolfe nodded, his expression serious. "When did you start blaming yourself for the abuse?"

Swallowing bile, Beth couldn't believe he'd read her so well. "I figured it was always me because I was blonde and pretty."

"Did you know many victims of abuse think that way?" Wolfe shook his head. "You were never to blame."

Taking a deep breath, Beth pulled herself together. She'd never spoken to anyone about this before. "Maybe we can talk some more. I'm so over talking to shrinks. But you're different."

"Okay, whenever you're ready. I'm always here to help, Beth. What we discuss is safe with me. This is nobody's business but yours." Wolfe walked toward the crime scene. "You can leave Cheyenne in my hands now. Go get her killer."

Beth looked up to see Styles heading their way, blood had crusted on the neck of his shirt and his eye was turning a nasty shade of blue. "Ready to go?"

"Yeah, sure." He looked at Wolfe. "Is Beth okay?"

"She'll do." Wolfe smiled at Beth and turned back down the path. "Take down this killer, before he strikes again."

FORTY

Rattlesnake Creek

The FBI chopper was missing from the top of the building that morning, and he wondered why they weren't investigating his murders. He liked that the media called him the Convenience Store Killer and watched every news report on his kills. He'd kept the TV turned down low in his bedroom so as not to disturb his mother, but since discovering the body of Cassidy, there'd been no follow-up news. Now the FBI had left town again, the sheriff was in his office, and the news was all about a holdup at the general store. Two men had been involved. Some idiot had drawn down on Agent Styles and the new woman agent, he didn't recall her name, had shot off one of his fingers, and the other dude had died. No one was saying how he died. All this going on in town and his skillful shooting had only gotten a mention on the news this morning and Cheyenne's kidnapping had been ignored. Did they know he'd murdered her? Perhaps they hadn't found Cheyenne's body. They should have by now. He checked his watch. It had been a couple of hours since he'd set her free and the crows would be flocking by now.

Determined to discover what was happening, he headed to the most reliable grapevine in town. The bell over the door at Tommy Joe's Bar and Grill jingled as he pushed inside. He went to the counter and ordered a coffee and a ham on rye to go and waited, leaning nonchalantly against the counter and staring into the seating area. He smiled at TJ when he came back from giving his order to the kitchen. "No FBI in for lunch today?" He raised both eyebrows. "I imagine they're out hunting down the Convenience Store Killer."

"I haven't seen them today." TJ filled a to-go cup with coffee and pushed on the lid. "There was a murder out at Mischief. Maybe they're out there investigating. Last time we spoke they said they might be away for a couple of days but didn't specify when that would be."

He shrugged. "The news didn't say if the general store holdup was the same guy or guys, did it? Maybe the sheriff has arrested him and they are on to something else now?"

"Maybe." TJ's eyes narrowed. "They don't discuss their cases with me. The sheriff did mention he'd sent the guy from the general store holdup over to County. He's knee deep in paperwork today over that incident because one of the robbers died." He leaned closer. "I heard from one of the hostages that they figure he drowned in liquid soap."

Unable to stop a laugh, he looked at TJ. "So real professional criminals, huh?"

"Seems that way." TJ turned as Wez, the chef, called out the order was ready. He handed him a bag. "You have a nice day now."

Now came the alibi. "I don't have to leave until one. I'm heading for the park to eat my lunch and watch the river. I'm hankering to do some fishing next weekend."

"We buy fresh-caught fish if you have a good haul." TJ

smiled. "Don't go over the limit now. The game warden is around."

He chuckled, always the nice guy. "I'll remember."

He walked out, checking his watch. He had time to go home and make some news. Killing Cheyenne hadn't satisfied him. He needed more. Climbing back into his van, he ate his sandwich and sipped the coffee. His mother's voice filled his head. It was like an earwig of abuse. Nothing he could do ever made her happy. With a gun, he could control the world, he could take any woman he liked and do whatever he wanted. No one could stop him but then he'd go home and his world would fall to pieces. It had to stop. He pushed the last bite of sandwich into his mouth and drove to the park. He dropped his phone into the bag, climbed from the truck, and placed it at the bottom of a garbage bin under a few candy wrappers and an old newspaper and then headed home. If anyone traced his phone, he'd been eating his lunch in the park as usual. He lived in an old ranch-style home surrounded by trees, and his closest neighbor was half a mile away. At home, he removed his clothes in the hallway, pulled on examination gloves and covered his head with one of his mother's stockings. He walked into the kitchen and heard her voice.

"Is that you?" She barked a laugh. "Lost your job, have you? You're useless just like your pa. Don't come in here making excuses. Get out and find another job. It's up to you to take care of me. I worked my butt off keeping food on the table so you could go to school, and what do I get in return? An ungrateful son."

He walked into the kitchen. As usual, she sat at the kitchen table with her back to the door, her feet up on a chair watching a soap on TV. "I haven't lost my job. I just came home to see if you needed anything."

"No, and stop whining, you're making me miss my show. Get back to work. I'm sick of having you around." She didn't turn or acknowledge his presence. One hand went into a box of candy and then her attention went back to the TV.

He slid open a drawer and lifted out a hammer. With her words filling his head, he picked up a cloth and wiped the hammer all over, polishing the handle and making sure it was clean.

"Are you still here?" His mom dug into the box of candy. "No, don't say anything. I can't stand the sound of your voice. Just go away and leave me be."

He weighed the hammer in his hand and stared at the back of her head. If only he could stop her talking. Even when she wasn't around, he could still hear her like an earwig in his ear, nagging him all day long. "You need to stop nagging me, Ma. It makes me angry."

"Angry?" His mom's eyes never left the screen. "Weaklings like you don't get angry. They get stomped on. You're weak just like your pa."

A red fog dropped over his mind. It was as if his arm had a mind of its own. Seeing everything as if from standing outside his body, he lifted the hammer and brought it down again and again on the top of his ma's head until her chest stopped rising. Emotionless, he stood staring down at her. She was quiet at last. A burst of elation filled him and his mind was suddenly clear, so clear he didn't have to think what to do next. He wiped blood from his body with one of her precious white towels and dried his bloody feet and then went to the bathroom and took a long shower. He tossed the soiled towels in the shower and doused them with bleach, dumped them into a bucket and then carried them to the washer. As the washer hummed away, he returned to clean the shower and then went back to the hall and dressed. Without a second look at the house, he drove back to the park, leaving his vehicle in the same secluded area. He climbed out and retrieved his phone. As he tossed the sandwich bag back into the trash, a woman walked by with two large dogs. He smiled at her. "Nice dogs."

"Thanks." She smiled back. "On your lunch break?"

What a perfect alibi. He nodded and checked his watch. "Yeah, and I'd better go, it's almost one and I'll be late back. Nice talking to you."

He headed for his truck and got onto the highway heading for Roaring Creek. He had a few deliveries and then he'd be done, but he couldn't go home, not yet. He had just one more thing to do and called his Aunt Helenja. "Aunt Helenja, could you do something for me? I'm on the road and won't be back until four. I just remembered Mom asked me to drop by on my lunch break and take her some cookies. You know how upset she gets when I forget things. Could you drop by and take her some?"

His aunt lived two houses over and knew how she treated him. He could rely on her finding the body and not being too upset. She didn't like his mom and would likely ask him to move in with her for protection.

"Okay, but not for her sake." Aunt Helenja cleared her throat. "I don't know how you live with that awful woman."

He sighed. "She's my mom."

"Okay." Aunt Helenja let out a long sigh. "Drive safe. I'll see you on Sunday for lunch."

Smiling, he accelerated along the highway, his next convenience store shooting at the front of his mind. His mom was history and he could play the grieving son just fine. He grinned. Free at last to do whatever he liked and he couldn't wait.

FORTY-ONE

Glad to see the blue skies had remained, Styles turned the chopper toward Rattlesnake Creek. "You sure we're not wasting our time? Cody might be in another town this afternoon."

"Not according to his schedule." Beth scrolled through her phone. "He was in town up until lunchtime and is due for a pickup out at River's Edge at two and will be back in town by four. This gives us plenty of time to get into position to apprehend him. He has a delivery for our general store. I figure we get him inside and take him down nice and neat."

Styles ran the layout of the general store through his mind. "There's an alleyway that leads to a roll-up door. That's where they take deliveries. We could hole up inside and wait for him to bring in the cartons and then jump him. It's unlikely he'll be carrying." Styles nodded. It made sense. "I'll run it by Cash when we get back to the office."

"I still feel the need to call him Sheriff Ryder." Beth stared at the scenery.

Laughing, Styles glanced at her blank expression. She'd been like an ice statue since speaking with Wolfe. "He likes you just fine, so don't overthink him." He sucked in a breath. "So what happened with Wolfe? Don't say nothing because you've been withdrawn since I left you alone with him."

"Wolfe? No, nothing happened, well not really." Beth chewed on her bottom lip. "He believes my memories of what happened the night my mom was murdered will come back. The idea is frightening, is all. I know he's there and you are too if I need a shoulder, but talking about it just brings back other memories I'd rather forget. You know, sometimes it's better to forget and move on rather than keep rehashing the same pain all the time."

Surprised Wolfe would bring up the subject, Styles nodded in agreement. "Yeah, I'm all for moving forward. We can't change the past, can we?" He glanced at her to see her watching him intently. "I'll be here if you need me, Beth. As a friend not as a superior, and if it's personal stuff, I could be waterboarded before I'd tell a soul."

"That's good to know." Beth smiled at him. "That goes both ways."

Glad to see Ryder's cruiser waiting in the parking lot of the FBI offices, he landed the chopper. "Good, there's Cash."

"As Cody is on the road somewhere—it's only twelve-thirty —we'll have time to grab a bite to eat at TJ's." Beth checked her watch. "I'm intrigued about Cody's mother. Is she the reason he's a psychopath? I figure we have probable cause for a search warrant and time to get one before Cody gets back to town. We need to go through his house before he knows we suspect him."

Styles powered down the chopper and climbed out. He let Bear out and grabbed his gear. "Okay, I'll open the door for Cash. I'll bring him up to speed while I take a shower. Meet you back at the office in ten."

"Sure." Beth headed for her apartment.

After waiting for Ryder to arrive in the elevator, Styles went to his apartment, giving Ryder the details of the case and what happened. "We'll have him by five at the latest. The dying woman's note and any evidence we find at his house will make the case."

"Okay, you get ready and I'll call the judge and explain what's happening." Ryder took out his phone. "I'll send him the pics of the murdered woman and the message. It should be enough for a search warrant and an arrest warrant."

By the time Styles was dressed and ready, Ryder had organized the warrants. "That's great. We'll go and collect them."

"I'll go." Ryder pushed on his hat. "I'll meet you at TJ's. I just hope Cody runs to schedule and we don't allow him to slip through the net. I have the sheriffs of three counties relying on me to bring this killer in. I've already called County and asked them to be on standby to collect a dangerous prisoner at five."

Styles pushed on his Stetson and shrugged into his coat. "I love your optimism. Let's go."

They met Beth in the hallway just as she was leaving her apartment. Styles walked to the elevator. "We have a search warrant for Cody's house. Just check again to make sure we know where he is right now."

"I already did that, Styles." Beth rolled her eyes. "I called his last two stops to see if he'd left yet and he's following his schedule."

Styles looked at her. She was always the professional unless she fell down a mineshaft. He'd discovered her Achilles' heel and it had surprised him. "It never fails to amaze me how serial killers are able to commit the most horrendous crimes and then just carry on as if nothing had happened."

"It's because they don't care." Beth raised one eyebrow. "It was fun at the time, but like a ride at a county fair, once it's over they look forward to the next one."

Grimacing, Styles shook his head. "That's brutal. Everyone cares a little at some point in their lives. You saying they never regret taking a life?"

"Never." Beth met his gaze and her expression turned serious. "This is why they're hard to catch, Styles. Outwardly, unless they're covered in blood, you could be standing beside a psychopath who has just walked away from committing a heinous crime and he'd be acting like nothing happened." She gave him a long look and shrugged. "You could be one for all I know."

Styles barked a laugh. "Okay, you've made your point."

"What's so funny?" Beth's lips curled into a smile.

Styles snorted and grinned at her. "That means you could be one too, right?"

"Like I said before." Beth's smile widened. "You'd never know."

As Ryder took off in his cruiser to collect the warrant, they walked across the road to TJ's and the smell of delicious food greeted them. Styles hadn't been hungry until he walked inside. He needed to refuel and always did during a case when the opportunity arose. The next few hours would be intense, so eating now was the best option. They stopped at the counter inside, both ordering the special of the day: pumpkin soup followed by a steak burger and fries. They sat opposite each other in silence. Styles was making a plan of action. He looked up as Ryder joined them at the table. "Are we good to go?"

"Yeah, but we need a plan to catch this guy." Ryder frowned. "He's a mass murderer. I don't plan on him getting away."

"I've been thinking the same." Beth held a fry between finger and thumb. "Styles is the best person to confront him, so he should be inside when Cody arrives. We can take position each side of Cody's truck to prevent him running. The three of us should be able to take him down."

Styles nodded. "That works for me. I had much the same idea, but I suggest Cash blocks the alleyway with his cruiser just in case Cody tries to use his van to make a break for it."

"That works for me." Ryder leaned back as TJ delivered his meal. "Thanks."

Looking at Beth over his coffee cup, Styles met her gaze. "We want him alive, right?"

"Sure, anything you say, Styles." Beth's mouth curled into a smile. "Just make sure you take him down, because he won't be getting past me."

FORTY-TWO

As Beth placed her coffee cup in the saucer, Ryder's phone buzzed. She leaned back in her chair and waited for him to answer. They needed to move along to catch Cody and she didn't want any unexpected delays.

"Calm down." Ryder took out his notebook and pen. "The Cody house?" He pointed to his phone to get their attention. "Give me the details, and are you sure she's dead?" He made notes and swallowed hard. "Okay, lock yourself inside your vehicle and head for the highway. We'll meet you there. A blue Nissan. Okay, we're five minutes away." He disconnected and stood. "That was Cody's aunt. She just found his mom beaten to death." He ran for the door.

"What?" Styles slammed his hat on his head and headed after him with Bear at his heels.

Beth rushed after them and climbed into Styles' red truck. Ryder's cruiser was already disappearing along Main with lights and sirens blazing. "You figure Cody has murdered his mom?"

"I'd say that's a distinct possibility." Styles took off at high speed. "This throws a cog in the works. It's unlikely he'll be doing his deliveries; he'll be in the wind."

Beth pulled out her phone. "Maybe not. He should be leaving his last stop by now and is planning on using his deliveries as an alibi." She made the call and, getting the confirmation from the store, disconnected. "Oh, this guy is smooth. He's carrying on as usual. He's not content to murder Cheyenne. He decided to kill his mom and make like he was at work all day." She checked his schedule. "He was in town at lunchtime, so he shot Cheyenne and came back to Rattlesnake Creek for lunch, killed his mom, and then left to make his next delivery."

"Odds are he set up a nice alibi in town." Styles shot her a glance. "Call TJ and ask him if he knows Cody. As this guy delivers all over it's likely he drops by TJ's as well."

Calling TJ, Beth waited a time for TJ to answer. It was busy at this time of day. Finally he answered. "Hi, TJ, it's Beth. Do you know Wyatt Cody, a delivery driver who lives in town?"

"Yeah, he drops by for lunch. Usually takeout. He was by earlier today. Mentioned he was going to eat in the park and watch the river."

Beth glanced at Styles. "Do you recall what time that was?"

"Sorry, I don't recall. Maybe around midday. It's always busy here between twelve and two."

Disappointed he couldn't pin down the time, Beth frowned. "Okay thanks. Catch you later." She disconnected before he had time to ask her any questions.

The truck slowed to a halt behind Ryder's cruiser and they jumped out to follow him to a blue Nissan. Inside an elderly woman was sitting bolt upright, her hands white-knuckled on the steering wheel. Beth looked at Ryder. "Do you want me to speak to her?"

"No, I know her. She looks afraid. Don't spook her." Ryder opened the vehicle's door and leaned in to speak to her. Moments later he closed the door and she took off like a jackrabbit, wheels spinning in the gravel.

Beth stared after her. "Is that the woman who found Mrs. Cody? Won't you need a statement?"

"I told her to go to my office and wait for me." Ryder indicated with his chin toward a driveway farther along the highway. "She said she came by to check on Mrs. Cody. She found her in the kitchen. Panicked and ran out. There's blood everywhere and she stepped in it. We'll need to suit up before we head inside. I figure, we'll need to call in the medical examiner. It's obvious she didn't murder herself." He looked from one to the other. "Do you figure Cody killed his ma so he could get away? As in, keep us busy so he could make a break for it?"

"It's possible." Styles shrugged. "We'll take a look and secure the scene. We can't wait around here. We have a limited time to take down Cody. We'll need to hand it over to the medical examiner."

The tension in the air thrummed around her. The need to move on Cody right now spiked Beth's adrenaline. Needing them to understand the urgency, she looked from one to the other. "If he's killed his mom, he's escalating. Like a rabid dog. He needs to be stopped. We'd better make this super fast. I agree our priority is stopping Cody before he kills again." She looked at Ryder. "It's your call, Cash."

"We'll check the victim real fast and then go catch Cody." Ryder checked his watch. "Let's move it."

Beth ran back to the truck with Styles and they took off following Ryder's cruiser down a tree-lined driveway to an older-style ranch house. The front door was wide open and bloody footprints led outside. They were small and obviously from the aunt who'd gone to check in on Mrs. Cody. Beth pulled on booties, gloves, and a mask and followed the men inside, stepping with care around the bloody footprints. In the doorway of the kitchen, they all stopped and peered inside. It was a bloodbath, and floating in the blood was a paper plate of cookies wrapped in plastic film. A woman was slumped to one side in a chair and had sustained massive head injuries. Beth stood back as Styles went closer and checked for life signs.

"She's been dead for at least an hour. The blood spatter is congealing." Styles shook his head. "There's nothing we can do for her now. Best we go and leave this to Wolfe." He led the way outside, pulling off his face mask and gloves. "Cash, we'll park away from the store and walk down. I'll call you if his vehicle is in the alleyway. Block his getaway. You and Beth go in from the alleyway and I'll go through the store." He looked from one to the other. "Put on your liquid Kevlar vests. We're not taking any chances with this guy."

"Gotcha." Ryder tossed his gloves into a bag Beth held out for them and then opened his door and pulled out his vest. He removed his jacket and pulled it over his head. "We'll need to tape up the door."

As Styles called Wolfe, Beth assisted Ryder to attach crime scene tape across the front door. She waited impatiently for Styles to relay precise details and the coordinates. Time was ticking by and the window of opportunity was closing. To make the arrest, they'd need to be in position to catch Cody. Heart pounding, Beth removed her booties, gloves, and mask and dropped them into a bag along with the others' protective gear. Sealing the bag, she climbed back into the truck and dumped it by her feet.

"I've explained everything to Wolfe." Styles slid behind the wheel. "He's on his way." He shook his head. "This is one twisted individual but I'm guessing you're right about his mother. He just couldn't take it anymore."

Zipping up her jacket, Beth shrugged. "It was just a hunch but that in there is overkill. He could have killed her with one strike but he wanted to make sure she was dead. Violence like that is personal, so maybe I'm right about him. Right now he's a barrel of gunpowder. One spark and he'll explode. You'll need to be very careful how you handle him. Don't turn your back on him."

"I've been taking down criminals for a long time, Beth." Styles accelerated back to town. "I'll make some excuse to show him something inside and cuff him in the back office. The loading dock is too open and anything might happen. You'll need to keep well out of sight until I've restrained him." He looked at her, his expression serious. "If everything goes as planned. I'll ride with Cash back to the sheriff's office. We'll need you to cover our backs when we transfer him to the cells."

Concerned, Beth nodded. "Don't underestimate him. He kills indiscriminately without a second thought. For him, you're just someone in the way. He won't see you as authority or anything else. You'll need to be on your game, Styles... even with us right outside."

FORTY-THREE

Trees flashed by as Styles took off at high speed, the newly budding vegetation blending into green and brown flashes as he accelerated. His red truck lifted and the engine roared as they flew along the highway. As they tore through the industrial end of town, Beth gripped the side of her seat. It wasn't the speed that concerned her but how close Styles passed the parked vehicles. She had confidence in his driving, and in fact, she preferred him to drive. She always had so much on her mind, and so many things to do between destinations. It had been a practical solution. They slowed as they reached Main and Styles stopped to back the truck into a space outside the drugstore. The vehicles angle-parked along Main on the busy side of town and alongside the curb opposite the river. Ryder had parked outside his office and she watched him climb out of his cruiser, check his watch, and then head inside. She checked her own watch. It was a quarter after three. She guessed Ryder was taking the time to check on Cody's aunt before getting into position.

Not taking her eyes off the road, Beth scanned back and forth, waiting for the delivery van to show. A few trucks went by and then the delivery van she'd spotted on Cody's webpage came into sight. It moved slowly past them and she could see Cody, with a phone plastered to one ear. The next moment, the van took off at high speed, barely missing an elderly couple crossing the road with their dog. "That's him. He looks in a hurry."

The next moment, Ryder burst from the sheriff's office and dived into his cruiser. Styles' phone buzzed and he frowned as Ryder took off along Main. Ryder's voice came through the Bluetooth on the radio.

"He'd just found out we know about his ma." Ryder swore under his breath. *"His aunt called him with the bad news she'd found his mother. He said he was heading out to the house. I'll follow him at a distance."*

"I'd say he's making a run for it." Styles started the engine and headed along Main after him.

Beth could make out the van in the distance, but it didn't turn at the crossroads that led to his mother's house. He went by and took the on-ramp to the highway. "He's heading for the highway. Go. Go. Go."

"Hang on." Styles mounted the sidewalk and drove along to avoid a line of vehicles heading for the local fresh-food market and they bounced back onto Main. Once out of town, he floored the gas and they shot off at high speed, following Cody onto the highway.

The wide blacktop wound its way through the mountains and was often busy midafternoon. Interstate trucks would spend the night parked at the roadhouse just outside of town rather than drive through some of the dangerous mountain passes in the dark. Rain and sleet were forecast for later, and from the sky, later would be sooner than expected. The higher they climbed up the mountain the colder it became, and soon, ahead of them Ryder's cruiser disappeared in a low cloud.

Driving at speed in this weather was suicidal and Beth called Ryder. "Can you see him ahead of you?"

"Just his taillights. It's like an ice rink ahead. The road is wet and freezing." Ryder sucked in a deep breath. *"It will ease some when we drop down the other side of this cutaway. Problem is Cody is overtaking everything in front of him. At least three eighteen-wheelers have passed me so far. I'm not following him. It's too dangerous in the cruiser."*

"We'll follow him." Styles gave her a confident nod. "My truck can handle the terrain. It's built for it and I have fog lights." He flicked on the lights and had caught up with Ryder's cruiser in a few minutes. "I'm passing you now."

Gripping the seat with both hands, Beth held her breath as they crossed over to the other side of the highway to pass Ryder. Seconds later an eighteen-wheeler sounded its air horns and its lights came out of nowhere. Styles held his ground, moving back into their lane just as the massive vehicle flashed past them, rocking the truck with its turbulence. Beth pressed a hand to her chest. "That was a little too close."

"Nah, we had heaps of room." Styles' eyes never left the road. "It's downhill now. There's a sweeping bend at the bottom and then we head back up the mountain."

As the fog lifted a little, sleet hit the windshield like buckshot. The wipers moved so fast back and forth, back and forth, it reminded Beth of being on a very fast train, everything out of her control. Ahead she made out Cody's vehicle fishtailing down the mountain. He'd just passed a slower vehicle and was having trouble righting the bouncing van. She glanced at Styles. "When we catch up with him, what are your plans? We can't ram him off the road, not here. He'll fall down the mountain."

"When we start to climb again, I'll get up beside him and push him into the rockface." Styles shrugged. "My truck is damaged anyway. It won't make that much difference. The department is taking their own sweet time replacing it." He glanced at her. "Maybe we should be driving your ride?"

Snorting, Beth shook her head. "My personal vehicle is for me. Unless it's an emergency. Since I've been here, this will be the second time you've wrecked your truck."

"I haven't wrecked it yet. Just a few scrapes, is all." He accelerated as the road began to climb again. "Here we go."

More eighteen-wheelers flew past and Beth held her breath as Styles waited for a break in the convoy to come alongside Cody's van. To her surprise, Cody swung the wheel of his van and tried to push Styles' truck in the path of oncoming traffic. Tires screamed, and suddenly thrown forward as Styles hit the brakes, Beth pressed her hands on the dashboard. The truck slid sideways then straightened and ran along the guardrail that prevented drivers from plunging hundreds of feet to their deaths. The metal on Styles' door screamed as it dragged along the guardrail, but he didn't stop. He yanked the steering wheel around and took up the pursuit again.

"He's onto us." Styles' expression was grim but he had a determined set to his shoulders.

Beth gaped at him. "You think?" She checked her seatbelt. "I figured we were going to take a ride on the front of that eighteen-wheeler all the way down to the bottom of the mountain."

"Don't be so dramatic." Styles flinched as the side mirror flew off his truck and took off high in the air like a missile. "He telegraphed his move. I saw him look in the side mirror, and knew he planned to pull out. We're fine and I'll stop him next time."

Trying to keep calm, Beth inhaled and blew out a long breath. "Must we stop him on a mountain pass? Can't we wait until he hits the interstate or something?"

"It will be too easy for him to get away." Styles gained on Cody as they reached the top of the hill.

Alongside the road were signs telling of a steep descent,

slippery roads, and winding bends. Beth pulled out her weapon. "Drive up beside him. I'll climb into the back seat and shoot him. It will be safer for everyone."

"Do you know just how difficult it is to shoot someone in a moving vehicle?" Styles flicked her a glance. "We'll try it my way just one more time. If it doesn't work, we'll follow him down the mountain and call Sheriff Bowman to block the highway."

Shaking her head, Beth gritted her teeth as Styles moved closer to Cody's vehicle. "He'll drive right through a roadblock. He's got nothing to lose." She gripped the seat again, so hard her fingers ached. "We'll need to call Bowman anyway if we leave Ryder's jurisdiction. Do you know where the county line is around here?"

"Not right now, no." Styles gripped the wheel and the engine roared as he pushed it to its limits. "I'll need to get between those eighteen-wheelers. Hang on, it's going to be a rough ride."

They approached Cody's vehicle at high speed, and through the mist Beth made out a convoy of eighteen-wheelers heading along the other side of the highway, moving fast despite the heavy sleet. Her heart was in her throat as Styles pulled the truck out and then attempted to tap the side of the van with the front of his truck. It was a familiar police maneuver that usually spun the other vehicle into the curb, but it didn't work. Instead, Cody hit the brakes hard, sending steam and shredded tires flying off in all directions as he bounced to a halt. Without warning, he reversed toward them at high speed.

Suddenly Styles wrenched the wheel to one side. They slid across the highway, wheels spinning. Beth gaped in horror. Trapped between two eighteen-wheelers, they were doomed. The one advancing on them hit the brakes so hard the front bounced. Spinning the wheel, Styles accelerated, sliding the truck back into the opposite lane. Breathless, Beth hung on for dear life as they shot along the highway. In the side mirror, she made out Ryder coming up close behind them. Now out of the fog, he was coming in hot, sirens blaring and lights flashing. Seconds later, he ducked between two eighteen-wheelers and flashed past them in pursuit of Cody. Relentless, and traveling at high speed, Ryder rammed into the back of the van. Watching in horror as the vehicles stuck together for a few seconds, Beth sucked in a relieved breath as Ryder's cruiser broke free and slowed alongside the guardrail. The impact sent Cody's van veering out of control across the blacktop. In a squeal of brakes, Cody's vehicle slammed head-on into an eigh-teen-wheeler in an explosion that shook the mountain.

Horrified, Beth gaped in disbelief as the front wheels of the massive vehicle swallowed up the van and ran over the top of it. In a relentless scream of metal, both vehicles careered twenty yards or more down the highway, leaving an oily slick. Cody's van was as flat as a pancake. Beth ducked as a wheel bounced across the highway, barely missing the truck before leaping the siderail and vanishing into the mist. Bits and pieces of twisted metal littered the highway and pinged off the top of the truck. Oil and gas ran in multicolored streams across the soaking wet blacktop. In front of them, Ryder was climbing slowly from his vehicle unharmed. The driver of the eighteen-wheeler was swinging down from his cab shaking his head. Only one person hadn't made it—Cody. Relieved everyone else had survived a horror wreck, Beth sighed and turned to Styles. "You okay?"

"Yeah." Styles removed his hat and ran both hands through his hair. "Dammit, I wanted to talk to Cody and find out how he ticks. We had no choice. He needed to be stopped. Utilizing the PIT maneuver is normal procedure." He turned to check Bear, but he was sitting up in his harness, eyes bright without a care in the world. "I'd better go and talk to people. We'll need witnesses and their details." He pushed on his hat. "This is Sheriff Bowman's county. Call him and he'll take over the investigation and get someone up here to clear the road." He indicated to Bear with his chin. "I'll leave him with you. There's glass and metal all over the road. I'm going to check what's left of the van with Ryder."

Deep inside, Beth wondered, just how many serial killers died by the hands of law enforcement without the benefit of a judge and jury. Cody's death hadn't been her doing but justice had been well and truly served for the many people he'd murdered and tortured. Strange how people perceived incidences like this wreck as natural justice but her way of removing monsters from society as a crime. Never, had she killed without absolute proof of guilt even if it meant becoming a victim. For her it was as simple as kill or be killed. The conception of normal people's idea of justice, by allowing people like Cody to walk the streets again, confused her, but she'd try harder to understand them. She nodded to Styles. "Sure, Bear is fine with me and I'll call the sheriff now." She needed to say something complimentary to him. That's what normal people did in situations like this to relieve the stress, didn't they? He'd kept her safe and she appreciated his skills. Taking a breath, she looked at his weary face. "Great driving, by the way."

"You weren't just a little bit scared, huh?" Styles zipped up his jacket against the rain and shook his head. "I don't believe I'll ever figure you out, Beth." Shoulders hunched, he headed into the mist.

She watched him pick his way around the debris strewn across the highway toward Ryder and smiled at Bear. "Just as well, huh?"

FORTY-FOUR

After turning the cleanup over to Sheriff Bowman's team, Beth and Styles followed Ryder back to Rattlesnake Creek. Their statements could be completed later but right now they needed to assist Wolfe with processing the Cody home. They wanted answers and searching his house was the only way to discover more about the Convenience Store Killer. By the time they'd arrived, Wolfe had removed the body and was doing a forensic sweep of the crime scene. She pulled on protective gear and followed Styles and Ryder inside the house. The smell of death had increased and seemed to crawl along the passageway. She went to Wolfe's side. "Find anything interesting?"

"If Cody killed her, he covered his tracks well." Wolfe waved a hand around the room. "He lives here, so didn't need to remove his prints. We found the murder weapon and it was wiped clean prior to use, and whoever wielded it wore gloves. They took a shower and washed everything in bleach. There are towels in the washer, which makes me lean toward Cody. Most killers wouldn't have bothered to launder the towels. Again, they've been saturated in bleach, so no joy there for trace evidence. The killer understood the need to destroy DNA." He moved to the kitchen sink and opened a cabinet. "This is a significant find because it ties in with the murders." He held up a bottle of PCR Clean. "It's not usual to have this product in a home in these parts."

"We've found evidence as well in the wreck." Styles held up a plastic evidence bag containing a gun with a suppressor attached. "If this matches the bullets taken from the victims, it will prove he was the Convenience Store Killer."

"And I found a bunch of scratch cards in a bedroom upstairs"—Ryder held up evidence bags—"a pile of panties, and a small selection of women's jewelry. If we can prove these belong to any of his abduction victims, it will be a home run on some of the cases at least." He handed the evidence bags to Emily Wolfe with a smile and looked at Wolfe. "Can you get DNA from panties?"

"Yeah, unless he sprayed them as well." Wolfe frowned. "I'll give it my best shot."

"Another thing, he called his aunt to ask her to drop by and bring his mom some cookies. I figure he wanted her to discover his mom's body before he finished work." Ryder pushed back his hat. "He'd set up an alibi. He went by TJ's for takeout and made a point of saying he was going to the park. It was probably then he murdered his mom. I'm guessing he went back to the park and made sure he was seen. I don't figure we need to look any further for another killer."

"Maybe not." Wolfe looked from one to the other. "I'll give a cause and time of death, but it will be homicide by person or persons unknown. Unless you can prove otherwise. From what we know of Cody, it is likely he murdered his mom, but he was very smart. I'm guessing we'll never really know the truth about him." He sighed. "Jo Wells would have loved to delve into his mind."

Trying to look sympathetic, Beth nodded. "Yeah, it's a shame, but at least he can't hurt anyone else now."

When Styles' phone buzzed, he indicated to her to follow him outside. "Who is it?"

"The director." Styles handed her one of his earbuds. "Yes, sir."

"The Tarot Killer has struck again. This time it's law enforcement: Deputy Branch Dryer out of Mischief. I believe you had contact with him recently when you figured the murders there might be connected to your current case."

"Yeah, he was one of the people at the sheriff's office we came into contact with. As far as I recall, he was just a regular guy. We went to Mischief on a hunch as the murders occurred close by and we couldn't ignore them. We examined the bodies to make a comparison." Styles flicked a glance at Beth. "The MOs were completely different to our homicides and we had expert advice from Dr. Shane Wolfe to validate our decision to return to base. Do you have some reason to believe they were the work of the Tarot Killer?"

"No, not the girls' murders. Dryer was found dead this morning, alone in his vehicle with a tarot card in his pocket. It could be poison. We've shipped his body out to Helena to undergo testing. Something was going down the night before his death. His cruiser is damaged, and at first we believed he'd suffered an injury or medical episode at the time, resulting in his death. When the doctor discovered the tarot card, the sheriff contacted me. No injury was found on Dryer, so I instigated further investigations into COD."

So they've found Dryer. Another vicious killer bites the dust. Thrilled her plan had worked, Beth moved closer to Styles, needing to get involved. "This is Agent Katz, sir. The Tarot Killer is more of a vigilante. It would be a complete turnaround for him to murder an innocent. Do you figure it's a copycat? He has been all over the media lately."

"I had the same thoughts, Agent Katz, but it's clear the Tarot Killer murdered him. The card on the body has been verified as

the same card he uses, and none have been found anywhere else, and trust me, we've tried to locate the manufacturer. So unless he's started murdering innocent cops, which doesn't make a whole lot of sense, something went down between them. There must be a reason the Tarot Killer targeted law enforcement. He has an uncanny ability to track down killers, so I'll need you in Mischief first thing in the morning to discover what the heck is going on there."

"We have a local murder here, sir." Styles stared up as sleet peppered his shoulders. "It's tied in with the Convenience Store Killer. It's his mom."

"Is there proof that he murdered his mother?" The director let out a long sigh.

"Not at this time." Styles looked at Beth and rolled his eyes.

"You'll need to leave it in the hands of the local sheriff. He can work with the medical examiner. You're off the case until you have proof to tie it in with the other murders. Right now, we have an ongoing federal case, Agent Styles, and it takes precedence. If the Tarot Killer is in Mischief, I want him caught. You leave first thing in the morning. Don't give up until you have answers for me." He disconnected.

Swallowing hard, Beth took in Styles' weary expression. She had mixed feelings about investigating the Tarot Killer. Getting involved with the case and covering up evidence against herself made her no better than Dryer. She refused to drop down to his level and in that second decided she'd present any evidence she found and suffer the consequences. Nervous but determined not to let Styles down, she pulled an energy bar from her pocket and offered it to him, glad to see him rip open the wrapper and eat it in two bites. "I guess we head back to Mischief in the morning." She caught his grimace and raised both eyebrows. "The director doesn't sound too happy and I'm surprised he didn't send Carter and Jo."

"Me too." Styles gave her a long considering stare. "I figure you have a crystal ball. You suspected something wasn't right in the Mischief Sheriff's Department. We should have followed up more when we were there."

Shaking her head and allowing the rain to spill from the brim of her hat, she squeezed his arm. "We did what we could, with the time we had, Styles. It would've taken too long to go through everything and check out every investigation. They all did the absolute minimum and that falls on the sheriff's shoulders. If Dryer was involved in a cover-up, we'll concentrate on him specifically this time." She offered him a smile. "We'll hand this crime scene over to Ryder to process. With Wolfe to assist him, he'll be fine. You need to get home and rest." She met his surprised gaze. "I'll do some groundwork on Dryer's cases this afternoon. Come over to my apartment this evening and we'll order in dinner and then get an early night. What do you say?"

"Thanks, I appreciate your concern. I wouldn't admit it to anyone but you, but I'm exhausted and my head aches and my ribs are on fire. I'd love to join you for takeout, but can we forget about work and just watch a movie or something? The workload is getting crazy. I feel like I'm on a carousel in a horror movie." Styles wiped a hand down his face. "I keep going round and round, faster and faster, and I can't get off."

FORTY-FIVE

SATURDAY, WEEK TWO

Mischief

The evening spent with Beth had been surprisingly relaxing. He'd refueled the chopper before heading back to his apartment to pack. He hurt all over, and bruised ribs aside, his exhaustion after the fall concerned him. He'd always taken flying very seriously, making sure he never flew if he became ill or injured. The last few days had been hell, but the fall had shaken him more than he'd admit to anyone. The preparation before the mission had been solid. They'd checked and rechecked the mineshafts in the area and they'd kept to what he'd believed to have been the safe area when trying to save Cheyenne. Falling into a mineshaft with his background was unforgivable and he blamed himself for nearly killing Beth and Bear. Somehow Bear hadn't been injured but he knew Beth was hurt. She covered pain well and he admired that about her.

His concern was validated when he found her dozing in the hot tub in the gym. They often used the hot tub after a long time out in the elements but rarely together. Beth liked her privacy but didn't send him away when he entered the gym.

They'd sat in silence most of the time just soaking in the hot water. They'd eaten pizza for dinner and just chatted about nothing until he'd headed for his apartment.

The morning met him clear with patchy clouds. The wind gusts had dropped a little. It was a perfect day for flying, and renewed after sleeping for ten hours straight, he enjoyed the flight. On the way, Beth made a few references to the Night Creeper murders but seemed determined to scour the hardcopy files they kept at the office. He dropped the bird over the top of the mountain range and Mischief came into view. They landed on the helipad at the hospital and made their way downstairs, and to his surprise, out front, Sheriff Lance Walker sat in his cruiser waiting for them. Styles turned to Beth. "So they're expecting us."

"Hmm, now the files will be sanitized for sure." Beth shook her head. "I can't believe he was prewarned by the director."

Styles nodded to Walker and climbed in the passenger seat. "Thanks for the ride. We'll need to check in at the hotel and drop off our bags."

"Planning on staying for a time, huh?" Walker eyed him suspiciously. "Do you have any intel on what happened to Dryer?"

Glancing around as they pulled from the curb, Styles shook his head. "The cause of death will come out in his autopsy. I'm sure the director will hand down the findings when they're available. Did you find his body?"

"I was called to the scene." Walker headed for the hotel and parked out front. "He was parked in the driveway of his house. Just sitting there, dead. It was darn creepy, I can tell you." He glanced at Styles. "I called the paramedics and they took him to the hospital but he was pronounced dead on scene. His vehicle was damaged, but he looked fine. Not a mark on him."

Interested, Styles turned to look at him. "Have you investigated the cause of the damage?"

"As much as there's been time." Walker heaved out a sigh. "It wasn't here in town around his patrol area. I have Boone scouting out around the saloon Dryer liked to frequent in his downtime. He did have a patrol later that night, but he often went by the Dancing Lady Saloon to pass the time. He didn't drink, just played pool or spent time chatting with people. It's not like he had a wife at home or anything. I figure he was a lonely guy." He nodded to the hotel. "You go and check in now and I'll wait here. I've arranged for a rental, as per your director's instructions. It will be delivered to my office by noon."

"Thanks." Beth climbed from the back seat the moment Styles opened the door for her. She looked at him. "I hate riding in the back of a cruiser. Being trapped inside with no door handles freaks me out."

Grabbing their bags out of the trunk, he dropped the handle on her suitcase and rolled it to her. "You'd better ride shotgun on the way to the sheriff's office. I don't want you freaking out and shooting out the windows." He chuckled and then looked at Beth's astonished expression. Clearly the thought had crossed her mind. "I didn't realize you were claustrophobic. How did you hide that during training?"

"I'm not claustrophobic." Beth lifted her chin and headed toward the hotel entrance, rolling one suitcase in each hand, more than enough clothes for a month's vacation, but that always seemed to be the norm for her. "It's a control thing. I don't like being out of control. I figure it's an echo from my past." She gave him a direct look that cut through him. "Being in foster care, at times I was forced to do things and had no control over my situation. I've overcome most of it but in some situations it comes back. During training, I was told to draw on the bad experiences to make myself stronger."

Nodding, Styles headed for the counter. "Me too."

Once they'd dropped their luggage off in their rooms, they headed back down to the sheriff's cruiser and climbed inside.

He drove them to his office and they made themselves comfortable around Dryer's old desk. This had made Beth happy. She
had full access to Dryer's computer and spent a good deal of
time going through the drawers. She found nothing of interest,
and Styles collected a pile of murder books and dropped them
onto the desk. "These are the Night Creeper murders." He
opened a file and took out two pieces of paper. "There's nothing
here. We're wasting our time."

"If the Tarot Killer murdered Dryer, then he had something
on him." Beth chewed on the end of her pen. "We need to find
what that was. From all the Tarot Killer cases I've read about,
he kills only serial killers who escape justice. If Dryer was
covering up evidence of his involvement in the crimes, it won't
be in these files. We need to look into him more closely."

Styles smiled. She always thought outside the box and
found angles he hadn't considered. "We don't need a search
warrant for a dead man. Once our vehicle arrives, we'll go and
search his house and see what Deputy Dryer was hiding."

"In the meantime"—Beth tapped away at the computer
keyboard—"I'm going to find out a little more about him,
starting from his upbringing and how he was in school. The one
thing about school records: I can hack them blindfolded. If he
scratched his backside, I'll know about it."

Styles stood and headed for the door. "I'll grab us a cup of
coffee."

Three hours later, Styles rubbed both hands down his face
in frustration. The murder books, where law officers were
expected to give details of crimes they'd investigated, were
useless. He went to another filing cabinet and pulled files out at
random. Flicked through them and then went back to the desk.
Beth was absorbed in her work and hadn't said much all morning. "Beth, got a minute?"

"Sure." Beth smiled at him. "Find something?"

Leaning forward on the desk, he shook his head. "It's what I didn't find that's a problem. A big problem. There's been a major cover-up but only on the Night Creeper files. It looks as if Dryer took the lead on all the cases and left Boone to do the grunt work, which because of the lack of evidence was negligible. I looked at a few other cases at random and they're as detailed as one would expect. In some cases, the murder books on the Night Creeper cases are one to three pages max."

"Suspects?" Beth leaned back in her chair, stifled a yawn, and stretched her arms over her head.

Styles shook his head. "A few but none of them panned out." He frowned. "I can't figure out why they were even considered as suspects. I mean, one guy happened to take a bus past the crime scene and walked a hundred yards or so to his home. It is as if they pulled in anyone just to have a few suspects on the books."

"Hmm." Beth checked her coffee and, grimacing, pushed it away. "I discovered a pile of information on Dryer. He didn't do well at school, was in counseling for being bullied. In high school he slashed a girl on the arm with a broken bottle, which he claimed was an accident. The report from the school counselor is quite revealing. He managed to extract information from Dryer. He'd been out on a few dates with her and they'd had some type of argument. The next day in the school canteen, all the girls were sniggering when he walked by. Dryer wouldn't elaborate on what had happened and insisted it didn't have any bearing on the incident with the bottle." She met Styles' gaze and a slow smile crossed her lips. "Okay, add to this he came from a broken home. His mom walked out and left him with a violent father. When he turned sixteen, his father was found dead at the bottom of an elevator shaft on a construction site. Dryer was sent here to Roaring Creek to live with his grandma. The year he turned eighteen, she died and he inherited the house. He joined the sheriff's department a short time later and has been living in his grandma's house all along."

Listening with interest, Styles nodded. "You managed to discover all that about him in three hours. That's remarkable. A violent father can cause damage early. Anything on his mom?"

"Oh yeah, she went into a shelter. The reports I have on her say she escaped with her life and just the clothes on her back. The husband was abusive. She wanted to go back for Dryer but was in fear of her life." Beth stared at him. "It's all there, isn't it? The groundwork for a psychopath. His father was most likely one, and I wouldn't mind betting Dryer pushed him down the elevator shaft." She smiled. "It wouldn't be the first time an abused kid has killed a parent. Then we have the first romance, which went sour. Why? Something happened on the date that made the girls at school ridicule him and then what does he do? He lashes out with a bottle." She shrugged. "It was probably too messy for him so he decided to teach women like her a lesson by raping and strangling them. The problem is, we know his problem. He couldn't rape them. Maybe the ridicule was he couldn't perform with his date either."

Styles rubbed the back of his neck. "That would have been his trigger, the humiliation at school. So how come he hasn't killed until now?"

"Maybe, he didn't date many women or it never went that far." Beth stood and bent to rub Bear's ears. "Until he tried again with the same result. I'd say most women would be sympathetic, but some can be mean-spirited. That would be the trigger, and once he'd started, he couldn't stop." She glanced at her watch. "I need a break. I figure so does Bear. We have some time before the vehicle is delivered. Mind if we grab a bite to eat and take a walk in the park?"

Styles smiled, surprised by her consideration for his dog. "Yeah, that's a great idea. I'll go and get Dryer's address and house keys from the sheriff. They'll likely be in evidence. Then we're good to go."

FORTY-SIX

Of course, Beth had discovered the information on Dryer weeks ago during her own investigation. Finding the rune cut into the fob on his keyring during her previous visit to Mischief and the fact he'd attempted to kill her had sealed his fate. Feeding the information to Styles now and having him agree with her findings filled her with a satisfaction she hadn't known existed. After grabbing burgers and fries and to-go cups of coffee from the local diner, they sat in the park and watched Bear round up ducks and send them waddling into the river. She laughed at his antics. "How come he likes ducks and hates chickens? They don't look much different, do they?"

"Ah, but we don't know if animals communicate, do we? As in speak each other's languages." Styles chuckled. "Maybe *quack, quack* means hello and a chicken's squawk means someone is coming to cut off your head. Who knows?"

Laughing, Beth shook her head. "And people call *me* crazy."

They headed back to the sheriff's office and found the rental parked outside, keys in the glovebox as directed. They climbed inside and headed along a tree-lined road toward Dryer's home. The sun had appeared at last and new leaves spread spotted patterns across the blacktop. It was an old suburb, with log-built homes. Most had long driveways and red-roofed barns out back. They climbed out and went to the porch. As Styles opened the dilapidated front door, she waited without luck for him to notice the distinctive keyring. An old-lady smell filled Beth's nostrils as she followed him into the house and, shuddering, she pulled on a face mask. The recognition came from living with an old lady and her son for a time and brought back memories she'd rather forget. The middle-aged greasy-haired overweight son had crept into her bedroom at night and watched her. Sometimes pulling the blankets from her and touching her legs. She'd wanted to kill him. The bread knife had been in her hand as he walked up behind her one morning before school and it had taken all her willpower to drop it into the sink. That morning she'd packed her lunch and a few meager possessions and run away.

Dragging her head back to the now, she pulled on gloves and followed Styles. They moved through the rooms and found Dryer's bedroom. It stank of stale sweat and the bed linen hadn't been changed for a year. They searched the drawers and beside her Styles whistled. She turned to look at him. "What?"

"Jackpot." He held up a small box filled with photographs. He turned them over in his hand. "Home-printed images of his victims. There are many here we didn't know about. It seems he took a few vacations in other states. He liked to spread his murders around. He has dates and places written on the back of each one, but no names."

Looking over his shoulder at the gruesome images, Beth shrugged. "They didn't have names to him. They meant nothing to him. It was all about domination. He needed to show them he was the man."

"Just a minute." Styles dove into the box again and pulled out a thumb drive. "What do we have here? Can you see what's on this?"

Beth went back to the small room Dryer used as an office and easily opened his computer. She stared at the videos, all neatly kept in dated files. "This is all we need to prove he was the Night Creeper."

"We'll keep doing the sweep." Styles dropped the thumb drive into an evidence bag. "He's not stupid enough to be in any of the videos and I don't want any doubt."

They spent some time hunting through each room and discovered a rolled-up yoga mat in the garage. Beth looked at it and raised one eyebrow. "We'll need to take that as well. It looks like it would fit the imprint in the weeds where we found Layla Cooper. This is Wolfe's case. He might find trace evidence on the mat. How confident was Dryer to keep this? He never believed anyone would suspect him."

"And yet the Tarot Killer did, didn't he?" Styles turned back toward the house. "There are garbage bags in the kitchen. I'll grab one and we'll take the mat with us. Take some images of the mat in situ before we leave."

After taking the images, Beth helped to bag the mat. "I can't see anything else of interest."

"Nope, we're done here." Styles tossed her Dryer's keys and then picked up the mat. "The keys will need to be returned to the evidence locker." He headed for the rental.

The perfect opportunity to prove the case against Dryer without any doubt, had just fallen into Beth's hands. She stared at the keys "Ah, Styles, wait up. I figure these keys need to go to Wolfe as well."

"How so?" Styles dropped the mat into the trunk and pulled the bag of photographs from his pocket and laid them beside it.

Walking to his side, Beth held up the metal stick with the rune etched into the end. "I think I found his branding iron."

"Well, I'll be darned." Styles examined the keyring closely.

"It sure looks the same. We'll need to get this to Wolfe ASAP." He smiled. "I'll give him a call."

Beth moved closer. "Put it on speaker. I want to be in the conversation too." She climbed into the rental.

"Sure." Styles slid behind the wheel and made the call. He brought Wolfe up to speed.

"Y'all have found a honey hole." Wolfe sounded impressed. *"I have some information for y'all as well. As I'm involved in the Night Creeper case, the ME out of Helena sent me the autopsy report on Deputy Dryer. He died of cyanide poisoning. It wasn't ingested. It was spilled on his pants. They found residue mixed with bourbon, so I guess he had a drink spilled on him at a bar. He had no alcohol in his system at the time of death. No other injuries were apparent apart from what could be scratches on his neck. They are old, maybe a week or so. As the Hooper girl was embalmed and is now buried, the chances of checking under her nails is remote. There was nothing under the fingernails of Layla Cooper. This would suggest the Tarot Killer was in a bar with Dryer the night he died."*

"Thanks, we know exactly where he was the night before he died." Styles glanced at Beth. "We'll check it out now. Thanks. We'll drop the evidence to you on our way home."

"I'll see y'all then." Wolfe disconnected.

Beth blew out a long breath. She'd be heading into the Dancing Lady Saloon to ask if anyone had seen her on the night Dryer died. Well, that had to be a first. She leaned back in her seat, trying to get her head around the problem. Of course she looked completely different. She wore no makeup and had blonde hair, different eye color as well. She gathered up her hair and, using the hair tie she kept around her wrist, pulled it into a ponytail at the nape of her neck and pushed on her Stetson. She liked the hat and pulled it low over her eyes. Her antics hadn't missed Styles' eagle eye.

"You don't like going into saloons, do you?" Styles flicked her a glance.

She shook her head. "Not really, no."

"It's all part of the job." Styles flashed her a smile. "Just keep it together. Guys in these small towns don't have a city filter."

Snorting, Beth shook her head. "And there I was worrying you might start a fight. Although, you've been tame of late. I must be a good influence on you."

FORTY-SEVEN

The drive out to the Dancing Lady Saloon seemed different than the last time, faster in the daylight, but Beth recognized the backstreet where Dryer had attempted to run her down. She had barely escaped with her life. As they pulled up out front of the bar, she zipped up her jacket against the wind blowing down from the mountains. She glanced up at the sky. "I hope it doesn't rain again."

"The way the climate is changing, I'm more concerned about a blizzard. I don't want to be trapped here for days." Styles pushed down his Stetson and headed into the saloon.

Beth followed him to the bar and waited for the bartender to walk slowly toward them. It was the same man who'd served her the night she poisoned Dryer. She pulled out her cred pack and held it up. Most people's attention went straight to the badge, likely he wouldn't even recall her face. "Agents Katz and Styles. We'd like to ask you a few questions about Deputy Dryer. He was a regular patron here, I believe."

"Yeah, Branch dropped by to pass the time before he went on patrol most nights." The bartender's face dropped. "I heard about him dying sudden. Shame, he was a good man."

"Do you recall him speaking to anyone the night before he died?" Styles leaned on the bar.

"He spoke to everyone." The bartender frowned. "Is there something about his death that we haven't been told about?"

"No, we're just trying to get a timeline of what happened. His vehicle has some damage." Styles shrugged. "Do you recall anyone spilling a drink on him?"

"He didn't take a drink, maybe a soda." The bartender shook his head. "I do recall a woman knocking her drink over. The glass smashed all over the floor. I swept it up and dumped it in the trash."

Although Beth knew the answer, she looked at the bartender. "You didn't touch the glass?"

"Where is the glass now?" Styles lifted his chin.

"Nope, I didn't touch the glass. I have a long-handled brush and pan. I don't like cutting myself and the garbage was picked up this morning." The bartender shrugged. "What does a broken glass have to do with Dryer's death?"

"Nothing at all." Styles tipped back his hat. "You mentioned a woman. Is she a regular here as well?"

"No, not a regular, but I figure I've seen her drop by before." The bartender scratched his head. "We have karaoke on Saturday nights. I can't swear on a Bible, but I figure she came last week. Dark hair and eyes, full figured, high heels and tight jeans. Every man's dream. If you know what I mean?"

Beth stepped closer. "Did she leave with Dryer?"

"Nope. She spoke to him and left." The bartender picked up a cloth and wiped the bar. "He left just after. Maybe he had something going with her, maybe not."

"Okay, thanks for your help." Styles handed him a card. "If you see her again, give me a call."

Beth followed him out of the saloon and frowned. "We all know the Tarot Killer is a man. This is a waste of time."

"We know the Tarot Killer is a master of disguise. I've seen female impersonators become the most beautiful women with the right wigs and makeup." Styles raised both eyebrows. "This is a lead we need to pursue."

Climbing back inside the rental, Beth shook her head. "No, it isn't. That woman is just a local. We know the Tarot Killer doesn't hang around and as sure as heck doesn't make himself known to the locals prior to the hit. He is long gone. We've found the corrupt cop and made a case against Dryer for the murders. Can we just go home?"

"Not yet." Styles looked at her. "If the woman shows tonight at karaoke, the barman will call me. This will prove she isn't the Tarot Killer. Like you said, he doesn't hang around to be caught. He's way too smart for that." He smiled at her. "One more night, Beth. You can relax, have a hot bath, watch TV. Order room service and a bottle of wine. All I need is a phone call and we'll be on our way home first thing in the morning."

Mind whirring with how she could escape Styles' attention to become the mystery woman again, Beth leaned back in her seat and sighed. "Sure. A night off would be wonderful."

At the hotel, Beth paced up and down in her room. She needed to show at the Dancing Lady Saloon, so that the bartender spotted her and called Styles. If she didn't, he'd be convinced the Tarot Killer was a woman and that would make her life considerably more dangerous. Right now, having an ambiguous persona suited her just fine. She changed into a leather jacket and pushed her hair under a black woolen cap. Before leaving, she ordered room service and then headed downstairs. Strolling out of the hotel she pulled on sunglasses and walked to a convenience store, went inside, and purchased a ton of candy. With her back to the CCTV camera, she slipped a burner phone from the display and took everything to the counter, hunching slightly to make herself look older, she left and sprinted along the sidewalk. Back inside the hotel, she removed her temporary disguise and used the phone to book a cab to pick her up at the corner at eight. She'd just opened the door to room service when her phone chimed. "Agent Katz."

"It's me." Styles laughed. *"Don't you look at your caller ID?"*

Beth pulled out some bills from her pocket and handed them to the server. "Ah, yeah usually, but room service just delivered my dinner and I was searching my pockets for a tip. What's up?"

"Nothing. I just updated the director with our progress." Styles answered a knock on his door. *"Hang on, my dinner has just arrived."*

Beth waited, hearing muted conversation. "What did he say?"

"He wants the evidence in detail and uploaded to the server ASAP. We'll wait for Wolfe's findings first. He was surprised Dryer was the killer, but he's not making any excuses for the Tarot Killer. He feels much the same as we do. As in, what did we miss the Tarot Killer noticed?" Styles blew out a long breath. *"Anyway, I'll leave you to eat your meal. See you in the morning. Do you want me to call if the bartender contacts me or wait for the morning?"*

Beth sighed. "Wait for the morning. I'm going to sleep right through. I'm exhausted."

"Night." Styles disconnected.

FORTY-EIGHT

Running a plan through her mind, Beth ate dinner so distracted she didn't notice if the food was good or not. It filled her belly and gave her energy and that was all that mattered. Now every second counted. She pushed the tray outside into the passageway and attached a DO NOT DISTURB sign on her door handle. She picked up her phone and called down to the desk. "I don't want to be disturbed. Please hold any calls until eight in the morning." She turned off her cellphone and left it beside the bed and checked the time. It didn't take her long to morph into the mysterious woman, and finding another suitable pair of heels, carried them in one hand and slipped out of the door. Unconcerned about CCTV cameras, as the hotel didn't have any apart from one on the front counter, but fully aware Styles could be walking the dog and meeting him at the elevator was too risky, she headed for the stairs. She took the fire exit from the hotel, pushed her feet into her heels, and walked the two blocks to an old redbrick building that offered apartments to rent. Five minutes later, a cab rolled to the curb, and she jumped inside. "Twenty-two Barn."

The address was close to the Dancing Lady Saloon and she

didn't want anyone knowing her real destination, just in case Styles got over-inquisitive. It was nine-thirty by the time she removed her jacket and walked inside. The Saloon was busy and karaoke night was in full swing. The bar was hot, and scents of perfume and male sweat mingled with beer hit her in a wall of stink. Wanting to be seen, she pushed her way through the crowd at the bar but didn't get far before a smiling guy in a baseball cap moved alongside her. Surrounded by tall men, she had to elbow her way to the bar. The stranger stuck to her like glue.

"Can I buy you a drink?" The guy smiled at her. "Or do you have a lazy boyfriend who risks sending you into a pack of miners to get him a drink?"

Not wanting to touch anything and a glass would hold her fingerprints, which were on record, she took the golden opportunity. She kept to her Southern drawl like before and raised her voice over the noise of the music. "Thanks. Whatever you're having will be fine."

The stranger ordered two beers and pulled out a seat for her. She climbed onto the barstool. "I'm Sue. Thanks for the beer." She didn't touch the bottle but stared right into the face of the bartender, who gave her a nod and then walked to the other end of the bar.

"Josh." He stood beside her giving her a slow once-over. "Do you sing?"

Smiling, Beth shook her head. "No, but I like being in a crowd of people."

"Me too." Josh took a long pull on his beer.

The bartender had help and the others moved up and down the counter serving the crush at the bar. The crowd was moving like ants over their nest, people changing places, getting drinks, and then moving away. She hoped the bartender had seen her and followed his back as he walked to the other end of the bar. Everything around her froze and her heart gave a jitter. Styles was sitting at the bar staring right at her. She avoided eye contact, but panic gripped her when he got to his feet and tried to fight his way through the crowd to get to her. She waited precious seconds for a large man to move in beside her and turned to Josh. "Watch my beer. I need to go to the bathroom. I'll be right back."

"Sure." Josh gave her a brilliant smile.

Pushing wildly through the crowd, Beth headed for the women's bathroom. The passageway led to the bathroom and farther down a light shone over an exit sign. She made straight for it, her heels clicking on the tile. Throwing caution to the wind, she dragged off her short brown wig and stuffed it into her purse. Her long hair dropped over her shoulders. The reversable jacket, she'd worn, she turned inside out and pulled it back on. Carrying her shoes, she sprinted for the cab stand. She jumped inside and was whisked away into the darkness. As the vehicle hit the highway, she pulled out the burner phone, removed the SIM, and wiped it clean before tossing it out of the window.

"Ma'am." The cab driver peered at her in the mirror. "You in any trouble? There's been a vehicle following us since we left the saloon. He's some ways back, but I took a back road and he was right on my tail."

Swallowing hard, Beth turned in the seat and peered out the back window. In the distance she made out headlights, not close but some distance away. "Maybe leave the highway and go back onto it again just to be sure. I left the saloon because a guy was being a pest. I didn't figure he'd follow me home. Maybe he's the Night Creeper?"

"Okay, I can do that, but all these changes of directions will cost more." The cab driver frowned. "You got the cash to pay for the ride?"

Starting to get frantic that Styles was on her tail, Beth nodded. "I'll give you double, just keep me away from that creep."

The cab took a few detours but the following lights stuck with them. Beth gripped the back of the seat in front of her. "He's persistent. Any ideas?"

"Maybe cover up that hair and pull up your hood. I'll drop you at the end of an alleyway. It's close to the address you mentioned. It runs alongside the hotel. Maybe go in one door and out the other to avoid him." He tossed her a black woolen cap from beside him. "Here, use this."

Beth pulled her hair into a ponytail and pulled on the cap. She reversed her jacket again and pulled the hood over the cap. As they approached the hotel at high speed, she took bills out of her purse and thrust them at the driver. "Thanks."

The cab slowed and stopped just long enough for her to leap from the vehicle. As Beth hightailed it down the alleyway, heart thundering in her chest, she chanced a glance behind her. The lights of the following vehicle hadn't turned the corner yet. She threw herself into the side entrance of the hotel and stood panting for a few seconds before peering both ways along the passageway to the stairs. Taking off at a run, she thrust open the door and, taking the steps two at a time, ran back to her floor. She opened the door a crack just as the elevator pinged its arrival. Frozen in place, she stared through the crack in the door as Styles walked out of the elevator and down to her room. Panic had her by the throat as he stared at her door for a few agonizing seconds before shaking his head and heading to his room.

As Beth put one hand on the door to push it open, Styles' door opened again and he walked out with Bear at his side and went to wait for the elevator. When the dog's head turned her way, Beth sprinted back down the stairs to the floor below. Behind her the sound of Bear's bark sounded like a hurricane siren. She burst into the passageway and went to the elevators. One was going down and she pressed the buttons like a woman possessed on the one going up. The doors opened and she fell inside, riding the elevator to her floor. Holding her breath as the doors hissed open, she looked both ways. The floor was empty and she made it inside her room in seconds.

Dashing into the bathroom, she scraped off the silicone disguising her features and flushed away the evidence before popping out her contacts. She had stripped and stowed away her disguises when a knock came at the door. Instinct told her it was Styles and she still had remnants of makeup on her face. Slapping on a thick coating of cream and pulling on her robe, she went to the door and peered through the peephole. "Styles, I refuse to let you see me like this."

"Just for one second." Styles cleared his throat. "It's important." She turned and noticed the wig peeking out of her half open purse and her stomach tightened. *Now what?*

Opening the door a crack, she stared at him in silence. When a smile lit up his face, she glared at him. "What do you figure 'do not disturb' means, Styles?"

"Sorry." Styles' grin hadn't left his face. "I followed a suspect, the one we figured might be the Tarot Killer. I'm not sure but I believe she came into the hotel via the alleyway. Just before, Bear was convinced someone was on the stairs on our floor, so I figured I'd better check you were okay."

Beth raised both eyebrows. "Do you honestly figure if some stranger burst into my room, they'd walk out alive?" She shook her head. "My weapon is always in reach, same as yours, and anyhow, the Tarot Killer murders serial killers." She indicated to her face. "Look at me. Do I look like a serial killer to you?"

"Nope." Styles cleared his throat, but he hadn't stopped grinning. "Do you wear that stuff to bed every night?" He made a few snorting sounds, his eyes dancing with amusement. "I thought that went out of style a hundred years ago."

She closed the door in his face. "Good night, Styles."

EPILOGUE

THURSDAY, WEEK THREE

Rattlesnake Creek

After Styles had pigeonholed her search for his sister, Beth brought up the subject again. "She could still be alive. Don't you want to know?"

"Yes and no. I figure if she's alive, she'll have a new life by now. If she was murdered, I don't want to know the details." Styles rubbed the back of his neck. "Leave it with me a little longer. Right now, we need to finish up these cases. I'm itching to get some downtime."

The paperwork and follow-up of the cases took some time. Beth had presented all her evidence on both killers. After the director had asked for more details, with reluctance Beth had requested a video hookup with behavioral analyst Agent Jo Wells. Each time she came into contact with Jo, she risked exposure. Her stomach cramped as she waited for the call to start. She'd agreed to speak with Jo only to please Styles. She didn't need Jo to tell her about why the Convenience Store Killer or the Night Creeper murdered women. It was all there for everyone to see, especially after a few interviews.

"Jo, great to see you again." Styles smiled and nodded to Carter. "Hi, Carter, any good fishing lately?"

"Yeah, I'm heading to my cabin in Black Rock Falls for a week's vacation real soon. Jo is taking her daughter, Jaime, and Bobby Kalo to Disney World. It's not for me. I like the quiet life away from noise."

"Me too." Styles chuckled and looked at Beth. "I'm hoping to persuade Beth to try fishing."

Beth looked from one to the other. "I'd love to go fishing with you, Styles, if I can bring my paints, but right now, do you mind if we talk about the cases? The director is expecting a final report." Keeping a neutral expression, she looked at Jo. "I've sent you all the background we found on both killers. We recently spoke to Cody's aunt. It shone some light onto why he became the Convenience Store Killer."

"He was exhibiting a number of different psychoses. The smooth typical charming front we see in many types of psychopath, covered a sociopathic nature." Jo let out a long sigh. *"I'm doubtful that anyone could have saved him. Rehabilitation was out of the question. He didn't want to be taken alive. I figure he was looking for death by cop all along. I am interested in what started him on this path. What was his trigger?"*

Leaning on the desk, Beth couldn't understand Jo's empathy for Cody. His acts of violence without regard to the suffering he caused for not only the victims but their families made him a monster in her book, but finding out what made him tick was what the FBI required. "The aunt gave us a rundown of his childhood. His father left for another woman, and Cody was abused by a number of his mother's boyfriends. When he complained to his grandma, she told his mom and he received a beating." Beth took a breath. "That was trigger number one. In all accounts he loved his mom—he cared for her, cleaned house, and provided for her. The aunt said the mom berated him constantly, telling him he was useless, and any girl he brought home was tossed out."

"*Hmm, plenty of triggers there.*" Jo pursed her lips. "*The killing of strangers in the stores was representing the strangers who abused him. The kidnapping of the girls and taking them away for the night was his way of dating them. He'd only known violence, so that's what he gave back. The panties and jewelry were his trophies. In that way he fell into the normal psychopath pattern. He needed a keepsake. I believe he had some under-standing of what he was doing was wrong because of the elabo-rate way he covered his tracks.*"

"The grandmother died suddenly." Styles cleared his throat. "There is a report by a paramedic a pillow was on the floor with spittle over it. So he could have smothered her. She was old and the local doctor recorded the death as natural causes. I'm sure he killed his mother."

"*If she nagged at him continuously, that would be likely. He wanted to shut her up and that was his only way to be free of her.*" Jo leaned back in her chair. "*He'd likely decided to take one more girl at that stage and then go out in a hail of bullets.*"

"That just about sums up Cody." Styles scrolled through files on his tablet. "Now the dirty deputy, Branch Dryer. We went back and found some of his old high school sweethearts. There's one or two women he dated for a very short time. He was deemed medically impotent. The embarrassment and bullying from girls he'd dated from his time at school, we figured these incidents are what triggered him."

Beth glanced at Jo. "I've sent you everything I know about him, but branding the women to prove he'd murdered them was significant. He made sure he'd marked them as his own. Killing them meant that no one else could have them, torturing them by strangulation and prolonging their death was payback for what they'd done to him."

"*I agree.*" Jo smiled. "*I'll cosign any reports you need me to. I think you've done a fine job on both cases. Shame the Tarot Killer slipped away, but without him, we'd never have discovered Dryer's crime spree."*

A cold shiver went down Beth's spine. It had been a close call and one she didn't need to happen again. She smiled. "Sometimes we just have to take the good with the bad."

"You sure you don't want to come to Disney World with us?" Jo smiled through the screen.

"Nah." Styles chuckled. "Someone has to mind the store. We don't know when the Tarot Killer will strike again but we're ready for him." He looked at Beth. "Isn't that right, Beth?"

Nodding, Beth smiled at him, wondering what intriguing case would fall into their laps next. "Go and have fun, you two. I can assure you the Tarot Killer is in safe hands."

A LETTER FROM D.K. HOOD

Dear Readers,

Thank you so much for choosing *Dark Hearts*. If you'd like to keep up to date with all my latest releases, just sign up at the website link below. Your details will never be shared and you can unsubscribe at any time.

www.bookouture.com/dk-hood

It's exciting to release another Special Agent Beth Katz book into the world of crime thrillers. I'm ecstatic by the feedback from all the positive reviews for my new series and glad that you enjoyed the cameo appearances from the Detectives Kane and Alton series. As both series are set in the same state, it was inevitable local law enforcement agencies would cross over from time to time. I've loved expanding the backgrounds of Beth and Styles to give you a small insight into their complicated past lives.

If you enjoyed my book, I would be very grateful if you could leave a review and recommend my book to your friends and family. I really enjoy hearing from readers, so feel free to ask me questions at any time. You can get in touch on my Facebook page, X, or email through my webpage.

Thank you so much for your support.

KEEP IN TOUCH WITH D.K. HOOD

www.dkhood.com

 facebook.com/dkhoodauthor
x.com/DKHood_Author

ACKNOWLEDGMENTS

Many thanks to my editor Helen and the fantastic #TeamBookouture, who have supported my dream for Beth Katz from the start.

Heartfelt thanks to Myrto, my publicist, for promoting Special Agent Beth Katz, and to all the wonderful bloggers who've supported my new series.

Many thanks to all my readers, especially those who take the time to share my posts and leave reviews. It warms my heart that you have all become friends. It's like a huge family of lovely people and I appreciate all of you very much.

PUBLISHING TEAM

Turning a manuscript into a book requires the efforts of many people. The publishing team at Bookouture would like to acknowledge everyone who contributed to this publication.

Audio
Alba Proko
Sinead O'Connor
Melissa Tran

Commercial
Lauren Morrissette
Jil Thielen
Imogen Allport

Cover design
The Brewster Project

Data and analysis
Mark Alder
Mohamed Bussuri

Editorial
Helen Jenner
Ria Clare

Made in the USA
Las Vegas, NV
22 February 2024

86113902R00157